THE JUBILEE PROBLEM

THE SHERLOCK HOLMES
AND LUCY JAMES MYSTERIES

The Last Moriarty
The Wilhelm Conspiracy
Remember, Remember
The Crown Jewel Mystery

Upcoming:
Death at the Diogenes Club
The Return of the Ripper

The series page at Amazon:
http://amzn.to/2s9U2jW

OTHER TITLES BY ANNA ELLIOTT

The Pride and Prejudice Chronicles:
Georgiana Darcy's Diary
Pemberly to Waterloo
Kitty Bennet's Diary

Sense and Sensibility Mysteries:
Margaret Dashwood's Diary

The Twilight of Avalon Series:
Dawn of Avalon
The Witch Queen's Secret
Twilight of Avalon
Dark Moon of Avalon
Sunrise of Avalon

The Susanna and the Spy Series:
Susanna and the Spy
London Calling

OTHER TITLES BY CHARLES VELEY

Novels:
Play to Live
Night Whispers
Children of the Dark

Nonfiction:
Catching Up

THE JUBILEE PROBLEM

A SHERLOCK HOLMES | LUCY JAMES
MYSTERY

BY ANNA ELLIOTT AND CHARLES VELEY

This is a work of fiction. Names, characters, organizations, places, events, and incidents are either products of the author's imagination or are used fictitiously.

Typesetting by FormattingExperts.com
Cover design by Todd A. Johnson

ISBN: 978-0-9991191-2-9

EPIGRAPH

Away, and mock the time with fairest show.
False face must hide what the false heart doth know.

—William Shakespeare, *Macbeth*, Act I

PREFACE

I give thanks that I am still alive to record these recollections. For reasons that will be readily apparent, they must not be published during my lifetime or in the next century.

John H. Watson, M.D.
London, December 31, 1897

Unlike my father, I have the utmost regard for Dr. Watson's skill as both a storyteller and Holmes's biographer. But there are some parts of this story Dr. Watson didn't know—namely, mine. I have added them to his account.

Lucy James
London, January 31, 1898

PROLOGUE

THE PROBLEM EMERGES

1. A MEETING WITH THE QUEEN

The occasion, on the 11th of November 1896 in Buckingham Palace, is etched upon my memory. We were in the Royal presence for a little more than two minutes, ushered in through a back door and led through circuitous hallways to a magnificent room, the details of which were obscured by my emotions at the time. The Queen, small, frail, and dressed in the plainest and nearly threadbare black silk mourning garb, sat in a wheelchair, dwarfed by her palatial surroundings.

Her voice came in a shrill, croaking whisper, as though each syllable cost her substantial energy and effort. "We have not many years remaining to us, Mr. Holmes," she said, "and Salisbury here"—she nodded towards the Prime Minister—"tells us that, if it had not been for your prompt and effective actions at the Radnar estate in Dover several weeks ago, my son Bertie would have preceded me in death."

Holmes inclined his head in a respectful bow. "No more than my duty, Your Majesty," he murmured.

"I am glad you take that view," she said. "For I am in need of your services once again. The sixtieth anniversary of my reign will fall within the next year. There will be a series of celebratory events. We shall refer to them as the Jubilee, as we did for the fiftieth anniversary celebration. Some of the arrangements have yet to be made. However, thousands of distinguished visitors from all over the world will attend, and interference of any kind would be a sign of weakness and insecurity within the Empire. I need you to prevent that. Do I make myself clear?"

"Amply, ma'am. I shall do what I can."

The Queen gave a little sigh, settling back into her wheelchair for a moment. Then she drew herself up again, with a visible effort. "That will no doubt be sufficient," she said. "You and Dr. Watson may go. Salisbury and I have other matters to discuss."

I had nearly died serving her in Afghanistan seventeen years earlier. I had returned with my health broken, and I carried within my memory the indelible recollections of the iron gates that I had passed though at the War Office to collect my pension. I remember too clearly the look of pity on the guards who admitted me and the perfunctory smile of the clerk who handed over the envelope containing the seventeen pounds, twelve shillings, and six pence that were to sustain me for the next thirty days. Had it not been for my chance meeting with Holmes, only the Lord knows what would have become of me. More to the point, I reflected, had it not been for Holmes's subsequent triumphs, I would never have seen the inside of the palace, much less have heard the Queen speak my name.

Now the Queen had given Holmes a mission. I was deeply moved by her small, frail figure and by the Royal will that she exerted with such determination. I had a far deeper appreciation of the loyalty that a sovereign can command than I had known in Afghanistan. As we left the palace, I resolved to assist Holmes in every way that I could.

Holmes never spoke of the meeting.

LUCY

2. A LETTER FROM LUCY JAMES

Exeter Street

February 7, 1897

Dear Mother,

That is wonderful news that you've been invited to audition for the orchestra at La Scala. *Of course* you will be selected; if not, they are clearly Philistines who don't deserve you.

I hate to spoil your happy news with my own less-happy thoughts, yet that appears to be what I am about to do, because I'm afraid. Those are some of my least favorite words in the entire English language—right along with, *I don't know what to do.* I'm using them now, though, in rapid succession, because I *am* afraid, and I have no idea how I ought to proceed.

I'm worried about Holmes. I've told you about the traitor he suspects exists in a position of power within the government? We have tangled with his web of agents more than once, but have yet to unmask the man in charge—or even catch a hint of his identity. Holmes has become even more obsessed about this, ever since he and Dr. Watson returned from Buckingham Palace last November. Neither one will say what occurred there, but lately he has been working himself to the brink of exhaustion. He is not using cocaine that I know of, but he is also hardly eating and scarcely sleeping or taking any rest. None of that is unusual for Sherlock Holmes, I know. As Dr. Watson keeps reminding me, that is more or less his *modus operandi* while on a case. Watson is worried, though. He has spoken to Holmes. *I* have spoken to him. Knowing Holmes, I'm sure you can imagine the results of those particular exercises in futility.

I've written three different versions of this letter and have torn up every one because I don't want to worry you. But if you have anything to suggest, any way of approaching Holmes with an argument that might actually make a dent in that monumental self-assurance of his, I would be incredibly grateful.

Even Sherlock Holmes is not entirely infallible, and I worry this may be the case on which he drives himself past the point of being able to exercise his best judgment.

With all my love,
Lucy

PART ONE

AWAY

WATSON

3. A PRIEST IN NEED

Even our first meeting with the doomed priest did not go smoothly. A slender, dark-haired young man in a black wool cassock, he had introduced himself as Keenan Mulloy. He sat in the chair normally occupied by Holmes, in front of our fireplace and opposite me. Holmes was at his desk, having recently put aside one of the many documents from the Foreign Office that he had been studying.

Holmes's daughter, Lucy James, had arranged the appointment.

It was ten o'clock on a cold morning early in February of 1897.

Holmes said, "You told Miss James that you wanted to discuss a matter of grave urgency to the Empire."

The young priest hunched forward, his elbows on his knees, looking down at his worn black shoes. His nervous fingers toyed with rosary beads and a dark metal crucifix that swung, pendulum fashion, illuminated by the warm yellow glow from our fireplace coals. Outside our rooms a raw wind tore at our bow window, rattling the panes.

"I have no proof," Mulloy finally said.

He ran his fingers through his close-cropped black hair. Clean-shaven, his round face bore a worried frown. His blue eyes were wide with importunate entreaty.

Then his words poured out—so rapidly that I imagined he had been rehearsing them in his mind and needed to be rid of them in the shortest time possible. "Yes, it was Miss James who suggested that I consult you. She has been kind enough to allow my sister Mary to share her flat on Exeter Street. Miss James said you were far more reliable and discreet than the police."

Holmes appeared to take no notice of the mention of his daughter. He leaned back slightly, pressing his fingertips together in his customary fashion. "Please start from the beginning."

Mulloy took a deep breath, exhaled, and then sat up, returning his beads and crucifix to his cassock pocket. In the firelight, the sheen of perspiration was visible on his forehead.

He took another deep breath and went on. "I have— I support—a shelter and school for orphan children at the church in Whitechapel, where I am employed. None of them has a family to protect them. My shelter is far from providing a family— we can offer little more than a roof and hot soup from time to time—but it makes a difference in cold weather especially. To obtain funds is difficult. London society is not particularly sympathetic to the children in Whitechapel, though they need help just as much as those from other parts of the country."

"The name of the church?" Holmes asked.

"The Church of the English Martyrs."

"Your parishioners are Irish," Holmes prompted.

"Yes. Therein lies my tale, I fear. Hard men are associated with the Irish. I am Irish myself, of course. But these hard men are different. They began to appear at my church in the ordinary way, dropping off clothing and tinned food. Leaving coins and occasional pound notes in the collection plate. I was surprised and delighted to see their support, naturally. I thanked them at every opportunity I had. Then I noticed that they would arrive at the same time, though from different locations and directions."

"Using the shelter as a meeting place," Holmes said.

"They would go into the chapel to pray at noon every Wednesday. On several occasions, I overheard them. They were not talking to God, nor were they talking about the children. They were talking about the government. They were talking about destroying it."

"What did you do?"

"It was a matter for the police, surely, I thought. I have a friend who is a constable. Miss James knows him too. His name is Kelly, and he is a most trustworthy fellow, with the sole duties of support for his younger sister."

"You sympathized with that, of course," I said. "Having a younger sister of your own."

The priest gave a tight smile. "It is a privilege to help one's family. But to return to my narrative, I told Constable Kelly. He did not seem overly concerned—at least that was my impression after our meeting. However, he evidently changed his mind as to the seriousness of the threat. He made a report to the Commissioner of Police."

"Indeed."

"Several days later I was in my booth at the church, hearing confession at my usual hour. A man entered, taking his place on the other side of the screen in the usual way. But this man was very different from my usual parishioners. From his speech,

I could tell that he was highly educated. Very cultivated. He said he could be of substantial help to the shelter if I would be so good as to do him and my country a service in return."

"He wanted you to inform on the hard men," Holmes said.

"He wanted me to—yes."

"Did you see who it was?"

"Oh, yes indeed. It was the Commissioner of the Metropolitan Police. I caught a glimpse of him as he was leaving."

"You had seen him before?"

"I recognized him from the picture sketches in the papers and in magazines. His white hair and white moustache were unmistakable. Also, the left sleeve of his coat was empty. I remember reading that the Commissioner had lost his left arm to a tigress in India. I was quite thrilled to be asked for help by so distinguished a gentleman."

"Did you ask how he came to be acquainted with the matter?" Holmes asked.

"I did. Evidently, he has a high regard for Constable Kelly. He said the young man had saved his life. He made me promise never to speak of the matter to Kelly, though. Even if Kelly inquires if there have been further developments, I am to say there have been none at all and that I must have been allowing my imagination to run away with me."

"And you have kept your promise. You make regular reports, informing on the hard men."

Mulloy nodded.

"How do you make your reports?" Holmes asked.

"In the confession booth. Each Wednesday a man comes to confess and says his name is Sir Robert. It is not always the same man."

"And this past Wednesday, no Sir Robert appeared, though you have fresh information to convey."

"How did you know?"

"Because you are here," Holmes said. "What is the new information?"

"The men are part of an organization called the Fenians. I believe they plan to disrupt the Queen's Jubilee."

WATSON

4. THE JUBILEE PROBLEM

I drew in a breath.

Holmes's grey eyes glittered. "How do you know this?"

"Because the men wanted to store four crates in the basement of my church."

"How large were the crates?" Holmes continued his questioning. His words came more quickly now, as though he was impatient to obtain each new detail.

"I saw them on a lorry, so I cannot be precise. But I would say each was large enough to contain a case of wine bottles."

"Were there markings on the crates?"

"None that I could see."

"Did you ask what the crates contained?"

"The men would only say that I was better off not knowing."

"But you have an idea the contents could be dangerous." He paused, looked carefully at the priest, and then continued. "You suspected explosives, perhaps?"

"The men had already prepared a place to store the crates far at the back of the church basement, in an obscure place hidden from view. I believe the contents need to be protected from water because they built up a stack of wooden pallets on the dirt floor. Even though we are situated on Tower Hill, our basement can flood sometimes after a long period of rain."

"How many men were present to unload the crates?" Holmes asked.

"Only two."

"Did they say how long the crates were to remain in the church?"

"Until June."

"And that is why you made the connection with the Jubilee?"

The priest hesitated, as though recalling something that disturbed him. "Yes, yes, it was the date. The June date. When they said they would take away the crates in June, I remembered that the Queen's Jubilee will begin in June, and I had a bad feeling that something was very much not right. I said nothing to the men about that, of course. But I told them I could not have my parishioners or the children in my shelter who are entrusted to my care involved in anything that was not open and above board. I told them quite firmly. They were very dissatisfied with my answer."

"But not surprised?"

"They understand my duties as a priest supersede what they believe to be my political views. They were dissatisfied, however, as I said, and I very much fear that they will no longer share their confidences with me. So I shall no longer be useful to the Commissioner as an informer."

"When did you refuse the request?"

"About a week ago."

"Can you be more precise?"

"It was two Wednesdays ago, now that I think about it. It was at the end of the day, and I had spoken with 'Sir Robert' earlier that afternoon. I remember my anxiety, that I would have to wait a whole week before letting him know this important information."

"And since the visits from 'Sir Robert' have apparently been discontinued, you wish me to convey this information to the Commissioner."

"You have it, Mr. Holmes."

"Is there anything else?"

"Only that I am being watched more closely now. It may be that my loyalty to the Fenians has come into question, now that I have refused them permission to hide their crates in the church. It may be that my betrayal of their trust has been discovered. Or that such a discovery may occur sometime in future. If that occurs, I know the revenge would be swift and conclusive."

"So if something were to happen to you—an accident, let us say—you are suggesting that the police might do well to investigate the Fenians."

The priest's fingertips went to his close-cropped black hair, massaging his temples. After a moment, he seemed to collect himself. "If it leads to their capture, my death will not be in vain."

"I have a better plan," said Holmes. "We shall follow you to the church, where you will identify the men who are conspiring in this manner. We will then have the police arrest them on some pretext or other and keep them imprisoned until well after the Jubilee celebrations have passed."

Mulloy smiled ruefully. "These men have stopped coming to the church. I cannot point them out, for I do not know when I will see them next."

"You said you were being watched more closely."

"It's more a feeling—a sixth sense, if you will."

"An example, please."

"A person who appears familiar crosses the street at an odd time. A stranger looks away or turns in the other direction when I look at him. But to point out someone solely on that basis—"

Holmes interrupted. "Yet it is possible that some firm evidence may appear. Now I have one more question. When did these Fenian fellows first appear in the church?"

Mulloy reflected for a moment. "It would be—let me see, I remember first noticing them when we were putting up the Advent wreaths. So ... the last week in November."

Holmes nodded. Then he spoke in that distracted manner he takes on when he has no further interest in a conversation. His words came briskly as he stood up from his desk and moved to our dining table. "Then if the situation changes, please send a note to your sister that you will be unable to visit her as planned. Or you might even use the telephone. And then look for me in your confessional booth the next time you receive confessions. For the safety of both of us, I shall have altered my appearance. I shall introduce myself as Sir Robert nonetheless, but before and after doing so I shall clear my throat. You understand?"

Holmes picked up Mulloy's cloak and tossed it to him. "Now, Dr. Watson, please escort Father Mulloy downstairs and keep an eye out for danger as he departs along Baker Street."

He then returned to his desk and busied himself with the papers in which he had been immersed.

Feeling somewhat awkward, and without taking time to get my overcoat, I nonetheless escorted the young priest out to the cold and wind-swept walkway. He pulled the hood of his cloak over his head. Mindful of Holmes's warning, I scanned the street for suspicious characters. I saw none. After our brief exchange of goodbyes, the young priest mounted a bicycle that he had left leaning against our front steps. He soon disappeared among the clamorous flow of vehicles along Baker Street.

As I returned to our sitting room, I was surprised to see Holmes had come away from his desk and was now holding the earpiece connected to our telephone. Holmes said, "Commissioner Bradford has confirmed my hypothesis."

I looked at Holmes, bewildered.

Holmes hung the telephone earpiece on the brass-plated switch hook of that instrument. "The Commissioner has never set foot inside the Church of the English Martyrs, and he has never heard of a priest named Keenan Mulloy."

I continued to stare at Holmes.

"It is as well that the weather is cold," he said. "You can conceal your features beneath your hat and a heavy muffler."

"Where are we going?"

"*You* are going. If you will agree to do so, of course. You will travel to the Church of the English Martyrs and wait there for Father Mulloy to return. If he does, bring him to the Diogenes Club, taking care to obscure his outer appearance with some non-clerical garb. If Father Mulloy has not returned by five o'clock, you are to meet me at the Diogenes Club all the same."

"What should I tell him?"

"You must warn him that his life is in immediate danger. You will have your service revolver with you."

I stared once more. "Who would want to harm a priest?"

Holmes spoke with an exasperating mixture of patience and impatience. "There are three possibilities as to what happened here this morning. The first, and the least likely, is that the man who came here is the real Father Mulloy and was lying to us. The second, and most probable, is that our visitor was the real Father Mulloy and has told us what he believes to be the truth—or as much of the truth as he is able to say and keep his vows. If so, he has been manipulated into telling us this easily discreditable story of a meeting with the Commissioner."

"But why would anyone make up such a story?"

"We do not have sufficient facts to formulate a reliable answer."

"I should have known you would say that. What is the third possibility?"

"The man whom we spoke with may be an imposter."

I stared again, trying to think why anyone would wish to impersonate Father Keenan Mulloy.

Holmes put on his heavy black wool ulster coat. He continued, "You will eliminate that third possibility, of course, if you see Father Mulloy at the church and identify him as our visitor of this morning."

WATSON

5. THE CHURCH OF THE ENGLISH MARTYRS

The inside of the church was cold and hard. Faint shadows cloaked the huge stone columns. In the great circular window above the altar, the colours of the stained glass were barely visible. I walked towards the main altar, passing a hooded woman in one of the pews to my right. A few candles flickered along the opposite wall, lit in memory of the departed. At the corner of a small altar rail, another woman—older than the first and with a black scarf covering her head—knelt in prayer before the candles. I turned around and walked back. Facing me on my left were the ornately carved wooden confessional booths. I had hoped to find Father Mulloy there, but both booths were empty. I waited for a moment while my eyes adjusted to the dim atmosphere. I loosened my muffler and took off my hat.

The woman who had been praying in the pew stood up and drew back her hood. She placed her index finger to her lips.

She was Lucy James.

The sight of Holmes's lovely daughter always has an effect on me—partly of gladness, partly of relief that she is safe. I was happy to comply as she silently beckoned me to follow her to the vestibule outside the sanctuary. When we reached the vestibule, she leaned close to my ear and spoke quietly.

"I'm waiting for Father Mulloy. What are you doing here?"

"The same. He was with us in Baker Street earlier."

She opened the door to the street. Cold wind ruffled her dark brown hair, and she put up her hood. "His rooms are in the building next door, although he is not there just now. I have his sister's key."

Concealed beneath her hood, she might have been anyone. In only a few moments she had unlocked the door to the building where Mulloy lived. Moments later we were inside his small room, a Spartan, anonymous affair on the ground floor. We saw stark white painted walls, a metal-framed bed with grey wool blankets and no pillow, a shabby wooden wardrobe, and a small bookshelf with a few tracts, a bible, and a prayer book.

Lucy locked the door behind us. "Yesterday he was at my flat on Exeter Street, visiting his sister. He looked furtive and ashamed, as well as worried."

"This morning he appeared to be hiding something as well."

Briefly I explained what had happened, concluding, "Holmes believes Father Mulloy's life to be in danger."

"Did he say why?"

"It was Holmes's conclusion. He did not enlighten me."

She sat down on the bed. "Let's see what *we* can conclude."

"Very well."

"We'll start with what we know. The priest told a false story. At least, the part about the Commissioner coming to see him was false."

"But he may not have known that. Holmes does not think that he was lying to us this morning, only that he was withholding something."

"So he looked furtive and ashamed when I saw him yesterday, and he was hiding something from Holmes this morning. But we assume that he was telling the truth about the visits from someone he believed to be Commissioner Bradford. Those visits really happened. So what do we conclude from these facts?"

I recalled Holmes's words. "Someone has gone to a great deal of trouble to manipulate him into telling an easily discreditable story."

"Because someone wants to ensure that he will not be believed if he tells whatever it is that he is hiding." Lucy stood up. "If he really is in danger, he will probably be killed in a manner supporting the idea that he is delusional." She bent over, gripping the top of the painted metal bedframe. "Help me turn this over."

"What are you doing?"

"If we cannot find Father Mulloy, we can at least try to find what he knows. Maybe he's left a clue."

But at that moment the door opened.

Keenan Mulloy stood staring at us open-mouthed.

There was no question that this was the man I had seen in our Baker Street rooms, but it was obvious that he had been in an altercation of some sort. His left eye was swollen, and there were abrasions on his left cheek. Moreover, there was a ragged tear at the right shoulder of his cloak, and it bore patches of mud, indicating that he had fallen.

Lucy said, "You were fighting."

The priest continued to stare, but his eyes took on a guarded look.

"Your knuckles are banged up," Lucy continued. "I hope you gave as well as you got."

Finally he spoke. "What are you doing here?"

Lucy tilted the bed back to its upright position. "We were trying to find you. We thought there might be a clue here in this room."

I added, "Holmes believes you are in danger. Your appearance indicates that he is correct."

Mulloy looked obstinate. "What grounds does he have for this belief?"

"The Commissioner has never heard of you. Holmes telephoned Scotland Yard."

Mulloy did not change his expression. "It appears I gave Holmes more credit than he deserves. Of course the Commissioner would say that. It was a matter of the utmost secrecy, not to be shared with anyone!"

I was about to protest that the Commissioner held Holmes in the very highest regard and would have trusted him with his life. Indeed, the Commissioner had done precisely that on several occasions. But Lucy gave me a warning glance.

To Mulloy she said, "Please don't think that we don't believe you. Quite the contrary. We were worried for you, however, since you might have been followed and since 221B Baker Street is known to the public. You don't have to explain your appearance if you don't want to. But Holmes does believe you would be safer if you came with us."

"To where?"

"To Pall Mall," I said. "There is a safe haven there."

The priest folded his arms across his chest. "My place is here. If something happens to me, my soul is prepared, as I told Mr. Holmes."

"You said he ought to look to the Fenians if some harm came to you." I said this for Lucy's benefit, as I did not recall telling her this part of our morning's interview.

Lucy said, "Tell me about that."

* * *

A few minutes later we were in the basement of the church, walking carefully, holding lighted candles. Lucy had asked Mulloy to show us where the Fenians had intended to store the crates that he thought would have contained explosives. The floor was dirt, and we were looking for footprints. "We won't investigate further," Lucy had promised. "I just want to see if there is something that might help us identify who brought in the crates."

Candlelight flickered on the mottled brown stones of the walls around us, flakes of whitewash curling and drooping where moisture and chemicals in the atmosphere had assaulted them over the past decade. On the brown dirt against the wall was an array of four wooden pallets set into a square. Between us and the pallets were several clear sets of footprints.

Mulloy said, "No one comes down here, as I told Mr. Holmes. So although three weeks have elapsed, these footprints are likely to be those of the Fenians."

Lucy said, "I am glad we can confirm at least *this* part of your story to Mr. Holmes. Now there is just one more question I have. We can wait until we are outside, however. This dank air is oppressive. I should like to see where the cart waited with the crates."

We reached the outdoor courtyard.

Mulloy pointed to a spot in the yellow mud near the hatchway that led to the basement. "There is where the cart bearing the crates was being unloaded. No trace remains, I suppose, since we have had three weeks of weather to obscure cart tracks and footprints. Now, what was your question, Miss James?"

"Forgive me, but I must be very direct with you, Father Mulloy. Other than the attempt to store explosives here, what else do you know about a plot to harm the Queen's Jubilee celebration?"

"How could I know such information?"

Lucy shrugged. "A priest hears many secrets."

Mulloy's face flushed deeply. "You are referring to the sacrament of Confession, I take it."

"Not that I—we—would ask you to betray the confidence of a penitent. You need not tell us anything you think—"

The priest was becoming more agitated. " 'Need' is not the criteria for judgment here, Miss James. I am bound to absolute silence by the highest, most sacred vows of the church—not just at penalty of my position as a priest, but under peril of my immortal soul. I can tell you nothing."

"Your manner indicates that you do possess some knowledge that would endanger those who would commit treason and, therefore, knowledge that endangers you. Someone may want you permanently silenced."

"I can tell you nothing."

Lucy's green eyes held a sorrowful appeal as she faced the priest. "I ask that you please reconsider. You should come with us to Whitehall."

Mulloy shook his head. "I fear I remain unable to accompany you, Miss James. My place is here."

"Not even to help your sister?"

"What does Mary have to do with this?"

"I came here today because she is not at my flat on Exeter Street and she did not attend rehearsal this morning. Whoever wants you to be silent may have taken her in order to gain a hold over you."

The priest relaxed and gave a wry smile. "Actually, I anticipated that possibility. Mary is quite safe. She has gone home to Ireland. Yesterday I took her to Euston Station and put her on the train for Liverpool."

Lucy's eyes narrowed. For a long moment she was silent. Then she said, "I hope you change your mind. If you do, please send word to Mr. Holmes."

We left immediately. In the cab on our way to the Diogenes Club, Lucy said, "Mary has an audition for the Duchess of Devonshire's ball tomorrow. There is no way on earth that she would consent to go to Ireland."

LUCY

6. AT THE DIOGENES CLUB

The Diogenes Club stood on Waterloo Place, its white columned entrance giving it a stately, neoclassical splendor. There was something about its dignified stolidity that always made me want, just a little, to do something outrageous, like set off a round of firecrackers or decorate the perfect alabaster-white facade with stripes of bright green or red.

Although tonight that could have been because worry and frustration over Keenan Mulloy, combined with the press of uncomfortable remembrances, were making me feel as though my blood were too hot, my chest too tight.

Sometimes London felt welcoming to me, with its fierce rush of life and streets that seemed to breathe with voices from every far-flung corner of the British Empire. Other times it seemed dangerous, mysterious, with its mazes of blind alleys and thick yellow fogs. Tonight, what it mostly felt was haunted, although I couldn't be sure whether that was because of the city's history or my own.

Our cab drew up in front of the club. I watched Dr. Watson— or Uncle John, as I had over the past months come to call him.

Shadows from the shrubbery and trees in the adjacent Waterloo Gardens pooled on the street, intensifying the growing darkness.

Less than two years ago and only a few feet from here, the late Colonel Sebastian Moran had emerged from the same shadows of the garden to light an incendiary bomb.

Now I wondered whether Uncle John was thinking of Colonel Moran, too. From the tense line of his mouth and the shadowed look about his eyes, I thought he might be. Unfortunately, I couldn't think of a way to comfort his remembered fears without revealing my own.

If I had learned nothing else in my twenty-two years in the world, it was that weakness was seldom rewarded—not ever, really, but particularly not in the life I had chosen.

I compromised by smiling as Watson offered me his hand to help me down from the carriage.

"The Diogenes Club. Famous refuge of the most unsociable and unclubbable men in all of London," I said.

Uncle John's face relaxed in an answering smile. "It's nice to know that at least one member of your family values my stories enough to quote from them."

"Of course. *The Adventure of the Greek Interpreter* had me absolutely spellbound."

It was just after sunset, with fog rolling in misty ribbons down the street, but I could make out the figures of two uniformed police constables guarding the Diogenes Club doorway and several more ringing the perimeter of the building.

"There must be a visitor of some importance expected here tonight," I murmured.

Uncle John looked momentarily puzzled. "Why should you … ah, of course. The police presence."

I studied the faces of the constables on duty as we approached, my heart quickening a little, but none of them were familiar.

I almost sighed, but gave myself a hard mental kick instead. I hadn't seen Detective Constable Jack Kelly in the last week, but tonight we had graver concerns.

I started up the club's front steps, then paused, fighting the urge to square my shoulders, straighten my spine, lock my jaw—or possibly all three at once.

"Is something wrong?" Uncle John asked.

"I was just bracing myself."

"You needn't worry about the club members. They may express disapproval of your being here, but they can't actually demand that you leave."

I shook my head. It was true that I wouldn't be entirely welcome inside the Diogenes Club. Actually, disapproval was rather too mild a word.

I had learned on my first visit here that being young, female, and possibly still worse *an American* inside its hallowed doors was somewhere akin to being as out of place as a fish on dry land—and approximately as welcome as a dead rat in the middle of the tea table. Everyone was perfectly capable of ignoring you, certainly, but they weren't really enjoying their cup of Darjeeling or Gunmetal Green, either.

"I'm not worried about the club members," I said. Their inevitable outrage was more or less their bother, not mine. "It's Holmes. I was just imagining what he'll say at hearing that I was at Father Mulloy's church today."

For the past several months, my father and I had been engaged in a kind of unspoken tug-of-war: Sherlock Holmes trying to protect me and keep me out of our investigation of a ring of German spies, and me refusing to leave him to face the danger on his own.

Now Uncle John patted my hand. "It's only because he worries about you, my dear."

"I know. Just as I worry about him. He's pushing himself too hard."

"As usual."

"But if he makes a mistake—if he lets down his guard because he's fatigued—"

"I worry too. But we must carry on."

Nonetheless, the memory of Colonel Moran returned. At the time, I thought it an unbidden warning of the ruthlessness of Holmes's opponents. They would kill him if they could. I needed to remain at my father's side, whether he wanted me there or not.

One of the uniformed constables at the door nodded to us as we approached, while the other raised a hand in greeting, showing the blue and white striped armlet that identified him as being on duty.

The club doorman, as stately and dignified as the club itself, bowed in greeting and ushered us in.

As expected, I heard a cacophony of outraged newspaper rattling and throat-clearing from the reading room as Watson and I passed by. Though as Uncle John had said, the same club rules that forbade any conversation whatsoever prevented anyone from actually shouting at me to be gone.

My father was waiting at the foot of the stairs that led to the club's upper floors, his sharp, hawk-like features unsurprised, but also slightly grim about the mouth at the sight of me.

Sometimes the best defense is a vigorous offense—another fact I had learned some time ago. I waited until we were on the stairs, out of earshot of the club members, before asking, "Why was I expected?"

The tight lines of Sherlock Holmes's face relaxed just a fraction, and he raised an eyebrow at me in silent question.

I made a quick, impatient gesture. "Obviously I was expected, otherwise the doorman would never have let me in the door."

In addition to the no-speaking rule, the Diogenes was a strictly male preserve.

This time, the twitch of my father's lips was just short of becoming a smile. He might not relish my putting myself in harm's way, but I thought he did sometimes permit himself to appreciate the fact that—for better or worse—our minds sometimes followed similar paths.

"A message was sent to your flat in Exeter Street, asking you to come here. The Prince of Wales evidently has a role in mind for you in the security arrangements for the Jubilee."

"The Prince? That is a relief."

Uncle John gave me a puzzled glance. "Why a relief?"

Holmes answered for me. "I believe Lucy is interpreting his willingness to involve her in matters of national security as a sign he has given up all thought of romantic pursuit."

The Prince had expressed interest in me last year—interest that had tempted me not at all. His Royal Highness wasn't a bad man, but he was a self-indulgent one, and aside from being old enough to be my father, he seemed to have difficulty remaining faithful to the same woman for longer than five minutes.

Fortunately he had lost interest before my rejection reached the point of being awkward, though whether it was me or my father who had frightened him off, I wasn't sure.

"Do you know what the job is?" I asked Holmes.

"Indeed," Holmes said. His jaw tightened, brows drawing together in a scowl that had been known to give grown men weeks of nightmares. "I am hoping you will decline, since it is likely to involve a not inconsiderable degree of danger. Though I do not for a moment expect those hopes to be realized."

I sighed.

I loved knowing that Sherlock Holmes was my father, especially as I had spent most of my life alone in the world, with no idea of who my parents might be. Looking at it from Holmes's perspective, though, I had to admit it was something of a cosmic irony that fate had delivered me to his door.

Sherlock Holmes was brilliant, self-sufficient, and utterly unused to anyone questioning his considerable authority.

Now he had a daughter who questioned his authority almost daily.

I matched him, scowl for scowl. So far tonight, there had been no sign that we were in immediate danger. But something—the thought of Keenan Mulloy's bruises? The memory of the Moran affair?—was making a nameless, formless anxiety crawl up the length of my spine.

"That is fortunate, because I do not for a moment expect to decline."

A servant appeared at the foot of the stairs and spoke in a low, respectful tone. "Dr. Watson? A gentleman is asking to speak with you on the telephone, sir. He gave his name as Father Mulloy."

Uncle John's face brightened—partly with hope that Keenan had changed his mind, partly with what I suspected was relief at being allowed to make his escape.

I turned back to Holmes, trying to speak in a conciliatory tone. "I assume you have deduced from the three drops of wax from the altar candles on the sleeve of my jacket that I was at the Church of the English Martyrs tonight. And from the way I am grinding my teeth together, that I failed to convince Keenan Mulloy to take steps to protect his own life."

"Indeed." My father's scowl faded, to be replaced by a look approaching resignation.

I breathed a covert sigh of relief. The war might be far from over, but this particular battle had been won.

"We must hope his telephone call to Watson is a hopeful sign."

We had reached the top of the stairs. At the end of the hall that stretched before us stood a pair of oaken double-doors. A tall man in a worn frock coat, hunched over with a stack of documents, hurriedly opened the doors and slipped inside without so much as a glance at us.

Holmes approached the same doors and knocked lightly.

A voice called from inside, "Come in."

LUCY

7. A FEAR TAKES SHAPE

The doors led into a small antechamber, lined with shelves of books and carpeted with an oriental rug, that opened out onto what looked to be a larger meeting room.

Mycroft Holmes sat in a winged armchair, just inside the door.

"Come in?" Holmes gave his brother a look of inquiry. "Without so much as a request that we identify ourselves?"

Mycroft's large hands gripped the arms of the chair as he heaved his bulky figure up to a standing position. "Of course I knew who you were, Sherlock." His voice was very like his brother's, though with the slight wheeze of the very obese. "The sole of your right shoe has an eighth-of-an-inch thick area of unevenness on the heel. It gives your step a distinctive and immediately identifiable sound as you approach."

My father's eyes narrowed just a fraction. "I see you have recently engaged a new valet."

"And you have been to the opera sometime in the last two— no, three—nights."

"I hope the letter you received from Manchester this afternoon contained no bad news."

"Not at all. And may I say, Sherlock, that I hope the remodeling work being done on the house next door to yours on Baker Street causes you no annoyance."

The brothers Holmes were fond of each other, I believed—or as fond of each other as they could be of anyone. Certainly they respected one another's intellect. But watching them in conversation was something like witnessing a match of lawn tennis played at a dizzying speed.

"The Prime Minister is inside," Mycroft said. "With Lansdowne and two of his assistants."

"And the man who just entered before us?" I asked.

"That was Captain Stayley, chief of staff to the Duke of Devonshire," Mycroft said.

I frowned. "I don't believe I know either of them."

"The Duke is president of the Queen's Privy Council and responsible for the Cabinet's Defense Committee. Stayley has been with him for nearly a decade."

Mycroft led the way into the larger inner room.

At the end of a long mahogany table sat Lord Salisbury, Prime Minister of England. His dark curly whiskers, so often caricatured in the press, were as capacious as ever, spreading out and downward to cover his shirtfront and necktie.

To his left sat the familiar tall and aristocratic figure of Secretary of War Lansdowne. I had met Lord Lansdowne before. In fact, Holmes, Uncle John and I might be said to have saved his life twice.

Now Lansdowne inclined his high-domed brow in our direction, smiling an acknowledgement beneath his gray mustaches.

Seated on Lansdowne's left were two watchful-looking men. One was heavy-set and florid in complexion, blond and obviously Nordic in ancestry. The other man was dark-haired and clearly Italian, with swarthy cheeks and a gray, unhealthful pallor about his lean features.

The two men might be clerks, but I thought it more likely that their job description was somewhere nearer to the neighborhood of bodyguard. Both had a taut, watchful air, as though constantly evaluating their surroundings for any threat.

A cheery coal fire burned in the fireplace, and to our right, a decanter and glasses had been set out on the sideboard.

Before the Prime Minister, a map was spread out to cover most of the table's polished wood surface.

Lord Salisbury spoke. "Gentlemen. Miss James. Please be seated." He gave a perfunctory nod to the man beside him—the same man Mycroft had identified as the Duke of Devonshire's chief of staff. "This is Captain Stayley. I have asked him to join us because the Duke is otherwise engaged. He works tirelessly on the Duke's behalf—some would say too tirelessly, eh, Captain? Captain, this is Mr. Sherlock Holmes. You know his brother Mycroft. And the young lady is Miss Lucy James, an associate of Mr. Holmes and of whom the Prince has spoken. You are all welcome to take refreshment. No? Well then, let us get to the business at hand. Miss James, you will understand the reason for your presence here in a moment. Captain Stayley and Mr. Holmes"—he nodded toward Mycroft—"will you please continue."

Stayley was a tall man, with pleasant, well-cut features, though at the moment he looked rather careworn, with shadows under his eyes and lines of tension bracketing his mouth.

He nodded to acknowledge the introduction and reached for a leather-bound box that sat beside the map.

"Certainly, Prime Minister. This morning the Master of the Horses Committee settled on a route for the Jubilee Day parade. I shall arrange these"—he opened the leather-bound box to reveal a set of ivory chess pieces—"to depict the route."

I watched Captain Stayley arrange the chess pieces on the map.

I was trying to keep my mind focused, but the nameless anxiety from before was growing, coalescing into a clump of ice that sat in the pit of my stomach, refusing to dissolve.

I couldn't shake the feeling that I had missed something, some fragmentary detail that I ought to have made note of or remembered—

Stayley set the chessmen up in rows, some straight and some curved to twist back upon each other, serpentine fashion, following the streets of London, describing the streets as he went.

As Stayley went on, I kept trying to identify what was making me feel so uneasy. I cast my mind back, all the way back to Uncle John's and my arrival, trying to pinpoint the moment when my sense of there being something wrong had begun.

The shadowed street outside ... the memories of Sebastian Moran ...

No, that wasn't what was troubling me.

Stayley set the last piece in place. "As you can see, these chessmen form a convoluted circle that begins and ends at Buckingham Palace."

"And you fear an attack may occur?" Holmes asked.

The Prime Minister gave him a startled look, to which Holmes responded with a brusque wave of one hand.

"We are presumably here in this meeting for a reason, are we not? It hardly requires a great cognitive leap to deduce anxiety over an attack."

I sat up with a sudden jolt. "The police constable on duty at the door!"

Lord Salisbury looked at me in some astonishment, as did all the other gentlemen in the room.

I turned to Holmes, speaking as fast and as urgently as I could. "Outside the door were two uniformed police constables. One of them raised a hand to acknowledge us when we came in, and I saw his armlet. It was on his right arm."

I had watched Jack get ready to go on duty dozens of times. I could picture it in my mind: the brass-buttoned navy police constable's tunic, the wide leather belt, a lantern, clipped to the belt on the right side, a heavy wooden truncheon on the left.

And the blue and white arm band that identified him as being on duty, invariably worn on his *left* arm.

The significance of what I'd seen registered instantly in Holmes's gray gaze. His head snapped up, and he leapt out of his chair—just as the doors to the outer room crashed open.

The constable from outside bore down on us.

He had abandoned the police helmet, leaving his face exposed. He was young, with a thatch of fiery red hair and a freckled face that should have been open and friendly, but now was set in a tense, white-lipped look, part terror, part furious determination.

Holmes was on his feet, already moving to intercept him. The young man raised a hand, which I now saw clasped a gun.

"No!" My lips shaped the word, but I wasn't sure whether any sound emerged; if it did, it was lost in the roar as the weapon discharged.

"*Erin go Brach!*" The gunman shouted the words as he fired.

I saw my father jerk back as though punched and then topple over.

I scrambled to my feet, but Captain Stayley was there before me, throwing himself headlong at the gunman, tackling him, and dragging him to the ground.

I caught just a glimpse of the young gunman's white face and wide, astonished blue eyes. Then they both fell in a scramble of arms and legs. Before I could move—before anyone in the room could move—the gun barked again. The young red-haired man's body convulsed once, then lay still.

WATSON

8. NĒWS

The Prince of Wales was about to speak when we heard the gunfire.

He had entered the lobby of the Diogenes Club just as I had set down the telephone on the club visitor's desk.

For an instant, both the Prince and I stood frozen. Almost as one, we both started for the stairs.

Two men appeared, barring the way—personal bodyguards of His Royal Highness, I surmised, from their military bearing and determined air.

"Your highness, we cannot permit—"

"It is not safe—"

I scarcely heard them. My attention was fixed on what I would find upstairs. Ducking past the guard, I made for the stairway and raced up, taking the steps two at a time.

A set of double-doors at the end of a long hallway stood open. I burst into the room beyond, my gaze taking in the scene before me at a glance.

On the floor sprawled the dead body of a man in the uniform of a police constable.

Immediately before me sat Sherlock Holmes, with Lucy wrapping an already blood-soaked white cloth around his arm. Holmes was speaking, though I caught only the last part of the remark.

"—scarcely alters facts. We knew already that the corruption had spread to a level that would allow someone among our adversaries to purloin a police uniform for our nameless Fenian here." He indicated the body. "Although it is perhaps significant that he knew of this meeting, which would indicate—"

Lucy drew the makeshift bandage tighter. Her hands were steady, but she looked rather pale. "Maybe you could wait to theorize until you're not in danger of bleeding to death?"

Holmes glanced unconcernedly at his bloodied arm. "I hardly think the wound has any possibility of proving fatal. The bullet scarcely grazed me."

Lord Salisbury's eyebrows rose. "Fenian? How can you be certain?"

Holmes gestured with his uninjured hand. "I admit we cannot identify his allegiance with absolute certainty. He did, however, use the Fenian slogan or battle cry, and—" Holmes glanced at Lucy. "What was that very colourful American expression I heard you employ the other day? Ah, yes. If it resembles a duck and vocalizes in the manner of a duck, one may be reasonably justified in assuming it to be a member of the anatine family."

Lucy still looked pale with the aftermath of fear, but her lips curved in a very small smile—a fact that I suspected was not lost on Holmes.

"Close enough."

By now the Prince's two bodyguards had entered the room. At the Prime Minister's nod, they bent over the fallen constable.

They lifted his body as easily as if he were a sack of potatoes. A few moments later they were gone. No traces of blood were on the carpet. Nothing remained of the incident other than Holmes's minor wound and the smell of cordite.

Lord Lansdowne turned to a tall, dark-haired man who stood to one side, appearing rather dazed. "Captain Stayley, we owe you a great debt. If not for your prompt and courageous action—"

Captain Stayley's eyes were fixed and slightly glassy. His hands shook badly. "Thank you, sir." He seemed to speak automatically.

"Go downstairs and get yourself something to drink, man," Lord Salisbury advised him. "Then you may go home. You've had a bad shock."

Captain Stayley swallowed visibly. "Yes, sir. Thank you, sir." The door closed behind him.

"He was with the Duke's younger brother in Dublin in '82," Mycroft murmured.

I saw Lucy open her mouth, but Holmes anticipated her question.

"The Duke's brother was sent to Dublin in May of 1882 as the Crown's Chief Secretary for Ireland. The day he arrived, he was brutally murdered in a knife attack by Irish partisans hostile to the Empire."

Mycroft added, "Captain Stayley barely escaped death as well. He hates the Fenians with a passion."

Lord Salisbury offered drinks once more and poured one for himself. "The Prince will be here soon," he said. "While we await his arrival, I suggest that Mycroft Holmes, who attended the Committee with me this morning, provide us with additional detail concerning the parade and the dangers we may anticipate."

Mycroft said, "The date of the parade has been set down as Tuesday, June 22. That will be the principal day of celebration. Fifty thousand troops representing military forces throughout the Commonwealth will ride on horseback to escort Her Majesty and hundreds of dignitaries throughout the parade, following the route you see here. The stack of documents the Captain has brought in contains the names of invitees from the various nations and provinces. Persons of highest rank will ride in open coaches, including, of course Her Majesty. She will carry a white parasol, and eight cream-colored horses will propel the Royal Carriage. There will be no mistaking our Queen, even at a distance."

Mycroft placed a pudgy finger on the top of one of the chess pieces, a bishop, that Stayley had set down on the map. "During the Jubilee celebration of ten years ago, the service of thanksgiving was held inside St. Paul's Cathedral. This year, however, the service will be held directly outside the cathedral. Bleachers will be erected for the principal attendees at the West Entrance. The Queen will remain in her carriage."

"Thus providing a large, convenient, stationary target for those who wish to cause harm," Holmes said. His voice was dry.

Lord Salisbury stiffened. "The palace is reluctant to show Her Majesty at a disadvantage. She cannot climb into or out of her carriage without assistance. Nor can she climb the steps to enter the cathedral. So two thousand Anglican churchmen and political dignitaries will be seated on bleachers outside the cathedral at noon on June 22, trusting to Divine Providence that there will not be rain."

Holmes gave him the half-lidded gaze that made him appear faintly bored, but in fact it meant that his thoughts were racing far ahead of anyone else's. Then he said, "If there is an attack, rain will be the least of our worries. Will Kaiser Wilhelm be invited?"

"He will not," Mycroft said. "The official position is that the Queen, being of an advanced age, feels herself unable to sustain the effort necessary to entertain any crowned heads of state at the level to which they are entitled or accustomed. Heads of state outside the Commonwealth are not to be invited."

"Then if Wilhelm knows he has not been invited—" Holmes began.

"Which he does—"

"Wilhelm may bankroll a group of assassins to create havoc without fear for his personal safety," Holmes continued. "Having failed twice before to undermine our government, he may find this third opportunity irresistible."

The Prime Minister turned up an empty palm. "We cannot know the inner workings of a madman's mind. However, it is our mutual task to see that the Jubilee proceeds."

At that moment, the door opened again, and in the doorway stood the Prince of Wales.

We rose as one. Holmes angled his torso slightly so that his bandaged arm faced away from the Prince.

"Evening, Salisbury," the Prince said. His clear gaze swept the table. "Evening, Lansdowne. Are we ready to meet?"

Lord Salisbury inclined his head respectfully.

"Then let's get on."

We all sat. The Prince took the chair to the right of the Prime Minister, next to Lansdowne.

He continued. "I understand that the assassin Arkwright is dead."

WATSON
9. DEVONSHIRE AND ELSWICK

We stared. I saw the glint of satisfaction in the Prince's eye. It was a far different expression we had seen from him last October, when only quick action by Holmes and Lucy had prevented Adrian Arkwright from exploding a bomb that would have killed the Prince and all of us as well.

"You lot look surprised. Didn't you tell them, Salisbury?"

"I was just about to ask Lord Lansdowne to do so."

The Prince shrugged. Lansdowne leaned forward.

"We have decided to keep this information secret, Your Royal Highness, apart from my two assistants here, Mr. Bretton and Mr. Greco. Each was privy to the communication when it arrived this morning, and each is, sir, completely reliable."

Lansdowne paused momentarily, turning away as the Prince, having lit up a fat cigar, puffed a cloud of tobacco smoke. Then Lansdowne took out a yellow telegraph message from his vest pocket. "As you know, I had given instructions for Arkwright to be interrogated after he reached the Andaman Islands. I had expected a long voyage in the brig of a warship would have undermined that defiant attitude of his. Today this came to me at the War Office." He read aloud:

COL B. RAWLINGS, PORT BLAIR TO SECRETARY LANSDOWNE, WHITEHALL. SIR:
AT YOUR INSTRUCTION THE PRISONER ADRIAN ARKWRIGHT WAS SUBJECTED TO INTENSE INTERVIEW PROCEDURE 9-11 AM THURSDAY FEB. 11 ON ROSS ISLAND. TRANSCRIPT OF INTERVIEW HAS BEEN SENT BY COURIER. TWO WORDS WERE OBTAINED WITH DIFFICULTY AND ARE PRESUMABLY IMPORTANT: "DEVONSHIRE" AND "ELSWICK." ARKWRIGHT WAS IN POOR HEALTH FOLLOWING THE INTERVIEW AND WAS PLACED IN SICK BAY THE EVENING OF THE 11TH. HE REVIVED AND ESCAPED EARLY THE NEXT MORNING, BUT WHEN ATTEMPTING TO SWIM TO A FISHING BOAT OFFSHORE FROM WHERE HE HAD HIDDEN IN A CLUMP OF MANGROVES HE WAS KILLED BY A SALTWATER CROCODILE. REMAINS WILL BE BURIED IN PRISON CEMETERY.

"How long until the courier brings the transcript?" asked the Prince.

Mycroft said, "Three days to Bombay, two weeks to Suez, a week more to London. Three weeks if they have good fortune with the weather and four weeks if they do not."

"Intolerable delay. The entire transcript ought to be sent by telegram."

"Secrecy is an issue, Your Royal Highness," Mycroft said.

"Can't you put the damn thing into code, military fashion?"

"Mr. Greco?" Lansdowne looked inquiringly at his dark-complexioned assistant and received a respectful nod in return. "Sir, we will send a wire to have that done immediately," said Lansdowne.

The Prince nodded. "Now. What do you make of the word 'Devonshire' in that telegram?"

"It could be anything," said Lansdowne. "It might refer to the county of Devon. Or to the Duke of Devonshire."

"It might refer to a plan involving the Duke," said the Prime Minister. "Arkwright was an assassin, after all."

"A plan to kill Lord Cavendish?" The Prince appeared sceptical. "I would think the stakes would be higher than just the death of one man—important though he may be. I'll tell you what occurred to me when I saw a copy of that telegram this morning. I think 'Devonshire' refers to Devonshire House. The Duchess plans a Jubilee event there." He paused and looked at Lucy. "Are you aware of that, Miss James?"

"The Duchess's costume ball is already the talk of the theatrical set," Lucy said. "A young actress friend of mine is auditioning."

"And I am obliged to attend," said the Prince. A shrewd glint appeared in his close-set eyes. "So if there is some plot afoot, I want it quashed."

Heads nodded respectfully. The Prince warmed to his theme. "The parade may not be the target"—he gestured at the chessmen on the map—"though of course it makes for a whopping great bulls-eye with Her Majesty and everyone of any significance in the Empire all concentrated in one location. But the parade may not be the only point of attack. At Devonshire House you'll have me and a lot of others who are worth an assassin's attentions. Including you, Lansdowne. And Lansdowne House is just next door."

"We shall have guards, of course."

"At night, with people running about in masks and costumes? You're going to have a devil of a time. How would it look to have armed guards interrupting a party given to honour the Queen? I'm sure my mother would not be pleased with that. We have to be sure before we take action." He paused, and the shrewd glint reappeared. "But I have an idea on that score."

All waited.

The Prince pointed his cigar at Lucy. "I've seen the abilities of Miss James, here. It strikes me that she would be the perfect solution to this problem. She can be one of the entertainers and mingle about, keep an eye on things, raise the alarm if there is real trouble. The ball will be the social event of the year, Miss James, which ought to do your acting credentials a bit of good. Not that they need it, of course," he added with a courtly smile. "What say you, Miss James?"

Lucy carefully avoided looking at Holmes. "Who could resist such an opportunity?"

"We shall see to it that you are hired," the Prince said. "I shall attend the audition."

"I should need to observe the preparations and identify risks," Lucy said. "Not just attend rehearsals in the ordinary way."

Holmes said, "A pretext must be found for that. Miss James must not be seen to be an investigator, or her ability to function will be compromised and her life will be endangered before the event even begins."

"I am certain you will be equal to the necessary arrangements," said the Prime Minister.

I shook my head in wonderment at the politician's ability to shift the responsibility for the Devonshire social event to Holmes.

The Prime Minister went on before Holmes could protest. "Now, however, I have another problem for you as well, Mr. Holmes."

Holmes said, "I presume you refer to the other word in the telegram: 'Elswick.' "

"What the devil are you talking about?" asked the Prince.

Lansdowne's face was pale. "We had a report at the War Office about a month ago. One of the naval cannons manufactured at the Elswick arms factory was sent to Liverpool for shipment to Japan. But the Japanese government lodged a formal complaint. The gun never arrived." He paused. "I do not yet have all the details, but I am reliably informed that the cannon can fire a shell with explosive force sufficient to obliterate this building, from a distance of eight thousand yards. That is four and one half miles, gentlemen. This missing gun might be brought in under cover of darkness and hidden anywhere in London. Imagine what it might do to the Jubilee celebration."

WATSON

10. A MATTER FOR THE POLICE

We left shortly thereafter. Lucy had a performance that night at the Savoy, so Holmes insisted that we accompany her to the theatre. I was looking forward to supper at the Savoy restaurant next door. However, Holmes bade me wait in the cab while he escorted Lucy into the theatre lobby.

Upon his return, he ordered the cabman to take us to the Church of the English Martyrs.

Less than an hour later, I raised my knuckles and knocked at the door to Father Mulloy's room in Whitechapel. I could hear Mulloy's agitated voice through the thin wood.

"Who's there?"

"Two friends," Holmes said quietly.

The priest opened the door. A Bible was in his hand. He had washed his face, but the dark bruising typically found after a sharp blow had begun to discolour the flesh around his left eye.

"You must trust us," Holmes said, keeping his voice barely audible. "Please get your cloak. Do not speak until we are outside."

Something in Holmes's manner must have gotten through to Mulloy, for he obeyed. Once outside, we made our way to Commercial Street, keeping to the shadows. "Where are we going?" Mulloy whispered.

"We are going to walk briskly for about fifteen minutes until we reach the Commercial Street Police Station. If we are fortunate, we may be able to speak there with Constable Kelly. If not, we shall leave him a message. The men who are following us at this moment—no, do not look around, Father Mulloy—will conclude that you have reported the attack upon your person this afternoon. They will realize they have nothing to gain by attempting to silence you. Now please, no further questions. Walk as quickly as you can, keeping between Watson and me. Watson, keep your revolver at the ready."

We were doubly fortunate. We reached the station—an oddly elongated structure of heavy concrete and brick—unopposed. Constable Kelly was also on duty there. We huddled around Kelly's small desk in a corner of the second floor, keeping our voices down so as not to be overheard. Holmes gave a brief account of the situation, though without mentioning a connection with the Jubilee.

Kelly promised to have Mulloy escorted safely back to his room, and the young priest agreed to the plan.

Then Holmes said, "By the way, Constable, when you first learned of the Fenian presence at the church, did you speak with the Commissioner?"

"I made the trek to New Scotland Yard to do just that before going home that evening," said Kelly. "But he was away. I left him a note."

"Do you recall the note?"

"Perfectly. It said that a priest that I knew had told me something of interest and that I wanted to discuss it with him."

"And what was his response?"

"There was none. He never responded."

Mulloy said, "He never responded to *you*. He responded to me."

Holmes gave one of his patronizing overly patient slow nods. "Be that as it may, Father, I have been thinking about your logic. It seems remarkable."

"In what way?"

"The Fenians wanted to store crates until June. The Jubilee celebration will be in June. Therefore, the Fenians are planning to attack the Jubilee."

"Nevertheless, that was my conclusion."

"The crates were the sole rationale?"

"Yes."

"Nothing else? No other event, or clue, or perhaps a warning from some other source that you are unwilling to disclose? Come, come, Father. We are long accustomed to discretion. You may rely on us."

Once more I saw a deep red flush spread upward from Mulloy's white collar to his ears and then to his face and forehead. He folded his arms across his chest, pressed his lips tightly together, and said nothing.

We were never again to see Father Keenan Mulloy alive.

PART TWO

AND MOCK THE TIME

LUCY

11. NŌNE SHALL PART US

Tonight was Monday, the 7th of June. A small, blonde-haired girl was singing, sitting beside me on the piano bench in my flat on Exeter Street.

"That was excellent, Becky," I said, when she had done.

Becky turned. "Really?"

"Really. You know, in a few years' time, you could speak to Mr. Harris about auditioning to be in the chorus of the D'Oyly Carte Company. He sometimes takes girls as young as sixteen."

"*Really?*" Becky beamed, her face turning pink beneath the scattering of freckles across her nose. She bounced on the piano seat, spinning around. "Jack, did you hear that? Jack! You haven't gone to sleep, have you?"

"No, I'm awake."

Detective Constable Jack Kelly of the London Metropolitan Police was young to have already risen in the police ranks; he'd turned twenty-three this past winter, which made him barely a year older than me.

Jack was tall and hard-muscled, with a lean, darkly handsome face, and as a rule, he radiated taut, tightly controlled energy, an air of dangerous competence that said he was extremely good at his job of enforcing the law.

We had met just over six months ago, when I was involved in one of Sherlock Holmes's cases—a case I would never have survived if not for Jack.

Becky whipped around, sending the loose pages of music from which I had been playing scattering. She had all of her older brother's energy and practically none of his self-control.

"Can I audition, Jack? *Please?*"

Jack's eyes met mine, and one side of his mouth tipped up. "Ask me again when you're sixteen, okay?" His voice was deep and attractive, with a touch of the East London where he had been born.

Becky's eyes narrowed. "*Exactly* when I'm sixteen? What if I'm fifteen and a half?"

I mouthed the silent word "*Sorry*" to Jack over the top of Becky's head.

"Let's try *I'm the Monarch of the Sea* next," I told Becky. "You almost had it last week."

Becky had a particular fondness for *HMS Pinafore*.

Now, though, she shook her head, setting her blonde braids swinging. "It's your turn to sing next!"

That was part of our agreement: She would sing, then I would perform a song of her choice.

Becky rifled through the basket of music beside the piano. "What show are you performing at the Savoy now?"

"*The Gondoliers.*"

"Which part are you playing?" Becky asked.

"I'm just in the chorus for this one. I can't always be at rehearsals, since I have to be free—" I stopped. I didn't want to think about my assignment to perform at the Duchess's ball. The date for the ball—July 2—was rapidly approaching. But tonight, with the lamps lighted and with Becky and Jack here, my flat felt insulated, safe.

I stood on stage almost nightly and received the applause of hundreds. I had even performed for royalty. Calling something a dream come true is a cliché. But in this case, my position with the D'Oyly Carte Company was, quite literally, everything I had dreamed of one day achieving when I had been Becky's age.

And yet, somehow, these quiet Monday evenings in my flat with Becky and John had become my favorite night of the week. It felt like ... family. That was the word that came to mind, although I had scant experience with one of those.

Now, with Becky rooting, terrier-style, through my music and Jack in his shirtsleeves, leaning back on my couch, I could almost forget to worry about German spies and Fenian plots. About missing artillery weapons and my father driving himself into an early grave with work—

"I'm afraid I may not be able to do our next week's lesson, Becky," I said.

"Oh." Becky looked crestfallen for a moment, but then brightened, "Are you working on a case? Is it dangerous? Do you need help?"

In addition to music, Becky's greatest passion in life was the stories Uncle John had written about my father.

I opened my mouth, torn between a desire not to lie and a profound wish to keep Becky as far away from this case as I possibly could.

"Nothing is definite, yet," I finally said. "But if I can't make next week's lesson, I'll make sure you can see the show. I'll have one of my friends in the company—maybe Louisa, you already know her—come round and collect you and bring you to the Savoy, all right?"

Becky beamed. She loved being allowed to attend performances at the Savoy. Mr. Harris, our stage manager, ran the opera company with all the strict efficiency of the famous Modern Major General, but even he looked the other way when I sneaked Becky in backstage.

"Here." Becky plucked a file of sheet music from the basket. "Sing this one next."

I took it from her, glancing at the first few lines. "This one is a duet, Becky. I can't sing it by myself."

"I know that. Jack can sing it with you!" Becky bounced up, turning to her brother. "Can't you, Jack? Please?"

Jack raised an eyebrow at his sister. "Terrific, Beck. I was just sitting here hoping for a chance to sound like an idiot."

"You don't sound like an idiot! *Please*, Jack?"

In addition to being a whirlwind in small-girl's form, Becky was also extremely difficult to resist. Jack pulled himself up off the couch and came to stand by the piano.

"Which one is it?"

"It's *None Shall Part Us from Each Other*. You know, from *Iolanthe*," Becky said.

Jack nodded, but I hesitated before starting to play the first chords of the piano accompaniment.

Jack had never had a roof over his head growing up, much less been to school. He had taught himself to read, enough that he could pass his police exams, but I knew he still struggled—and no one would call Sir William Gilbert's libretto's easy to read at first sight. I knew trained actors who still stumbled over the words.

But Jack sang without hesitation or a hitch.

All in all since that fond meeting
When, in joy, I woke to find

Given how musical Becky was, I shouldn't have been surprised to find that Jack had some of the same in-born talent. His voice was untrained, but he had a pleasant baritone, with a strong sense of pitch.

What did surprise me was that he seemed to already know both the music and the words. The D'Oyly Carte Company had performed *Iolanthe* earlier this year, and both Jack and Becky had attended the show one night. But he couldn't possibly have heard the song often enough to have it memorized ... could he?

None shall part us from each other,
One in life and death are we

As I played the final chords on the piano, I happened to glance up at Jack. He was watching me, an expression I couldn't read in his dark eyes.

"Lucy!" Becky's small, piping voice beside me made me startle. "Who is that photograph of? The one on the mantle there. I haven't seen it before."

"Oh." Turning to follow where Becky was looking, I said, "That's a photograph of my mother."

"Your mother? Really?" Becky jumped up to study the portrait more closely. "She's beautiful!"

"Thank you." I smiled. "I think so, too."

The photograph was a recent one and had been taken of my mother while she was playing her violin. The photographer had captured not only the loveliness of my mother's features, but also the look of pure joy that always transformed her face while she played.

Although tonight, looking at the photograph made a fresh worry squirm through me. A few weeks ago, acting on impulse, I had set a plan into motion—one to which I had absolutely no idea how Sherlock Holmes would respond.

"She's very pretty." Becky was still studying the picture. "But I think you're even prettier, Lucy. Don't you think so, too, Jack?"

Jack opened his mouth.

Prince, the Kellys' enormous white and brown mastiff unfolded himself from the hearthrug and let out a short, peremptory bark.

"Prince thinks it's time to go." Jack glanced at the clock. "He's right. I have to be on duty soon."

Jack usually worked a night shift as a detective constable so that he could be with his sister during the day.

"All right." Sighing, Becky picked up the leather lead that she had left hanging on the coat rack by the door.

I stood up, too. "I'll walk you out."

When we reached the building's main entrance and stepped onto Exeter Street, Jack paused.

"What you said about next week," Jack began. "Has anything happened?"

"No." I watched a fish vendor pushing his half-empty cart along the street. He was moving slowly, which could be due to fatigue, or it could be—

I stiffened, running my gaze over the man and his cart, and then relaxed. The fish vendor had fish scales glittering on the cuffs and front of his overcoat and dried fish's blood under his fingernails. In my experience—and with the possible exception of my father—agents in disguise hardly ever strove for quite that degree of verisimilitude.

"Boots," Jack said in a quiet voice.

"What?"

Jack nodded towards the vendor. "The sole on one of his boots is split. Someone up to no good might put on a disguise, but they wouldn't make it impossible to run if they could help it."

Jack was right; the sole on the man's left boot flapped with every step he took.

"I missed that," I said. "One point for you. Did you see his fingernails?"

"No, just the fish scales on his coat."

"Oh, well, maybe I'll only give you half a point then."

Jack grinned.

It didn't surprise me that he had read my thoughts or evaluated the fish vendor as a possible threat, too, though the thought flitted through my mind to wonder what it would be like *not* to regard any and all such persons as potential assassins.

Nearly four long months had passed since Keenan Malloy had arrived at 221B Baker Street, seeking my father's advice—and even longer since the German spies we were pursuing had attempted to assassinate the Metropolitan Police Commissioner.

Regardless, despite Holmes's tireless efforts, we had made practically no progress whatsoever in tracking them down or the Fenians, with whom Keenan Mulloy suspected they were working.

"The Jubilee's coming up," Jack said.

"In two weeks."

Jack seemed to hesitate, then said, "Look, I know you can take care of yourself, but if you need anything—"

I stopped him. I trusted him more than anyone, but I still shook my head. "Getting involved in any of this is even more dangerous for you than it is for me. They—whoever these people are—have already tried to see you hanged for a murder you didn't commit."

It had taken all of Holmes's and my combined efforts to win Jack his freedom in that case.

I nodded towards Becky, who was squealing and dancing to and fro with Prince. They earned a few startled looks from the other pedestrians who hurried past, but mostly smiles.

"Becky needs you to stay alive."

"Yeah, well." Jack caught hold of my hand, his voice lower now. "Maybe I need *you* to stay alive, too."

My heart sped up.

Jack sometimes looked at me as though he admired me. But he had never said anything.

Holmes, with his usual gift for clinical analysis, had given it as his opinion that Jack felt he didn't belong in my world. I had grown up in exclusive finishing schools and performed on stage for royalty; Jack had fought his own way to adulthood while living homeless on the streets and now patrolled the most dangerous neighborhoods in London for wages of twenty-six shillings a week.

To be fair, I had never told Jack how I felt, either. My whole life, I had longed for a family, and now I had come to know my mother, my father, Mycroft, and Uncle John. I had also learned the terrifying part of family: You had people you were constantly terrified of losing.

I wasn't sure I was brave enough to add Jack to the list of people I couldn't bear to lose.

I tilted my head back to look up at him, arching an eyebrow. "Only maybe?"

Jack's eyes were grave, but he smiled. "It's possible." He was still holding my hand, and he tugged me a step forward, towards him.

"Lucy!" The shrill voice that made me drop Jack's hand and turn wasn't Becky's this time.

My flat mate, Mary Mulloy, had returned and was mincing her way quickly towards us along the pavement.

She was about my height and age, with black hair and thickly lashed blue eyes. She would have been pretty if she had not habitually looked as though the entire world were something nasty she had found stuck to the sole of her shoe.

She scowled more deeply at the sight of Prince frolicking up and down the street with Becky.

"*Please* tell me that you haven't been letting that *disgusting* animal into our flat?"

"I wouldn't dream of it."

Mary huffed out a breath and pushed her way past me. "I need to go and change for the show tonight. It's *vital* that I be there on time."

Mary had won the part of fourth peasant girl in the current production, which meant that she sang only with the chorus and never as a solo.

I sighed, looking after her as she entered our building. "I should go and speak with her. Ask her whether she's heard anything from her brother recently."

Although speaking with Mary about her brother was tantamount to hitting one's own head against a brick wall: painfully unproductive, and also your own fault if you thought it would accomplish anything.

We had been out of Mary's hearing when I had advised Keenan Mulloy to see my father. Mary knew nothing of her brother having consulted Holmes, and since I trusted her to keep secrets about as much as I would trust Holmes to write an advice column for the lovelorn, I couldn't tell her.

For the past months, any attempt I had made to subtly find out whether Keenan might have confided something of value to her before he put her on the train to Ireland had been met with spite-filled ramblings about Keenan's attempt to send her away and her glee that he believed her to still be abroad.

Still, she *might* have heard something.

Jack nodded. "We'll see you later, then."

"Yes." I looked up at him and added, "Be careful."

Jack raised one hand and brushed my cheek with the back of his knuckles, in a gesture so light I might almost have imagined it. "You, too, Trouble."

WATSON

12. AN EMPTY CAB

It was the morning of June 8. Four months had gone by since our encounters with Father Mulloy, and we had heard no news of him, either good or ill. I continued to hope that the Fenians intended no further mischief towards the young priest after all.

My heart was far from light, however. I had been awakened by a thunderstorm just before dawn and dozed only fitfully for the next hour. My mind whirled with useless speculations and emotions as well as a feeling of gloomy foreboding. I feared that our enemy was biding his time and that a trap that we had failed to discover would be sprung when it was too late to prevent disaster.

Two weeks from today the Jubilee parade would set off from Buckingham Palace. Already the streets, restaurants, and shops of London bore witness to the colourfully exotic uniforms and costumes of new arrivals from the far-flung corners of the Empire. As more and more visitors came in, I knew there would be more confusion and even less likelihood of our seeing the pattern of evil beneath the chaos, thereby preventing disaster.

Holmes had worked tirelessly, but every thread of investigation that he followed seemed to break off in his grasp. He had pored over the transcript of Arkwright's final interview in the Andaman Islands' prison and pronounced it devoid of clues to the tantalizing words "Devonshire" and "Elswick." He and I had travelled the nearly three hundred miles to Newcastle, interviewing employees at the Elswick works, examining manufacturing and shipping records, and returning, I thought, with no better idea of the whereabouts of the missing cannon than when we had set out.

Each night in Baker Street, Holmes would open yet another fresh box of documents, mainly correspondence, that Mycroft had sent over from the Foreign Office, resolutely continuing his search for clues to any connection with German correspondents that might lead to Kaiser Wilhelm or the Kaiser's senior minister and strategist, Bernhard von Bulow. Each morning the documents would be packed up again and exchanged for another box.

But after nearly four months, the process had contributed nothing of value to Holmes's understanding of the shadowy forces that manifested themselves in the case. Or so I thought at the time.

Lucy had attended early rehearsals at Devonshire House in London for the Duchess's ball. Her role had been selected. Mary Mulloy also had a role; as Lucy had expected, Mary had appeared on time for her own audition, having gotten off the train from London at the first stop and never getting on the boat for Dublin. She had begged Lucy not to tell her brother that she had disobeyed. As far as I knew, Lucy had complied with this request.

Holmes, in his frustration, had occupied himself with other cases. However, he would drop everything to follow any lead having even a faint connection with what he referred to as "The Jubilee Problem." He was working so intensely that I had become concerned for his health, for even a constitution as strong as his, I knew, could not withstand extended periods of unusually strenuous activity. On one occasion, I argued that even the most powerful racehorse must be given adequate food and rest.

"You will observe, Watson," he replied, "that I am not a horse," which only made the situation more worrisome.

Such was my state of mind when I came downstairs, expecting to take my customary breakfast in the sitting room. Holmes stood at our bow window. The sky had not yet cleared, and only pale, misted daylight came through the panes of glass. On our carpet, I could discern only the barest outlines of a shadow emanating from Holmes's tall, lean figure. The previous night's cardboard box of correspondence from the Foreign Office had been repacked, bound with stout twine, and set down neatly beside the entrance to our hallway door, a forlorn testimony to our lack of progress.

Holmes was staring intently at the street below.

I asked, "Have you eaten breakfast?"

Still looking outside, he gestured vaguely in the direction of our table, where Mrs Hudson had set down covered containers of what I was sure were her customary sausages, boiled eggs, and toast. The silver gooseneck coffee pitcher was also in its accustomed position, between our usual place settings of Mrs Hudson's floral-patterned china and silver utensils.

"Your unused plate and coffee cup speak for you, Holmes."

His gaze remained fixed on whatever pedestrians and vehicles were passing on the street below. If anything, he seemed more interested in them than previously, for he was leaning forward towards the window, his face nearly touching the glass.

"So it appears I must set you the example," I went on.

I was about to sit when I saw him straighten up. At the same time, I heard the ring of our outside doorbell.

Holmes was at the open door to the stairway, calling down for Mrs Hudson to admit our visitor.

I quickly went to the window. Directly below I saw on our walkway an empty and driverless hansom cab and a horse tethered to the nearest hitching post. At our door stood a man, his cap in his hand. On his trousers, on the legs and chest of his horse, and on the sides of his cab were splashes of yellow mud.

I turned to Holmes. "You will see him?"

"When an aging London cabman is concerned enough to press his horse to a five-mile journey without a passenger— you noticed, of course, his stooped shoulders and the particular yellow mud common in Whitechapel after a rain such as we had earlier this morning—and then risk a citation from the police for leaving his cab on the walkway, such behaviour indicates an urgency for which we ought at least to hear the underlying motive." Holmes gave a nod towards the door leading to my upstairs sleeping room, adding, "Provided we take the usual precautions."

I understood. Quickly I climbed the steps and retrieved my service revolver from the drawer of my dressing cabinet. I returned to our sitting room with the weapon tucked into my waistband and concealed by my jacket. I arrived just as Holmes opened our sitting room door for the cabman.

True to Holmes's earlier estimate, our visitor appeared to be nearing fifty, a hunched, grey-haired, ill-nourished fellow with a sallow, wolfish face adorned by a wispy, unkempt beard. He had taken off his grey cap and was twisting it nervously in his hands. Beneath his unbuttoned jacket he wore a frayed black waistcoat and a greasy shirt that appeared to have gone several days without laundering.

"I won't sit, sir," he said, gesturing apologetically at the mud that clung to his trousers and at his dirty brown boots. "I must persuade you to come with me."

"Your name?"

"Owens, sir. And you are Mr. Holmes?"

Holmes nodded. "This is my friend and colleague, Dr. Watson. Now pray tell us where it is you are to persuade us to go and who has sent you."

"You need have no concerns about the fare. I have already been paid." From his jacket pocket Owens produced a somewhat tarnished silver crucifix, roughly four inches in length.

Holmes's manner remained calm, but I saw a flash of concern in his grey eyes. "A priest has sent you?"

"He took this off the chain he wore around his waist. He said it was all he had." So saying, Owens held the small icon out for Holmes's inspection. "Feel it, Mr. Holmes. It has a substantial heft to it. Even melted down it will fetch more than I would hope to earn in a day."

Holmes turned the crucifix in his palm. "I hesitate to disappoint you, Mr. Owens. However, on the journeys of life the truth is generally the better companion. This crucifix has been cast in lead, with a silver coating electrically applied. You can see where the silver has been worn through at the back. It is worth two shillings, possibly three."

The cabman gave a brief sigh, and it struck me that he was accustomed to disappointment. Then he shrugged. "Still," he said. "A shilling's a shilling."

"Precisely." Holmes turned the crucifix towards me. It was of an unremarkable appearance, save for the skull and crossbones moulded in relief below the effigy of Christ. Holmes touched the skull delicately with a fingertip.

I saw that the initials "KM" had been scratched into the base immediately below.

I nodded to Holmes, indicating that I remembered Keenan Mulloy. Holmes tapped the crucifix a second time. "The skull beneath the feet of Christ is intended to represent a triumph over death, Watson," he murmured. "Let us hope it is an omen more auspicious than the leaden composition of this artefact itself."

Then he turned to the cabman. "Now, Mr. Owens, please tell us what happened when you received this crucifix and your instructions. Where were you?"

"On Commercial Road, heading back to my post after droppin' off a fare in London Hospital."

"You helped your passenger out of your cab. The mud on your trousers is still damp."

"I did get splashed, yes. Just before I climbed back up to my seat."

"What time?"

"It was a bit after seven-twenty when I left the hospital. I wrote that time in my book. I came straight here, quick as I could."

"It took you one hour and"—Holmes consulted his watch—"ten minutes. What happened?"

"A man—this priest fellow—runs right up to my horse and stops it, and then comes back to me, wavin' a scrap of paper, and sayin' he needs to borrow the use of my pencil, what I use for my fare book. I gives it to him, and then he looks round quick-like and says your name."

"His exact words, if you please."

"He said, 'Go to Sherlock Holmes at 221B Baker Street. Take him to St. Paul's Cathedral.'"

Holmes's grey eyes glittered. "You are certain he said St. Paul's."

"As sure as I'm standin' 'ere. He says, 'St. Paul's Cathedral. Tell him to come at once.' Then he shoved the crucifix into my hands and scarpered."

"On what was he intending to write?"

"I don't know. But when he gave me the crucifix, he wrapped it up in this scrap of paper." Owens took from his pocket a tattered, stained, yellowing piece of cheap newsprint and passed it over to Holmes.

"It is the first page of a tract railing against the evils of drink," Holmes said, sniffing the stained area. "Quite evidently not effective in its purpose, for it reeks of ale in its latter stage of decomposition and has been trodden on—hardly a mark of sincere reformation or even feigned respect." He folded the paper and put it into his jacket pocket. "Now, Mr. Owens, what else can you tell us about the holy man who presented you with these two very different articles and gave you such a very direct instruction?"

"I don't know, sir. He was a priest, like I said."

"A young man?"

"Maybe forty."

"Blond hair?"

"No, it were black. Or maybe dark brown."

"Was his hair long or short?"

The driver merely shrugged.

"His voice?"

"A man's voice."

"Surely you can do better than that, Mr. Owens. Was his voice deep or shrill? Did he have a cough? Was he pleading in his tone, or did he order you as if he were invoking his moral authority? Did he speak with an accent as though he were from another part of London—or from another country?"

"I don't remember none of that, sir. But I do know two things. He was in a hurry, and he was afraid."

"Did he return your pencil?"

"He didn't, come to think of it. Just ran off."

"Which way?"

"Towards the river. I had the thought he might have been bound for the church on Tower Hill, him bein' a priest an' all." Owens then added, "He did say 'at once,' Mr. Holmes."

Holmes nodded. "You will take us to St. Paul's. I will keep the crucifix and the paper. Here is a gold sovereign. It should be ample compensation for your time this morning. Please go downstairs and turn your cab southward. We shall join you momentarily."

We heard the man's footsteps descend the stairs. We heard the outer door open and shut.

"Please telephone the cab company," Holmes said. "See if badge number 914A21 is registered to Mr. Owens. Also see if Mr. Owens has been reported missing."

I picked up the earpiece and twirled the magneto crank. I heard only silence.

Mrs. Hudson's voice came from below. "There's no telephone this morning. I found out when I tried to call the butcher's. I think it was that thunderstorm."

Holmes motioned me to the window. "Young Flynn is across the street," he said, pulling the blind downward and then slowly letting it roll up again.

Flynn, one of the ragged street urchins Holmes employed from time to time as his watchers and searchers, had not been outside when the cabman arrived. Normally he was stationed outside Lucy's residence on Exeter Street. Plainly he had noticed the movement of the blind at our window. He lightly touched his index finger to a battered beaver top hat that looked wildly incongruous above his ragged cotton shirt and torn trousers. Then he quite deliberately folded his arms across his scrawny chest. That pose, I knew, signalled that Lucy was neither at her residence nor at rehearsal at the nearby Savoy Theatre.

Then Flynn lifted his top hat in a kind of brief salute, replacing it a long moment later atop his untidy blond curls. That signal meant he had seen something on Baker Street to indicate that we were in danger.

Moments later Holmes and I were racing downstairs. Holmes called to Mrs. Hudson that she must not open the door to anyone that she did not recognize.

I was about to open our front door when I realized that Holmes had gone in the opposite direction, past the astonished

Mrs. Hudson in her sitting room rocker, and was heading for her kitchen.

"This way, Watson," he said over his shoulder. "The mud on Owens' boots was brown, not yellow."

WATSON

13. A NEW DOORWAY

Like many London residences, our Baker Street home has an exit to a rear alleyway, enabling tradesmen to enter or leave from behind Mrs. Hudson's kitchen. There is also a small garden. The door leading from the kitchen to the alleyway is heavy oak, reinforced after Holmes returned from Reichenbach, and fitted with a stout Chubb lock.

Holmes had taken out his key and was about to open that door.

Then it opened, pulled from the outside.

Lucy James appeared, replacing her own key in her reticule.

She gave a momentary glance at the key in Holmes's hand and asked, "How did you know?"

"I saw the hansom driver's boots. They indicated he was wearing trousers taken from another man. Also Flynn gave a danger signal. You?"

"I saw three men waiting outside your doorway. They do not appear to be clients."

"Why were you on Baker Street?"

"I tried the phone, but I couldn't get through. Keenan Mulloy came to the flat last night looking for Mary. She hid. He said he'd written repeatedly to her in Dublin but hadn't heard from her and was worried. Then he said he had important news that he had to deliver to Sherlock Holmes. That was when we tried the phone. I asked him what the news was, but he wouldn't tell me."

"Where is Mary now?"

"In our flat. She likes to sleep late."

Holmes nodded. We left the house, Holmes carefully locking the outside door. He led us to rear entrance of the building next door, which contained a restaurant. We entered and walked quietly past a cook who barely looked up. Then we were amidst the white-draped tables at the front. Baker Street was visible through the plate glass window.

"Let us see if the three men are still waiting for us," said Holmes.

I saw a laundry van stopped directly across from our doorway. The cabman who had called himself Owens was now in the driver's seat of the van. His hansom cab was still standing empty on the sidewalk, the horse still waiting patiently.

Lucy said, "The three men intend to wrestle you both into the laundry van."

Holmes eased the door open and leaned out slightly. "They are still on either side of our doorway. One is trying to pick the lock."

Lucy said, "The restaurant has a telephone."

"The police cannot reach us in time. We cannot have those three men dragging Mrs. Hudson into this. Watson, see what you can, and then we must move."

I peered out at Baker Street. In front of our door were three shadowy figures, two on the far side. They wore long coats. Their hands were in their pockets. It was impossible to know whether they carried guns or knives. The hansom still blocked the sidewalk. I now realized that it had been intended to cut off our attempt to escape, had we come out by way of our front door.

Then the man nearest me turned in my direction.

"Holmes," I said, "they have seen me."

"Draw your pistol." He moved past me and opened the restaurant door wide. "Lucy, you stay here."

I stepped out to the pavement. The three men broke into a run, coming towards us. I tried to pull my revolver from my pocket, but it caught on the fabric. One of the men tackled me. I hit the ground and saw the other two pulling Holmes down as if the pavement alongside Baker Street had suddenly been transformed into a rugby field. I heard one say, "Dead or alive, Mr. 'Olmes. It's all the same to us."

My adversary was pulling my still-tangled pistol from my pocket.

Then I felt a rush of air as, in a blur of black silk fabric and black leather, Lucy's boot heel connected with the jaw of my attacker. His body, now dead weight, slumped over me. Before I could roll my attacker off me, Lucy kicked one of Holmes's two attackers in the mouth. The man gave a roar of outrage and lashed out with a knife. Lucy dodged, then landed another kick. I heard a dull hollow crack as the man's head hit the pavement. The knife had fallen from his hand. Lucy stamped hard on his fingers, and I heard them break. The man moaned as the pain reached him, even in his unconscious state. Around us, a few onlookers had begun to gather, but no one interfered.

Holmes had the third man in a wrestler's hold. There was another crack, the sound of breaking bone. Holmes pushed the man away. The man's arm dangled uselessly at his side. He took one look at his two inert associates. Then he saw my pistol, which I had finally managed to pull from my coat.

But from my left came a clatter of hoof beats on the pavement. I turned and saw a police carriage approaching on our side of the street. Up front on either side of the uniformed driver were two uniformed constables. Another pair stood in the back, on the footman's perch.

The effect on the third man was immediate. He turned away from his two associates, stumbled across the street, and climbed into the laundry van, his broken arm rigid at his side.

Owens—or whatever his name may have been—was already whipping up the horse. The van pulled away, leaving us with two unconscious thugs and a rapidly growing group of passers-by. I tried to determine whether any of them were connected with the assault, but they all seemed only passively curious. On the fringe of the small crowd I could see Flynn, hovering watchfully.

The first man Lucy had kicked was now retching onto the pavement. The second, the one who had lashed out at Lucy, remained motionless, the side of his head nestled into the pavement as if it were a pillow. Blood oozed from underneath. The knife lay beside his ruined hand. The hansom remained on the pavement, its horse apparently oblivious to the activity around it.

The police carriage came to a stop a few feet from where we stood. Two constables jumped down from the front and began to disperse the crowd. Traffic resumed.

Inspector George Lestrade clambered out.

The little detective's cheeks were bright pink with excitement. Beneath his black bowler hat, jammed down against the wind, his beady eyes sparkled. He stepped forward. "Mr. Holmes, you must come at once to St. Paul's Cathedral."

WATSON

14. A FALLEN PRIEST

I drew in my breath.

St. Paul's. The location for the Jubilee thanksgiving service two weeks from now. The place where the false cabman Owens had said Keenan Mulloy wanted to meet us as soon as possible. Could Owens have been telling the truth after all?

Holmes said, "Why do you come to me?"

"Orders from the Commissioner." Inspector Lestrade paused for breath, taking a momentary glance at Lucy. "This morning, a Jesuit priest fell to his death from the southwest parapet of the cathedral. Your card was in his pocket."

Lucy said, "I'm going with you."

Lestrade left two of his constables behind to deal with our wood-be attackers and learn what they could about the failed abduction. Lucy rode in the police wagon across from Holmes and me. Lestrade sat at her side. Along the way Holmes enumerated the details of the visit from the man calling himself Owens. After a half-hour ride, we reached Ludgate Hill. The carriage stopped, and we climbed out to stand on the damp pavement in a chilly wind.

Above us, the huge bulk of the great cathedral known to all the world loomed high and dark. I felt quite small beneath the soaring walls and columns. Blackened with the soot and smoke dust that had accumulated over more than two centuries, the great landmark seemed to me to have the forbidding aspect of a great prison rather than a house of worship.

"For the Jubilee," Lucy said.

She was pointing towards the wide stone steps at the western end of the cathedral, where in two weeks thousands of churchmen would stand on bleachers specially erected for the thanksgiving ceremony.

I clung to my hat as gusts of wind billowed off the pavement and the walls that towered above us. Small particles of city dust and roadway grit assaulted my eyes. I had the irrational thought that the forces of both men and nature stood in opposition to our visit.

Holmes, his jaw clamped and lips pressed tightly into a thin straight line, appeared not to notice. His gaze was fixed on a row of uniformed policemen that now parted before us.

Lestrade said, "They're City men of course."

At Lucy's puzzled look, Holmes explained, "St. Paul's is not in the jurisdiction of the Metropolitan Police. We are in a one square mile district called the City of London, the historic centre of our metropolis, from which most of the financial activity of the Empire is controlled. The boundaries correspond roughly to the original settlement that dates back to Roman times, nearly two thousand years ago."

"You generally take no interest in history," Lucy said.

"The City has its own police force."

Lestrade was engaged in a conference with a sergeant of the City Police, a tall fellow who was obviously in charge. Moments later Lestrade returned to us. "They've not moved it," he said.

The row of City policemen parted to allow us passage, following the sergeant, around the blackened stone corner of the cathedral and along the south wall. We walked a few paces on the gravel. Directly before us, perhaps thirty feet away, was the distinctive curved array of columns that enclosed the south entrance to the great building. On the gravel beneath the columns, perhaps ten feet from the base of the towering wall, was a misshapen dark mass.

Beneath the dark mass, the gravel was stained with a large circular halo of red.

"You found no identification papers?"

The sergeant said, "Only your card. We called the Commissioner straight away."

"You called Commissioner Smith?"

"Correct. Sir."

We walked closer to what had once been Keenan Mulloy, man of God. The black cassock shrouded the contorted curve of the body. Protruding from the nearer end were black-laced boots and thin shanks of legs obscured by black stockings and black trousers. After a few more steps I saw the open red tissue, grey bone, and clumps of short black hair into which the man's head had been transformed by its collision with the gravel at the edge of the building. His arms and hands were outstretched and forward on the pavement, as though in final supplication.

"Constable on patrol saw the fall," said Lestrade.

"I should like to interview the Constable," said Holmes.

Lestrade nodded to the City sergeant, who nodded towards the line of uniformed patrolmen we had passed through. One of them, a tall man of about thirty, came our way.

"He was praying," the Constable said, after introductions had been made. "All the way down."

"What gave you that impression?"

"Had his hands clasped, he did. Clasped right afore him, tight against his chest. Must have been crazy, tryin' to pray while he was jumpin' off like that."

"Were his knees bent?"

The constable shook his head. "Can't remember."

"Did he cry out?"

"Not a sound. I see what you're getting' at, though. You think he might have been kneeling, in his mind, like. Well I don't remember. I was looking at his hands, and those hands were clasped, all the way till he hit. Were only a couple seconds, though, of course."

Holmes indicated the body. "And yet now his hands and arms are far apart."

"Must have been the impact. Splayed them out."

"From where did the man fall?" Holmes asked.

The constable glanced upward at a blackened stone balustrade. Our angle of vision was such that we could barely see the great dome, far above. "Likely he was near the clock tower. Right up there on the walkway."

"Did you see anyone on the walkway with him?"

The Constable shook his head. "I came around to the south entrance from the west. Something moved and caught my eye, and I looked up. He must have just gone over the rail, and I could see he was a priest and his hands were clasped. It flashed through my mind that he was holding a rosary or a crucifix. Like I said, I thought he was crazy. He must have known committin' suicide was a mortal sin and that he wouldn't have a chance to confess and obtain forgiveness."

Holmes received this information with a distracted nod. Now he was bending over the body, walking around it. "By the way, Constable, what is your name?"

"Griffin, sir. Constable James Griffin."

"Thank you. And at what time did you see this man fall?"

"Oh, that's in my report, sir. Just before 6:30 this morning. I called the Yard straightaway, after I found your card."

"Ah. And where is the card?"

"I gave it to my sergeant."

"And you have secured the upper gallery walk and the stairs?" Holmes asked.

"I have."

"Have you found a bicycle in the area?"

"We have not looked for a bicycle."

Holmes received this news with stoic indifference. He gestured at the man who lay at our feet. "Is this Father Keenan Mulloy?" he asked Lucy. His question puzzled me, for I could tell even from where I stood that this was the man Holmes and I had both seen less than four months before.

Warned by a look from Holmes, however, I kept silent.

Lucy bent over the body, peering into the face, which was partially obscured due to the prone position. Holding the cuffed sleeve of the man's coat between thumb and forefinger, she lifted the right arm. She bent over the hand, and then turned her head to look directly at the dead man's face. Then she lifted the other arm in the same fashion. Then she stood.

"We must find Mary and tell her. Are you going up to look at the walkway?" She gestured up towards the spot from which the priest had fallen; however, I noticed she was edging towards the wall nearest the entry columns.

Holmes nodded. "Thank you. Now, Constable Griffin. I should like to see where Father Mulloy gained access to the upper walkway. Once there, we can examine the spot from which he fell."

I noticed that Lucy continued towards the wall and was taking an envelope from her reticule. As Holmes and the Constable left us, I saw her bend and pick up what I thought might be a long piece of string. She placed it into her envelope.

LUCY

15. RETURN TO WHITECHAPEL

Ever since I met Sherlock Holmes, I had vacillated between a wish that I could be more like him and the fear that I would grow to be all too *much* like him if I continued in the business of detection.

At the moment, I was hovering somewhere between the two.

Sitting across from me in the jolting police carriage, Uncle John cleared his throat. "I haven't had the chance yet to thank you, Lucy, my dear, for your speedy intervention in Baker Street."

I glanced up, startled, and Uncle John smiled.

"You were flexing your ankle slightly." He gestured. "I deduced that you were recalling the kick you delivered to our attacker's jaw and the kidnapping attempt you thwarted."

After spending so much time in Holmes's company, some of my father's techniques had rubbed off on Uncle John. And he always looked so delighted when he was able to demonstrate his skill.

It was impossible not to return his smile—even with my ribs feeling as though they ought to be creaking with the effort to contain my anger.

We had left St. James behind and were on our way to visit the Church of the English Martyrs, where Keenan Mulloy had been a priest.

"I only helped to thwart it," I told Watson. "If Lestrade and his officers had not arrived when they did, things might have turned far uglier." I glanced at Inspector Lestrade, who was seated beside Uncle John. "What will happen to the men who attacked us?"

Lestrade opened his mouth, but it was Holmes who answered.

He had sat wrapped in silence since we climbed into Lestrade's carriage, staring impassively out the window. But now he turned, his voice biting. "They will be taken into custody and questioned. Whereupon we will discover that they were hired anonymously, paid anonymously, know nothing, and can offer no hint as to the person or persons who instigated the attack."

Holmes could be forgiven for his pessimism. That was more or less how every possible lead in this case had turned out, up until now.

In addition to carving out deeper hollows beneath his cheekbones and leaving the shadows of too many sleepless nights beneath his hooded eyes, the long string of investigative dead ends had left him in a perpetually foul mood.

Another wave of anger rose in me. Though in truth, I welcomed it.

When I stopped being angry, I was going to have to think about Keenan Mulloy. I would need to find somewhere inside me where I could keep the memory of his shattered body, and I knew from experience that the process would hurt.

With a rattle of carriage wheels, the driver drew to a halt.

Uncle John cleared his throat pointedly, looking at Holmes, and my father frowned.

"What is it, Watson?"

Watson inclined his head towards me.

Holmes's frown deepened. "What? Ah, yes." He turned to regard me with clear gray eyes. "That was well done, Lucy."

His expression was by now familiar to me: one part paternal pride, three parts horrified disbelief that I was once again caught up in the dangers of an investigation.

At least, I hoped that the paternal pride was there.

The Roman Catholic Church of the English Martyrs was on Tower Hill, practically in the shadow of the Tower of London, the famous castle where Queen Elizabeth had been imprisoned and her mother Anne Boleyn had lost her head for the unforgivable crime of failing to give her fat oaf of a husband a male heir.

Lestrade followed Holmes out of the carriage, and then Uncle John offered me his hand as I climbed down as well.

"Thank you, Uncle John."

Instead of releasing my hand, he drew it through the crook of his arm as we followed Holmes and Lestrade towards the church's front doors.

He glanced at me, his kindly face furrowed in concern. "Are you all right, Lucy?"

Evidently Uncle John's powers of observation were even sharper than I had realized.

"I was thinking about Mary. She'll need to be told."

Right this moment, Mary Mulloy was probably back at our flat, either still sleeping late or brewing a pot of her syrupy-sweet hot chocolate, with no idea whatsoever of the hole that had been ripped in her life today.

Watson cleared his throat. "You know, there is nothing wrong with being upset by sights such as we have seen today. Rather, I believe it would be of greater cause for concern if we were *not* troubled by the tragedy of a good man's untimely demise."

The speech encapsulated Uncle John's character in its essence. It was remarkable, really. He had accompanied Holmes through the twists and turns of cases that laid bare all the basest, most venial elements of human nature—cases that would have turned Sir Galahad himself into a crabbed and bitter cynic. And yet Doctor John Watson's goodness and basic human decency remained entirely uncorrupted.

"Do you think Holmes allows it to upset him?" My eyes were on my father's tall, straight back.

At the moment, he and Lestrade were speaking to the robed priest who had come to the door, asking when Keenan Mulloy had last been seen on the premises and requesting to be shown to the dead man's room.

A faint smile touched the edges of Uncle John's mouth. "I think that there is only one Sherlock Holmes—which is likely no bad thing, since I doubt that there is room enough in the world for two." He stopped, glancing at me. "What was it you picked up from the ground outside Saint Paul's?"

I imagined that he did truly want to know. But he was also trying to distract me from unpleasant memories.

I squeezed his arm lightly. "Holmes would probably leave you in suspense until the end of the case. But since, as you point out, I am *not* Holmes, I will tell you."

I took out the envelope I had used to collect the evidence and opened it, allowing Uncle John to look inside.

"Thread?" Uncle John's brows drew together at the sight of a length of beige-colored thread, the sort that a seamstress might use for sewing on buttons.

"There were marks on Father Mulloy's wrists, too—faint, thin indentations in his skin."

"As though his hands had been bound together." Uncle John's frown deepened. "You think that he was a prisoner, held captive somewhere before he was killed?"

Since—also unlike Holmes—I would never, ever hurt Uncle John's feelings by expressing overt impatience, I suppressed a sigh.

"Not exactly, Uncle John, I—"

Up ahead of us at the door to the church, Holmes turned to look back. His thin lips were compressed in a scowl. "By all means, Watson, take all the time you like. It's not as though we are in any sort of hurry."

"It's not Uncle John's fault," I said quickly, accelerating my steps. "And we're just coming."

LUCY

16. THE PRIEST'S ROOM

Keenan Mulloy's room had not changed from when we had spoken with him in February. Small, bare, and spartanly neat, it contained a narrow bed that was little more than a cot, a writing desk, a washstand, and a single hard-backed chair.

The only touch of extravagance—if one could call it that—in the room was a large gilded crucifix, which hung on one wall. Beneath it stood a dark wooden *prie dieu*, where the dead man must have said his prayers. A bible stood open in the holder at the top, and an onyx string of rosary beads hung across the open page.

Nothing out of the ordinary. But as I looked around the small, bare chamber, I had to curl my fingers to stop my hands from shaking.

Keenan Mulloy had deserved to keep living in this quiet little room, doing good amongst the people of his parish, saying his prayers. We should have done more, found some way of protecting him—

I took that thought and folded it tightly away, stuffing it into the same internal space where I was keeping the memory of his lifeless face. After this was all over, maybe I would dig it out again and let myself feel guilty over having failed to save him. But first we needed to catch his murderers.

"Here, Holmes, have a look at this!"

Lestrade's startled exclamation made me look up. The Inspector was bent over the writing desk, but moved aside to allow Holmes to see what he was looking at.

Holmes peered down. "Holmes must die." He read the words in the same tone of voice one might use for reading out a weather report, which somehow only made them all the more shocking.

I felt my jaw drop. "*What* does it say?"

Holmes shuffled a few of the papers on the desk, looking not at all surprised. "There is a great deal more of it here, as well. *Holmes must die. His face hides the devil's eyes. Forgive me, Lord.* And other miscellaneous ravings in a similar vein."

I stepped closer so that I could see the papers and found the sheets covered with scrawls written in a frantic, shaky hand. Some of the words were so badly splattered with ink as to be almost illegible. In other places, the writer had dragged the pen across the page with enough force to tear the paper.

Lestrade pursed his lips. "Looks like he went barmy, poor devil. Not surprising, really, there's got to be all kind of religious nutters in places like this."

His expression still distasteful, Lestrade looked round the room, his glance finally landing on the gilded crucifix. "Spend enough time with a whole congregation thinking you're God's mouthpiece on earth and you start to believe it yourself."

"Must have gone off his head and done himself in, poor blighter," Lestrade continued. "Though I'd say you'd had a lucky escape, Mr. Holmes. Judging by what's in these papers, he could just as easily have tried to take you with him when he jumped." Watson had been listening with an expression of increasing indignation and, at that, burst out, "But that's absurd! Father Mulloy was no madman, nor did he commit suicide. His hands—"

I was about to interrupt, wishing that Uncle John had not chosen this precise moment to realize the significance of the thread and the marks on Keenan's wrists.

But Holmes spoke first. "His hands were badly broken in the fall, so that it will be difficult to determine whether he was right or left handed, though clearly these papers were written by a right-handed scribe. That is what you were going to say, isn't it?"

"What?" Uncle John looked at Holmes blankly. Then I saw realization dawn in his eyes. "Oh—yes, yes, of course."

I would hate to suspect Lestrade of being part of an organization of traitors, too. But the fact remained that we knew already that there were spies inside the police force. At the very least, Lestrade might easily pass crucial information on to the wrong set of ears, and it would be safer for all concerned if we appeared to believe in Keenan Mulloy's suicide.

I looked over at Holmes and, for a brief moment, his clear gray eyes met mine. His head moved in a barely perceptible nod.

I cleared my throat. "Inspector, my flat mate is actually the dead man's sister. If you like, I could take one of these notes to her and ask her to confirm that it is indeed written in her brother's hand. It might allow you to close the case more quickly."

Lestrade looked at me, irresolution etched on his thin, sharp-featured face. He might welcome Holmes's involvement in his criminal investigations, but I suspected that he only barely tolerated mine.

At last he nodded, though. "Fine. Here, you can have this one. It's the least likely to upset her." He handed me the sheet of paper that was scrawled with *Lord have mercy on my soul.* "Just let me give you a receipt for it."

Lestrade patted his pockets, frowning. "Now where the blooming—where's my notebook got to?"

"Perhaps you accidentally left it in the carriage?"

Lestrade made an irritated *tsk*-ing sound under his breath and strode out.

I carefully didn't look back at Holmes as I followed, though I did take Uncle John's arm again, drawing him with me as we left the late Keenan Mulloy's room behind.

LUCY

17. THE PRIEST'S LETTER

Lestrade was just signing his name to a sheet of paper when Holmes emerged from the church. His countenance was as inexpressive as ever, but he gave me another fractional inclination of the head before turning to the Inspector.

"Ah, Lestrade. The missing notebook was indeed found in the carriage, I see?"

Lestrade grunted. "Must have fallen out on the ride here. There you are, Miss James." He handed the receipt to me. "I think we're by and large done here. Want a ride back to Baker Street?"

Holmes shook his head. "I think not. It is such a fine day that I feel inclined to walk and enjoy the spring weather."

Anyone well acquainted with my father would know that he had never in his life cared about the weather—except perhaps as it affected whether the ground was muddy enough to take footprints. But Lestrade only shrugged. "Suit yourself."

I waited until the police carriage had rattled away before turning to Holmes. "You found something?"

"Indeed."

Uncle John looked from one of us to the other, startled. "Found something? What do you mean?"

"I have been making a more thorough—and private—search of Father Mulloy's rooms than could be made under Inspector Lestrade's watchful eye."

Holmes drew a paper out from the inner pocket of his overcoat. It had been tightly rolled up into a cylinder.

"Found in the hollow metal leg of the dead man's bed. A reasonably astute hiding place. Whoever it was that planted the insane ravings on Father Mulloy's desk had also looked in all the drawers and had even slit open the underside of the mattress. But they obviously missed seeing this."

Uncle John eyed the paper with appreciation. "I say, Holmes. Lucky that Inspector Lestrade dropped his notebook."

"As you say. Though I believe it had less to do with good fortune and more to the fact that Lucy had the foresight to pick the good Inspector's pocket as he climbed out of the carriage."

Uncle John's head snapped round to look at me, his eyebrows shooting up.

"I thought that we might need an excuse for getting the Inspector out of Keenan's room," I said. I glanced at Holmes. "Though obviously I need more practice as a pickpocket, if you saw me."

The barest fleeting trace of a smile curved the edges of my father's mouth. "Perhaps we can enlist Flynn to give you lessons; he is past master of the art. Now." He unrolled the paper. "There is little here, but since it is the only tangible clue in our possession, we must make of it what we can."

I moved to look. The sheet was plain writing paper, of medium quality, with a London seller's watermark. The same paper that had been kept in a top drawer of the dead man's writing desk.

"*My dear Miss Jones.*" Watson was also looking over Holmes' shoulder and read the words aloud. "*While the confidences with which you entrusted me are and will ever remain sacrosanct under the rule of confidentiality surrounding the confession, I am not easy in my mind as to the nature of what you have told me. The unholy trinity to which you refer should be brought to the attention of the authorities. I must strongly urge you—*"

Watson stopped. "And there he breaks off. I suppose he was writing to this lady with the intent of urging her to go to the authorities with whatever she knew."

Holmes nodded. "One may assume so. In any event, we may take this to be a genuine sample of Father Mulloy's handwriting. And the scrawled ravings we previously found bear little resemblance to this letter to Miss Jones."

I made a face. "*Jones*? We can't possibly hunt down every Miss Jones in London. That has to be the most common surname possible."

"Not as common as Smith," Holmes murmured, "which outdoes Jones in commonality by a factor of roughly twenty percent. However in this case, we have at least the starting point of the parishioners here." He gestured to the church behind us. "And failing that, we can begin to comb through the registries of other nearby Catholic parishes."

I said nothing, but he nodded as though reading my thoughts.

"The proverbial hunt for a needle in a haystack, yes. However, to reference another proverb, beggars cannot choose the nature of their clues. Mycroft's resources may be of some value in obtaining parish registries."

If anyone could identify a single Miss Jones among thousands, Mycroft could.

"Did you find anything else inside Keenan's room?"

"Only this."

Holmes produced an envelope, of the type left in church pews to collect donations. A glance showed me that this one was stuffed with Bank of England notes.

My eyebrows went up. "You cannot possibly believe that Keenan Mulloy was stealing from the church collection box." I was watching my father's face as I spoke and shook my head slowly. "No, you *don't* believe that. But what do you believe?"

Holmes, in typical fashion, ignored the question. "I believe a visit to Cragside, the Northumberland estate of Lord Armstrong, is in order. If an attack on the Jubilee is planned, our time grows short to hunt down the missing artillery weapon."

"Of course." Uncle John straightened his shoulders. "I can be ready to leave within the hour, if need be."

"Capital." Holmes fell silent for a beat before turning to look at me. "And you, Lucy—"

I nodded. "I will do my best to ingratiate myself into the Duchess of Devonshire's household. But first, first I must go and tell Mary Mulloy that her brother is dead."

My voice was steady, but all the same, Holmes looked at me for a long moment, an unreadable expression in his gray eyes.

Did he feel that we had failed Keenan Mulloy, too? Maybe. He was just better at channeling that sense of failure into determination.

"I also found this," Holmes said. "It had been pushed to the back of the uppermost desk drawer, wedged between the drawer and its frame." He drew a sheet of stiff paper from his coat pocket. "His sister might like to have it."

I took the paper from him, which proved to be a photograph, worn and frayed around the edges. The image was of three children, grouped together in front of the painted screen of a professional photographer's background.

The photograph must have been taken twelve or more years ago. Keenan Mulloy was instantly recognizable as the oldest child: a handsome boy of around twelve, with dark hair and a serious, steady expression. Another boy, slightly younger, but with the same dark hair and handsome features, stood beside him. And between them—

I looked down at the photograph, feeling something cold clench the back of my throat.

Mary, too, was instantly recognizable; she was only nine or ten in the photograph, but had the same smooth black hair and pretty, delicate features that she did now. But she was smiling, her head thrown a little back, her eyes crinkled at the edges. She looked *happy* in a way that I had never in all the time of our acquaintance seen her appear.

I swallowed, then nodded. "Thank you. I'll see that she gets it."

WATSON

18. ARRANGEMENTS

We left the church after searching Father Mulloy's sad little room and rode in a four-wheeler with Lucy to her flat on Exeter Street. I was grateful that I had my revolver with me, for although several hours of daylight remained on this June evening, the Whitechapel area was no place for a lady and, under the circumstances we had seen that day, no cab driver could be trusted. Nonetheless, we reached Exeter Street without incident. There, over her protests, we escorted her up the three flights of stairs to the door of her flat. Then we said our goodbyes.

Holmes and I then set out along the Strand for the Diogenes Club. As we walked, I tried to make sense of what we had seen in Mulloy's apartment. We had uncovered ravings apparently written by the priest, filled with hate, threats, and rage at Holmes. I knew Lucy and Holmes believed that the writings, like the string Lucy had recovered from the pavement outside St. Paul's, had been employed by someone in order to portray Father Mulloy as a suicidal unbalanced religious zealot, and I quite understood their suspicions.

Still, the words continued to occupy my thoughts. How, if they were truly Mulloy's, could Mulloy have changed from the conscientious, benevolent priest? What could have occurred during the past months? I recalled the intensity of emotion he had shown when Lucy had questioned him in February. But that emotion, I thought, had been a zealous reverence for his duty as a clergyman. If he had written the letters, then how could he turn his pen so hatefully on the one man whom he had come to for aid in his perplexing circumstances?

Mycroft was waiting for us in the Diogenes Club lobby. Grim-faced, he beckoned us to a corner room where we would not be overheard. We sat on three of the club's leather chairs. Mycroft's voice was barely audible. Without pausing to ask us what we had found at the Church of the English Martyrs, he said, "A firebomb was detonated at your doorstep."

Holmes's grey eyes remained steady, but he blinked rapidly several times. That was his only visible reaction.

Then he said, "Is Mrs. Hudson safe?"

"She is packing her suitcases. I took the liberty of arranging for her transportation. She is prepared to travel to Chelsea and to remain there with her aunt until the Jubilee celebrations have concluded."

"All one could ask for, considering the circumstances."

"You are welcome."

"Watson and I will be traveling as well."

"Quite wise."

"We found a clue in the room of the unfortunate priest. I believe it will lead to a connection with Wilhelm."

Mycroft nodded, leaning back in his chair, his arms folded across his waistcoat, resting on his capacious middle. He said,

"Every trail, if it be a true one, must eventually lead us to Wilhelm."

"Agreed. Wilhelm has furnished the funds for two previous attacks. There is no reason to suppose that he has given up."

"Where will you go?"

"To Elswick works."

"But you have been there and found nothing."

"The last time I went there armed with only a letter from the Commissioner, addressed to the manager of the Elswick works. This time—if you can arrange it—I should like a letter of introduction to Sir Robert Armstrong himself, written by the Duke of Devonshire. He and Sir Robert are both Fellows of the Royal Society."

"Rank has its privileges," said Mycroft.

Holmes's mouth twitched in one of his tight, momentary smiles. "Perhaps Captain Stayley might prevail on the Duke to write the letter."

"So you trust the Captain with knowledge of your whereabouts."

"He is already aware of our mission and our difficulty. I am not entirely sanguine about sharing my whereabouts with the Metropolitan Police under the circumstances. It is as well to keep the circle of knowledge as limited as possible."

"How will you travel to Elswick?"

"On the Newcastle Express, departing at eleven o'clock."

Mycroft nodded. "Then you may look for me at King's Cross Station at ten-forty-five. I shall bring the letter." He sat forward. "Now, tell me about the clue."

LUCY

19. CONDOLENCES

"Mary?" I tapped on the bedroom door. "Can I do anything for you?"

I could hear a muffled sob from inside the room, but Mary didn't respond.

Not that I could blame her. Even as I spoke the words, I could hear how inadequate they sounded—all the more so because it was at least the fourth or fifth time I had repeated them.

But I couldn't seem to find anything else to say. All the usual platitudes about our dear departed being in a better place or time healing all wounds seemed even more inadequate and insulting.

Mary and I had been given time off from performing at the Savoy so that we could attend rehearsals at Devonshire House. After Holmes and Uncle John had taken me to Exeter Street, I had found Mary out and the flat empty. I had waited for hours, with my imagination painting nightmarish images of Mary, too, being set upon and killed. Thrown off a bridge or shoved in front of a train, her death to be chalked up as another suicide.

I would have gone out and looked for her, but I had no likely place even to start searching.

Finally, just as the clock on our mantle was showing nearly ten o'clock, Mary had come home.

Now I heard a fresh burst of sobs come from inside the bedroom. Mary had been home for nearly an hour. I had broken the news to her about her brother, and she had run into the bedroom, banging the door behind her—and then spent every one of the past fifty-odd minutes weeping and sobbing and wailing so loudly that I was halfway expecting the neighbors to complain.

I leaned against the door panel. Maybe I should just give up and leave her to vent her grief alone. Except that felt heartless, somehow.

"Mary? May I come in?"

She hadn't locked the door; I would have heard the key turn in the lock. She didn't answer, so I cautiously turned the knob and opened the door.

Mary was on her knees beside the wardrobe where she kept her clothes and didn't look up as I entered. There was a large, silver music box on the floor beside her, a very fine, antique-looking piece, with ornate silver scrollwork and a small sculptured figure of a girl playing a harp on the top. I had seen her bring it out only once before, when her brother was here.

"That's very pretty," I said softly, coming to stand beside her. "I've never seen—"

With a gasp, Mary snatched up the music box and almost flung it back inside the wardrobe, shutting the door after it. Then, burying her face in her hands, she broke into another torrent of sobbing.

I patted her shoulder helplessly, biting my tongue before I could say that I was so sorry for a sixth time.

It wasn't really Mary's fault. She was truly grieving her brother's death. After being onstage with Mary night after night, I knew her acting capabilities—or lack thereof—well enough to be certain that she wasn't pretending. Her eyes were swollen and bloodshot, her nose was red and running, and her whole body was hunched forward, trying to curl around bitter inner pain.

But I also knew from experience that those who made acting their profession often lived their lives as though they were *always* on an invisible stage.

Their only way of processing the cruelty of life was to find an audience for whom to enact their reactions. At the moment, I was serving as Mary's audience of one as she struggled with the shock and pain of her brother's loss.

"How *could* he?" Mary raised her tear-streaked face, her voice so choked that I could scarcely make out the words.

I sighed. I was also confronting the unpleasant truth that being incredibly sorry for someone unfortunately didn't make you like them any better.

Mary dashed a hand across her reddened eyes, her mouth twisting. "How could he *do* this to me? He was my *only* family, how could he leave me entirely on my own?"

"I told you, remember? As far as I know, the police are not certain that your brother killed himself."

Mary rubbed her eyes. "How do you know all this?"

"From Jack—Constable Kelly," I said patiently.

Mary sniffed, hiccupping slightly. "Oh yes, your pet policeman." She opened her mouth, but then closed it again without saying anything more, her shoulders slumping.

Another mark of genuine grief; she couldn't even bother with her usual sniping remark about Jack's and my friendship.

"Yes."

I had told her all of this already, but I couldn't honestly blame her for not having paid much attention the first time through; I had only just broken the news of her brother's death, after all.

This was also the part of my story that I had to be very, very careful about telling.

Uncle John had never announced to the world that Sherlock Holmes had survived his meeting with Professor Moriarty at the Reichenbach Falls. His return to London was not a secret, but neither was it generally known.

There might come a time when I had to tell Mary of Sherlock Holmes' involvement in her brother's case, but I couldn't bring someone who liked to talk as much as Mary did into the secret without first obtaining Holmes's consent.

"Inspector Lestrade of Scotland Yard was the investigating officer on the scene, but Jack heard of your brother's death." I hurried on before Mary could ask exactly *how* he had heard. "Inspector Lestrade had no idea that Keenan even had a sister; the other priests at his church didn't know he had any family. But Jack heard his last name and wondered whether there might be some connection to you."

And I would sometime very soon have to relate all of this to Jack, so that—just in case Mary ever had the chance to question him about any of the story—his version of events would match mine.

"Jack is telling Inspector Lestrade," I told Mary. "But I asked for the chance to be the one to break the news to you. Tomorrow you'll want to go and claim the … his body. So that burial arrangements can be made."

Mary squeezed her eyes shut, tears leaking from the corners of her closed lids.

"I can go with you, if you like," I said gently. I hesitated, then asked, "Have you—did you and Keenan have any other family? Anyone that you need to get into contact with? I can help—"

"No." Mary interrupted, her voice still clogged with tears, but final. "There's no one. Keenan is—was—all the family I had left."

"I'm sorry." The words were still inadequate, but they were all I had. "If there's anything I can do—"

Mary raised her head again. "If Keenan didn't kill himself, what do they think happened? An accident, or—"

"It could have been an accident," I said carefully. This was another area in which I would have to be very selective in which parts of the truth I told Mary.

It would actually be much simpler to let her believe—along with Inspector Lestrade—that her brother had taken his own life.

But Mary didn't deserve to live with the pain of thinking that she might have stopped her brother from jumping if only she had realized what he intended in time. The grief she would already have to carry was bad enough.

"The police are not certain," I said. "One possibility is that he jumped to his death. But they are also exploring the possibility that his death may have been caused by a group of … Fenians."

For a moment, I wasn't even sure that Mary had heard me.

Then the blood slowly drained from her cheeks, leaving her face ashen to the lips. "Fenians." Her lips shaped the word, but no sound actually emerged.

"Yes."

I couldn't tell Mary of Keenan's meetings with the false commissioner of police. "Some men with Fenian connections—or so the police believe—approached your brother and asked whether they might use the basement of his church as a place to store some crates. They wouldn't say what was in the crates, so your brother refused. The police are looking into the possibility that the Fenians may have killed him out of revenge or to stop him from going to the authorities."

I allowed myself a fervent, silent hope that it wouldn't occur to Mary to ask *how* that story had come into the hands of the police.

Though she didn't look in any state to question it. Mary's face was still blanched, her hands clasped and twisting on a fold of her skirt.

"*Fenians.*" This time, she almost spat the word, her sobs actually stuttering to a halt as anger suffused her face. "How could he have had anything to do with them?"

"But he didn't, not—"

I might just as well not have spoken.

Mary sat up, her back ramrod straight, her mouth thinning with anger. "Keenan should have found another way. He ought to have turned them over to the police at once. He ought—he ought—"

Her voice broke and she covered her face, digging the heels of her hands hard against her eyes. Then she raised her face again, grinding the words out through clenched teeth. Bright spots of anger burned on her cheekbones.

"If you ask me, Keenan should have taken a gun and shot every last one of those filthy men *dead* the second they set foot on his church's property."

Pointing out that Keenan Mulloy's bishop might have taken issue with cold-blooded murder would be pointless. Instead, I squeezed Mary's hand.

Mary went on. "Keenan knows—he *knew*—what the Fenians are, what they've cost—" She stopped abruptly, clamping her mouth shut.

"What they've cost ..." I finally asked.

Mary looked at me, and for the first time that night—almost the first time since I had known her—her expression was no longer petulant or irritable, but flat, as though someone had wiped all trace of feeling away with a cloth.

She shook her head. "Never mind." She stood up abruptly, turning towards the washroom. "I'm going to bed."

I frowned. I had thought that she would wish me to remain her captive audience for another hour at least.

"Of course," I said slowly. "You should try to sleep if you can."

I hesitated, then drew out the photograph that Holmes had given to me—the one of Mary with the boys who must have been her brothers.

"This was found in Keenan's desk," I said. "I thought—that is, Jack thought that you might like to have it."

Mary took the photograph and looked at it, her chin jerking up and down and her swollen eyes flooding all over again. But instead of the fresh sobs I was expecting, she wiped her eyes, swallowing.

"Thank you." Her voice sounded choked. For a moment she stood motionless, looking down at the floor, and I thought I caught a flicker of indecision cross her expression, as though she were debating whether to say more. But then she shook her head, raising her gaze to mine. "Thank you." She spoke with finality. "Good night, Lucy."

WATSON

20. DEPARTURES

Mycroft left us after we had told him of the half-completed note that Father Mulloy had written to "Miss Jones." Holmes and I then ate a quiet supper at the Diogenes Club. Holmes wanted to inspect the damage at 221B Baker Street, but I persuaded him that no benefit could come from his exposing himself to those who had planted the firebomb and who were surely watching. We stayed the remainder of the night in rooms at the Diogenes Club, without incident.

The next morning at breakfast we received a note from Mycroft. He reported that his valet had entered our Baker Street rooms via the back door and packed our luggage with clothing and other necessaries for a journey of several days. The suitcases had already been loaded aboard an earlier train and sent on to await our arrival at Newcastle Station.

All seemed in readiness for an uneventful journey.

At ten-forty-five we entered the soaring expanse of King's Cross Station. We could hear the steady rhythmic chuffing of several trains as they sat waiting, idling their steam engines. Clouds of acrid coal smoke hung in the air above us, clinging to the high ceiling and the great rafters as though trying to escape. Travellers and uniformed railway attendants manoeuvring their loaded luggage carts bustled to and fro.

Surprisingly enough, however, there was no sign of Mycroft. We made our way through the crowd toward the platform where the Newcastle Express awaited its passengers.

Then behind us I heard a familiar voice. "Mr. Holmes!"

We stopped. Behind us stood Inspector Lestrade, along with a tall gentleman dressed in a top hat and neatly tailored dark suit, a maroon silk cravat beneath his crisply starched white collar, who was nervously glancing at the crowd, twisting his head like a small, timorous bird fearful of predators. For a moment I did not recognize this second man as Captain Stayley, one of the three officials we had seen at the Diogenes Club with the Prime Minister. No longer burdened by stacks of papers, he now appeared less of the downtrodden underling.

Lestrade appeared tired and somewhat put-upon. He nodded a greeting. "You know Mr. Stayley here," he said. "Mycroft Holmes asked us to escort Mr. Stayley. He has something for you, and Mycroft wanted to be certain that it reached you safely."

Stayley leaned towards us, raising his voice so as to be heard over the din of passengers, relatives, attendants, cabs, and horses that crowded the station in a confused jumble. "Pardon the surprise, gentlemen. Mycroft told me you have requested a letter? I have it with me. I thought it best to spare your brother the journey."

"I am sure my brother appreciates not having to deviate from his daily routine in Whitehall," said Holmes.

"Actually, I have two letters," Stayley continued respectfully, pulling two envelopes from his inside pocket. "One is to Lord

Armstrong, as you requested, but the other is to Sir Andrew Noble, Lord Armstrong's partner, who is presently in charge of the company's business affairs. Sir Andrew will be more likely to be in a position to assist your inquiry at the armaments works. You should enjoy better access and greater cooperation than you encountered on your last visit. Both letters bear the Duke's signature and seal."

Holmes pocketed the letters. "Thank you, Captain."

Stayley smiled and nodded. "Well, that concludes my mission. I hope you enjoy Cragside, gentlemen. I understand it is quite lovely this time of year."

"My men will be staying behind to keep an eye on you, Mr. Holmes," Lestrade said, with an air of menace that I thought was somewhat exaggerated.

Holmes merely nodded.

After we bade our farewells, we walked in the direction of the platforms and the waiting trains. Less than five minutes remained until the scheduled departure of the Newcastle Express. We had not gone far, however, when, in the disorganized jumble of cabs and carts crowding the platform to pick up or discharge their passengers, I saw two large brown horses stamping their feet and jostling each other before a small black omnibus. The horses and the omnibus were turning around so as to enable a quick exit from the station.

I heard a familiar, oily voice up above us.

"Goin' somewhere, are we, Mr. 'Olmes?"

My heart raced as I saw that man above us on the driver's platform was Owens, the false cabdriver who had attempted to abduct us barely twenty-four hours earlier.

The door of the black omnibus opened. Four rough-looking men stepped down.

PART THREE

WITH FAIREST SHOW

WATSON

21. ESCAPE

The ruffians closed in on us, blocking our way.

Our adversaries were clad in dirty workmen's garb and flat workers' hats. All were unkempt, their beards and moustaches scraggly, untrimmed, and food-stained. All were younger than Holmes and me, however, and with that air of tension and excitement common to criminals about to show their true colours.

I took little comfort in the small Webley revolver in my jacket pocket, for at such close quarters in a crowded station there was a serious risk of unintended consequences. It would be difficult enough to control the direction of any bullet in a hand-to-hand struggle. Even with a direct hit, the bullet might pass through its intended target to injure or kill any of the travellers around us. Yet I was determined that these men would not succeed in abducting us. I was certain Holmes felt the same. Lestrade had said his men had been alerted, but I knew we could not rely on that. I tried to judge which one of the ruffians would be the better target for a wrestler's rush or a diving tackle.

Holmes had leaped toward the nearest horse. Holding it firmly by the bridle, he looked coolly up at Owens. "Who is paying you?"

A malicious grin split the man's dirty face. "Oh, it's the Good Lord's payin' me, Mr. 'Olmes. It's the Lord's work I'm doin,' after all, ain't it?"

Then the shrill high-pitched shriek of a police whistle pierced the din around us. I felt a surge of relief.

"If you trouble yourselves to look beyond our little gathering," Holmes said, "you will observe that several patrolmen are about to apprehend you."

Owens did not take his eyes from Holmes. "We're not to be gulled by that old trick, Mr. 'Olmes. You're coming with us."

"I think not," said Holmes, his manner still offhand. Letting go of the bridle he called out, "Officers!"

I turned. There were indeed two blue-uniformed patrolmen coming towards us at a run, and another two running behind them.

"Scarper, boys," said Owens. The evil grin flashed again across his face as he added, "We will find you again." Then he whipped up his horses and the omnibus surged past us and into the crowd, scattering all the pedestrians in its wake.

The four ruffians ran off. The patrolmen turned and ran in pursuit.

Looking back in the direction from which the patrolmen had come, I saw Lestrade and Captain Stayley, about a hundred feet away, only partially visible in the shifting crowd. Both men were looking towards us. Lestrade raised his hand in a friendly wave. The Captain drew himself up to stand at attention. I felt warmed by gratitude. Then the Captain clicked his heels together and saluted. I returned the salute. For a moment I felt like a soldier again.

"Our foes surround us at every turn," said Holmes. He turned abruptly and marched in the direction of the waiting trains with his characteristic swift stride, leaving me to follow.

We reached our train with seconds to spare. Before we entered our first-class compartment, Holmes looked behind the door, as if he suspected that our very last refuge might already have been invaded.

Once inside, however, he took out his pipe and shag tobacco, placed them on his lap, and settled back into his seat, closing his eyes as our train began to move. I waited until our train had cleared the station. Then, anticipating that he would soon be puffing away at his pipe, I raised our compartment window slightly at top and bottom to allow for the outflow of smoky air and the inflow of fresh. I waited for Holmes to open his eyes. So many questions welled up within me. Determined not to ask Holmes something to which the answer was obvious, I tried to marshal my thoughts.

First, it was plain that we had been followed from the Diogenes Club. What assurance did we have that we were not being followed even now? Well, I knew the answer to that one. We had no assurances whatsoever.

Would Elswick and Cragside be safer than London? I went over the obvious facts. The factory town of Newcastle was far smaller than London. The management would have better control over the workmen than the police would have over the millions of Londoners and the additional millions of visitors. The Elswick workmen would know each other. Strangers could not expect to pass unnoticed. And Cragside was a Lord's estate, fenced round and guarded. To attack Holmes there would be a difficult proposition once we were within the grounds. Though of course we would be traveling to and from the Elswick works, and possibly the docks from which the products of the factory were shipped. We might also, I realized, be visiting the shipyards, exposed to riverboats and marksmen from the opposite riverbanks. There was no escaping the danger. We would have to be on our guard everywhere.

I glanced at Holmes. His hawk-like features were stilled, reminding me of a statue or a mummified Egyptian king. His eyelids drooped, very nearly shut, and his hands were clasped atop his pipe and tobacco pouch. His spare frame appeared to have moulded itself into the plush seat of the railway coach, moving only slightly each time the carriage rocked on its springs or clattered over a switch point. His chest rose and fell slowly and regularly with each breath. I concluded that he had fallen asleep.

My thoughts strayed back to the Jubilee preparations and to the enormous difficulty of policing the hundreds of thousands of onlookers who would be crowding and jostling each other to see the Queen at the parade, not to mention the other events that had been scheduled, each of which represented a potential target. I wondered what had drawn the priest Keenan Mulloy to St. Paul's Cathedral. Did it have to do with the great thanksgiving service? Or had he been forcefully taken there in order to convey some message intended to mislead us?

The train was slowing. I heard the hiss of steam and the screech of brakes being applied. Looking out our window, I saw several small buildings and the sign for the Stevenage station, the first stop on the Great Northern Newcastle line.

Holmes was beside me at the window. His voice was tense. "There. On the platform, Watson. Do you recognize Bernhard von Bulow?"

22. A FAMILIAR ADVERSARY

The German diplomat entered our compartment a few minutes later, carrying a lit cigar and looking just as confident as he had appeared less than a year ago when our train first entered Germany. This time, of course, we were on British soil, but this did not seem to affect von Bulow. Grey haired, elegantly tailored, urbane, he appraised us both with cold blue eyes. "I come here to satisfy my curiosity. And to deliver a request."

Holmes interrupted. "Are you in England for the Jubilee, Mr. Ambassador?"

"I am."

"On an official basis?"

"As an observer."

"Observing what, exactly?"

"I interest myself in your country's greatest asset for the defence of your far-flung Empire."

"And what might that be?"

"Why, your Jubilee ceremonies themselves, of course. You have a love of ceremony, and you perform it extremely well. Those who govern your colonies take pride in the grandeur, the music, the medals, the splendid pageantry. They come here knowing the events of the Jubilee will all be reported. Their subjects will read, and envy, and kow-tow—some of them actually assuming that ridiculous pose."

"Your Kaiser seems to value that precise method of instilling respect and demonstrating political power," Holmes said.

"He does indeed. But he also values heavy weaponry. However, we were not discussing the All-highest, His Imperial Majesty. Were we? We were discussing the illusions that enable a pathetic, crippled, old toad-like caricature of a queen to create the emotions of affection and awe before her great majesty and power. But what happens if the bubble bursts?"

"You speak as though you plan to disrupt the Jubilee," I said.

"I?" His grey eyebrows lifted with feigned innocence. "I shall create no disruption whatsoever. I shall merely observe, to see for myself what others may do and to report to my ruler so that he can decide what course of action to pursue. There is no shortage of disgruntled colonials in your Empire, as you well know. Every day your newspapers report an uprising of some sort—whether in India or Egypt, South Africa or Ireland. Imagine what would happen if on a fine day in June in merry England the world were to see that the great British Empire had been humiliated, brought to its knees or worse, even at the apex of what was to have been its most prideful moment?"

"You can imagine whatever you wish," said Holmes. "Now, what is the request that has brought you here to this railway carriage?"

"Always the practical fellow, are you not, Mr. Holmes?" Von Bulow took out a silver box of small cigars and lit one. "There is something you might do for me. There are two German citizens who went missing in London last November. You know the two men. They were with us in the Kaiser's Schloss in Bad Homburg. Your government has officially denied any knowledge of their whereabouts. I should be grateful if you—"

Holmes cut him off. "I cannot help you there. I have not seen them since I was in your country."

"A pity. Do you know the whereabouts of Mr. Arkwright?"

"I am told he died in the Andaman Islands," Holmes said.

"I had heard the same."

"You hear a great many things. For example, you had the information about which train Watson and I would be taking this morning, as evidenced by your presence here."

"Obviously." Von Bulow took on a more wary look.

"Did you hire the men who tried to abduct us at King's Cross Station?" Holmes asked.

"I hired no one."

"You expect me to believe that, when your government invested heavily in two previous assassination attempts?"

"My government has categorically denied any knowledge of those. And I give you my word, my personal word as a gentleman, that neither I nor my government has paid to abduct you or to interfere in any way with the Jubilee celebration or your attempts to protect it. On this you have my word as, I repeat, a gentleman."

Holmes said nothing. An awkward silence ensued.

Then von Bulow continued. "Even if you mistrust me, you might also put yourself in the place of my Kaiser. Assuming that your accusation is true—that he had invested heavily twice before—which I certainly do not admit, except as a hypothetical example for illustrative purposes—"

"Arkwright said he had been promised a dukedom and a castle in Bavaria."

"The word of a traitor, eager to cast blame wherever he could." The German took a long pull on his cigar and blew smoke towards our carriage window. "But, as I said, let us assume what you say to be the truth. If you were the Kaiser, would you be inclined to invest after two previous failures, throwing more good money after bad?"

Holmes merely shrugged.

"There is no shortage of adversaries within your own colonies who have the capacity to do the things you are afraid of. The Pashtun in India, your rabid foes, have their dynastic treasures, antiques, and artefacts that are readily converted into cash. The Boers have their diamond mines. The Fenians have their anonymous American financial supporters. Why should the Kaiser risk any of Germany's resources when he can merely sit back and watch the many others who will inevitably challenge British rule?"

"Who is your intermediary at the Bank of England?"

"There was a senior clerk. His name was Perkins. He was not my contact but—"

"I said 'is,' Mr. Ambassador. Who is your agent *now*?"

"You strike a most undiplomatic tone, Mr. Holmes. Particularly for one who has said he cannot help me in what I came to ask, a very humanitarian request that would enable my government to end the worries and uncertainties of the grieving relations of Herr Richter and Herr Dietrich."

"I find it difficult to sympathize, Mr. Ambassador," said Holmes.

"Will you help me, or will you not?"

"I have already given you my answer."

Von Bulow left our compartment moments later.

Holmes sat silent, in deep contemplation.

After the train had gone a few more miles north, we stopped at Peterborough Station. I looked out our window.

"Holmes," I said, "von Bulow is outside. He is striding briskly across the platform towards a waiting southbound train. He is not looking back."

Holmes spoke as though the matter were of minimal interest. "He has fulfilled his intended purpose."

"Which is?"

"To convince us that he hopes we will not reach Cragside."

"I do not follow."

"He wants us to believe that we are on the correct path, so he makes protests of innocence that are obviously false. Did you believe he really wanted to provide information to the grieving relatives of his two missing thugs? Did you believe claim that he has had nothing to do with our attempted abduction at the station?"

"No," I said.

"Precisely. And he could not have expected us to believe him."

"So what was he attempting to do?"

"He wants us to redouble our efforts to reach Cragside instead of following other leads."

His lofty tone was beginning to get under my skin. "So what does that mean?"

"It means, old friend, that we cannot entirely trust Mr Arkwright's Andaman Islands prison confession that the word 'Elswick' is somehow an important clue. We must take a different path. Whether it is the path von Bulow wants to conceal from us or not—well, that is uncertain. As the future always must be."

I detected in his voice a note of resignation, but also a note of excitement, as though something in the German diplomat's words or manner had put him onto a fresh new scent.

"What path?"

"I shall tell you more when we reach Newcastle. That will be"—he consulted his watch—"in two hours and twenty-one minutes."

Whereupon he leaned back against the corner of the carriage seat and pulled his deerstalker hat down over his eyes.

23. A DIFFERENT PATH

"Newcastle Station, Watson."

Holmes's words woke me from that drowsy state frequently induced by a long railway journey. He was standing at our window, his pocket watch in his hand. As though obedient to his direction, the rhythmic sway of the carriage and the click of the steel wheels going over the rails began to slow. Moments later came the harsh sound of the brakes being applied.

"We are four minutes late," Holmes continued. "Provided the Newcastle Station is not too crowded, there should be ample time to collect luggage and board the local train to Morpeth. Eight minutes remain until its departure."

Holmes's prediction proved to be correct. We reached the platform for Morpeth with our luggage cart in tow by a uniformed attendant. We stopped beside the first-class carriage. Holmes directed the man to place my luggage on the platform. The man did so and reached for Holmes's two suitcases.

"Those will remain here for the moment," he told the attendant. "I shall carry these other two. Please wait here."

He picked up my suitcases and took a few steps to the carriage, indicating that I should follow. I did so. He placed my suitcases inside the carriage, then turned back to me. Lowering his voice he said, "I must leave you, old friend."

I was not about to show surprise. In fact, I had suspected something along these lines. "A different path," I said. "I suppose you will not tell me where."

He gave one of his tight smiles and handed me a small blue bound book. "According to this travellers' guide, the name 'Morpeth' derives from two words: 'murder path.' I trust that is not an omen."

"What do you want me to do at Cragside?"

"We need to uncover why Arkwright said 'Elswick' when he was interviewed at the Andaman Islands' prison. Question Sir Robert Armstrong. Find out if any unusual events occurred the first week of February this year. Find out if he has had any contact with foreign visitors since then. At the Elswick factory, look to the inventory of cannon parts. Perhaps the missing cannon was never assembled. Watch to see who observes you at the factory and at Cragside. If you have news, wire Mycroft. Prepare to return to London on the 18th. I shall meet you in Cragside before then. If I do not arrive, you are to return to London without me and act in accordance with certain instructions that I have given to Mycroft."

I yielded to my anxious curiosity. "Holmes, where are you going?"

"It is better that you do not know."

Then he clapped me on the shoulder and turned to the waiting attendant.

So I was to be kept in the dark once more. A hot rush of righteous indignation filled my mind and clouded my vision. I boarded the train without looking back.

24. A STUDY IN ARTILLERY

The sun had nearly set as I neared the end of my journey some three hours later. A coach and four had met me at Morpeth. The driver had told me I was expected for supper that evening at Sir Robert's table, and he did not spare the horses. We fairly flew over the narrow bumpy road, so that I had to hold on to the bar installed for the purpose within the plush interior of the carriage.

The driver slowed as we reached the crest of a hill. "Cragside," he called out. Through the carriage window I saw across a deep ravine, both sides thickly wooded, a huge castle-like estate, topped by a Tudor-like beamed triangular structure, as if some gigantic builder of Elizabethan homes or chalets had perched his favourite upper-storey structure atop a Scottish castle of olden times. Perched high and set into the mountaintop, and now bathed in the gold of the setting sun, the grandeur of Cragside made me stare with admiration and awe. How many men and how many years had it taken, I wondered, to have erected such an imposing structure? Had any of Holmes's other cases taken him to so grand a venue? Possibly his visits to royalty, I mused. But no case on which I had accompanied him had involved such an extraordinary setting. I hoped I should be equal to the task to which I had been assigned.

We were soon at the sheltered entryway. I was met by the butler, a venerable old gentleman who gave me a respectful nod. "Miss Hollister will show you to your room. Please take but a short while to refresh yourself following your journey. Supper is served at seven. It is now six-thirty-five."

Then he added, "Lord Lansdowne and his assistant will join you and Lord Armstrong."

I came downstairs as quickly as I could don my dinner apparel and make myself presentable, arriving about ten minutes before seven. The old butler beckoned me inside. The great wood-panelled dining room was equally as imposing as the exterior of Cragside. The ceiling must have been fully thirty feet high. Electric chandeliers bathed the table in a pale yellow light from above. At the side of the room there was an enormous fireplace, set within an even larger alcove. There was no fire, owing to the temperature outside.

On the other side of the room three men stood huddled over a high sideboard-like table.

I recognized Lord Lansdowne and his assistant, Mr. Greco, whom we had met at the Diogenes Club. The third man was obviously Lord Armstrong. He looked up as the butler introduced me, his wide round eyes bright and alert beneath his high-domed forehead and framed by his white side-whiskers. He appeared steady on his feet, though a bit stooped with age. I had heard that his wife had died four years previously. Perhaps it was my imagination, but he gave me an impression of sadness. Or resignation. Or possibly both.

I had brought with me Stayley's letter of introduction, but Lord Armstrong waved it aside. He spoke without hesitation in a near-Scottish Northumberland accent, though his tone was somewhat reedy and tremulous due to his advanced years. "No need, Dr. Watson. Lansdowne here knows you, and I have a clear recollection of Mr. Holmes's visit in February. We will take supper first, and then I have arranged a small display in the library to put your little Jubilee problem into perspective."

At the table it became apparent that this was a business meeting rather than lavish entertainment. The cooking was simple fare: roast beef with Yorkshire pudding, pickled beets, and boiled turnips. There was no wine served with dinner, only water.

From the conversation, I soon realized that Lansdowne and his assistant had not travelled to Cragside simply to assist in the investigation to which Holmes and I had been assigned. Rather, they were discussing the business arrangements that Armstrong's company would have with the British government after the merger with a former rival. The new company would be the largest manufacturer of weapons and warships in the Empire. Lansdowne was intent that the vast size of the new cartel would not lessen the Crown's ability to obtain favourable terms. Huge sums, huge quantities of weapons were at stake as the Empire grew and faced ever-increasing challenges from those who wished it harm, particularly Kaiser Wilhelm. Lansdowne seemed intent on keeping Armstrong weaponry out of Wilhelm's hands. Lord Armstrong was clearly a patriot, for he put up no objections whatsoever on that score.

Finally, dinner concluded, without dessert or brandy.

We adjourned to the library, which was also a wood-panelled high-ceilinged space, equally imposing and with an equally graceful air. To my surprise, on the great dark-stained oak table at the centre of the room were models of artillery, ranging from perhaps three inches in length and height to nearly two feet. There was also a map and a large copper-plated yardstick with holes drilled through it at regular intervals. Beside the yardstick lay a thick grease pencil.

Lord Armstrong stood at the side of the table, his right hand resting lightly on the smallest of the three models. Each had been cast in lead. Each looked as though it could have been taken directly from a boy's toy soldier set, only substantially larger.

"Gentlemen," said Lord Armstrong. "I realize that there has been some talk of a missing artillery weapon, of the type we have prepared for the naval fleet of His Majesty the Emperor of Japan, modelled along the lines of the big guns currently installed in Malta and on the Italian warship *Duilio*. But I hardly think that it would present a threat to the Jubilee. It is far too large. The barrel of the new gun is more than ten yards in length. It weighs over one hundred tons. It requires a crew of thirty-five men dedicated to its function, seventeen of whom are needed simply to handle the ammunition. And, as I told Mr. Holmes last February, the gun is not missing. We have delivered the only two guns that were ordered."

"Yet one was declared missing," Greco said.

"Falsely declared, as nearly as I can determine. A written communication was sent here from Tokyo claiming that a third gun had been ordered and invoiced for, but never delivered. That is the basis of the declaration. Yet I tell you that there was never such a gun. And to believe that such a behemoth of a weapon could be brought within range of London without Her Majesty's government being fully aware of the circumstances is ludicrous. To imagine that a crew of thirty-five could be trained in secret and operate it without being noticed and apprehended—" He broke off, shaking his head. "Well, that is beyond ludicrous, gentlemen. Beyond ludicrous. However, you are welcome—Dr. Watson is welcome—to examine anything and everything at the Elswick works or the naval works or anywhere else that bears the name of Armstrong or Whitworth, since we two firms are soon to be united."

"I appreciate your cooperation," I replied, though my heart sunk at the futility of the task before me and the knowledge that Holmes, who had been here earlier, must surely have known of the absurdity of the threat that I was to investigate.

Then I remembered his words. *See who observes you.*

Perhaps that was the real intention of the visit. Very well, I would take that as my working hypothesis.

"But why, then, are these little models here?" asked Lansdowne.

Armstrong gave an ironic smile. "Because these guns, gentlemen, might indeed threaten the Jubilee. They are Armstrong field guns, relatively easy to manoeuver and operate. Breech loaded and rifled. This one is a twelve-pounder, meaning that it can fire an exploding shell of twelve pounds in weight. The second is a twenty pounder, and the largest—here—is a forty pounder. Any one of these is capable of firing its shell up to two miles, provided that it can be set so as to have a clear firing line at an elevation of forty-five degrees. If not, if it needs to be set at a higher angle of elevation, the range is proportionally decreased."

He placed the tip of the yardstick on the map, positioned the black grease pencil, and deftly manoeuvred the yardstick, sweeping it in a smooth arc so as to trace a large thick black circle on the map.

"So, gentlemen. I have drawn a circle with a radius of two miles around St. Paul's Cathedral, which I am given to understand is one of the focal points of the Jubilee celebration. You have an area of roughly twelve square miles. Within it are several parks that would readily allow for the optimum elevation angle. As would the river, of course. And any one of thousands upon thousands of rooftops. On the twenty-second of June, anyone with such a weapon at any point within this circle could send an explosive shell raining down upon the Queen and all those around her."

Lansdowne drew in his breath. "It will be difficult to police all that area. But perhaps not impossible."

Beside him, Greco said, "We might get at the problem from the other direction." He hefted the smaller of the artillery pieces. "Have any of these gone missing from your factories or not been received by your intended customers?"

Armstrong shook his head dolefully. "You plainly do not understand what I am attempting to demonstrate. These are common field artillery guns. They can be disassembled and their parts concealed within innocent-looking crates or hogsheads. And they have been manufactured since the 1860s. In the last thirty-five years, thousands of these weapons, and tens of thousands of similar weapons from other manufacturers, have been produced and shipped all over the world. They could be used by anyone who is able to bring them into London."

"I do not see how that helps us," said Greco.

"You have limited resources," Armstrong said. "It would be best that you not waste them in pursuit of a heavy gun that has supposedly gone missing, according to a spurious and unsubstantiated Japanese claim."

"With all respect," Greco said, "I would point out that ignoring that Japanese claim is in the interest of your company."

Armstrong bristled. Quickly, Lansdowne intervened. "That will do, Mr. Greco. Lord Armstrong, we have every confidence in you and your integrity."

"Your confidence will be fully justified. My records and all my activities concerning the new heavy gun are open to your inspection. However, I believe you would do well to consider the dangers from the smaller weapons."

"We shall give them every consideration," said Lansdowne.

"The British Army has spent many millions of pounds to purchase those weapons in their thousands over the years," Greco added. "We have ample experience."

The responses of both men clearly indicated that they were unconcerned with the threat from smaller weapons. However, Lord Armstrong did not appear at all put off. "No doubt. I won't tell you how to do your jobs, gentlemen." He smiled brightly. Then he went on, "However, I would like to show you something new in the field artillery line. I have arranged a demonstration tomorrow morning, so you can attend and still have time before the eleven o'clock train to London."

Lansdowne coughed delicately. "Regrettably, urgent government business mandates our return before that," he said.

Greco added, "We have chartered a special train that leaves tonight. It awaits us at the Morpeth Station."

Lansdowne said, "Perhaps Dr. Watson could attend your demonstration tomorrow. When he makes his report on the missing naval gun, he can inform us as to the particulars. We shall return in a few days. Are you agreeable to that, Doctor?"

Respect for the positions of both parties, and my own, left me with no choice. I consented.

WATSON

25. ON THE FIRING RANGE

The field artillery demonstration took place in a driving rain outside Morpeth, with me holding an umbrella against the downpour, standing ankle deep in cold mud. Lord Armstrong had not come, due to the weather. We were at the edge of a farmer's field, perhaps two hundred yards from the edge of a cliff. The artillery gun was trained on a wooden bulls-eye target the size of a small shed, set approximately twenty feet back from the cliff's edge. Behind the target was an expanse of shapeless lumps that appeared to have been shrouded by a huge amount of heavy sailcloth, perhaps two or three layers. The white fabric billowed up and down in the wind and the rain.

A young officer—or, I should say, former officer—in the 66th regiment had been assigned to escort me to and from Cragside. His name was Crenshaw. Stocky and red-bearded, he looked to be a Scotsman, though he spoke with a Northumberland burr. "You were with the Fifth Northumberland Fusiliers, I understand," he said.

"Till Candahar. Then with the Berkshires. Till Maiwand. Then home."

"Carrying a jezail bullet, I understand."

"I was more fortunate than many," I said.

"Many didn't come home."

"Indeed."

Crenshaw indicated the artillery piece that was to be demonstrated this morning. "Would have been different if you'd had a few of those."

Rain splashed off the dull grey steel of the long barrel and the flat, angled gunnery shield. The wheels, carriage, and the remainder of the weapon in its entirety took up less space than a hansom cab.

"We had muzzle loaders," I said.

"The enemy had a dozen breach-loaders for every one of yours. More firepower, better accuracy. Small wonder at the outcome."

"I would have gladly paid for better weapons. I would imagine our government would have too, in hindsight."

"They're a tight-fisted lot. Not easily impressed, either. Others are more forthcoming in their praise."

"Indeed?"

"The Japanese, for example. We had a high official of the Emperor's here six months ago. We were testing one of the new Japanese shells in one of our twelve-pounders. Worked a treat, and the Japanese man all but jumped for joy and shook my hand. But the British gent he was with kept a stone face, even though it was our British gun we were demonstrating and hoping to sell!"

"He wasn't an Armstrong man?"

"Oh, no. A higher-up assistant to a cabinet minister."

"With Lansdowne?"

"Not War Office. Queen's council, I think it was. But look, they're ready now. You'll want to put your fingers in your ears. After the shot we'll go inspect the target."

The attendants to the gun stood aside, save for one of the four who now crouched behind the gun and leaned forward, his lanyard—a heavy woven leather cord of perhaps six feet in length—in his hand.

"Fire!" one of the others called.

The fourth man yanked savagely at the lanyard. There was a heavy *crump-boom* from the gun that shook the ground and forced the breath from my chest as though I had been struck by a hammer. There was no smoke.

"You see how it didn't buck or slew about," Crenshaw said. "Recoil's all absorbed in a new hydraulic mechanism. So it doesn't have to be re-aimed. Watch it—plug your ears again."

I crouched down slightly as the sound buffeted me once again.

"Now, have a look at the target through these field glasses."

"There appears to be only one hole in the wood. Directly at the centre of the bulls-eye."

"Both shells went through the same hole. You'll see for yourself when we get there. Just proves that the new anti-recoil mechanism works."

We walked side by side toward the wooden target. The four men who had handled the gun walked ahead of us.

Crenshaw explained. "Both shells were the new Japanese type, with a percussion fuse and an interior charge made of trinitrocresol and ammonium cresylate instead of picric acid. The percussion fuse is on the shell tip. It detonates on impact, of course, as it passes through the wooden target. Then just a fraction of a second later the shell explodes and delivers the payload over whatever is beneath."

"Shrapnel."

"Better than shrapnel. You'll see."

We reached the target. Clearly visible were two slightly overlapping holes in the wood.

Beyond the target, the expanse of white sailcloth was now shredded as though it had been stabbed repeatedly with a thousand knives. The ruined fabric was mottled with widening red stains throughout.

"See the impact of the payload."

The four men peeled back the disintegrated layers of sailcloth, to reveal the remnants of perhaps two dozen hay bales, the surface of which had been painted red. The red surface had been pulverized and was barely visible, exposing the straw-coloured interior. Most of that had been mangled.

Above and behind the demolished sailcloth and hay bales, the cliff rose up. Crenshaw pointed at a jagged hollow opening—perhaps six or eight feet wide—that had been gouged into the rock and dirt. Bits of soil and shale were still crumbling away, falling from the upper edges and sides of the huge new crater.

"The crater in the cliff was made by the second shell, which passed cleanly through the wooden target without detonating the percussion fuse. That's because the first shell had already made a hole for it. That's why the second shell only exploded when it hit the cliff."

I stared.

"There's your proof of accuracy," said Crenshaw.

Then he swept his arm around to indicate the shredded, red-mottled ruins that had once been hay bales, covered by layers of heavy sailcloth.

I turned away, but another ghastly vision filled my mind. I saw eight cream-colored horses standing at the front of a carriage and a white parasol held by a frail, elderly Queen who had entrusted Holmes with her safety. I saw the flash of a shell, bursting white-hot in the air above them.

"And there's your proof of power," Crenshaw was saying. "If the payload cuts through tough canvas like that, imagine what it will do to a man's skin."

LUCY

26. A CLUE AT DEVONSHIRE HOUSE

"And furthermore, the color scheme in this room is all *wrong*," Mary snapped. "Yellow and white brocade walls and all this gilding." She waved her hand at the elaborate plasterwork medallions and cornices that adorned the ceiling and walls. "We shall all look positively *jaundiced*."

Captain Hunter Stayley, secretary to His Grace the Duke of Devonshire, was waiting with us. He regarded Mary and nodded. "I will be certain to inform His Grace of your opinion."

Mary flushed—surprisingly, because she wasn't usually perceptive enough to pick up on subtleties like sarcasm, or if she did, she didn't care what the person thought anyway.

Nearly a week had passed since Keenan Mulloy's fall from the parapet at St. Paul's Cathedral. With my help, Mary had claimed her brother's body and made arrangements for him to be buried in the small churchyard associated with the Church of the English Martyr's.

Now rehearsals for the Duchess of Devonshire's ball were to begin.

At nine o'clock this morning, Mary and I had taken a carriage from Exeter Street to Devonshire House in Piccadilly, the London residence of the Duke and Duchess of Devonshire.

The rest of the D'Oyly Carte Company who were to take part in the performance would be arriving within the hour, but Mary and I had come early so that we might inspect the premises and formulate plans for the practical details of staging a production here.

Well, *I* was here for that reason.

I was not sure what strings His Royal Highness the Prince of Wales had pulled with Mr. Harris, our production manager. But Mr. Harris had entrusted me with the task of consulting with the Duke and Duchess's staff on where a stage might be erected, costumes and scenery stored, and which rooms might be conscripted for use by the players as dressing rooms.

Mr. Harris was probably now convinced that I was either a mistress of the Prince of Wales or well on the way to becoming one, His Royal Highness's flexible morals with regard to his marital vows being one of the worst-kept secrets in the Empire.

But the task I had been given would conveniently allow me to familiarize myself as much as possible with the Duke's household.

Mary's presence was *not* convenient, especially because she had prevented me from detouring through St. Giles on my way here and visiting Becky or calling on Jack at his station house.

I had spoken to Jack on the telephone to tell him about Keenan's death, but had only seen him once in the past week. Mary and I had gone to meet with Jack and Becky on the embankment, where we had walked along the river and Jack had given Mary the edited police report of her brother's death, as I had asked him to.

It seemed the least I could do for Mary to help give her peace of mind.

Today, though, I had hoped to time a visit to the Commercial Street station house so that I might catch Jack as he was returning from his nightly round of patrolling the streets. Not that I had any reason in particular for wishing to see him.

I shook my head, trying to dislodge that thought.

This was *exactly* why I kept trying to persuade myself that friendship with Jack was enough: Life was far less frightening when I didn't have a family I was afraid of losing.

But Mary had asked to travel to Piccadilly with me, and I had not had the heart to leave her behind, especially since she was herself due at Devonshire House for rehearsal in a few hours with the rest of the players anyway.

She looked a little pale this morning, her eyelids slightly red as though she had been crying last night in bed. But she was far from subdued.

She tossed her head, her lips compressing into a thin line. "I was only offering my opinion," she told the Captain. "I thought the Duchess was determined to make this *the* social event of the year—which it won't be if all the ladies in attendance look as though they ought to be treated with a course of liver pills."

Also inconveniently—and also surprisingly—Mary seemed to have taken an instant dislike to Captain Stayley.

He was not young—I would guess his age to be somewhere in his middle forties—but he was very attractive still and looking far less careworn than when I had first seen him at the Diogenes Club during our meeting with the Prime Minister. He had a broad-shouldered, athletic frame, brown hair just beginning to go gray at the temples, and brown eyes. His face was handsome, with high cheekbones, chiseled features, and a quick, ready smile.

He was exactly the type that I would have expected Mary to simper and swoon over, but from our first arrival, she had been cross and petulant, doing her level best to antagonize him at every turn.

Captain Stayley had offered to take us to the ballroom and wait for a member of the household staff to give us a more complete tour. It was early on when she had first castigated him for referring to us as *players*.

Players, as she stridently informed him, were to be found in medieval mummer's plays. We were *actresses and sopranos*.

She had found fault downstairs with the entrance hall, which she proclaimed too plain. The saloon, however, was too elaborate, and she had just finished telling him what she thought of the ballroom's color scheme.

In Captain Stayley's shoes, I would have been tempted to eject her from the house, if not from an upper-story window. But he had shown commendable patience with Mary. I wondered why he would be so polite with someone whose social importance to a duke's assistant had to be negligible at best.

I had stayed up late last night after Mary had gone to bed, reading through files that Holmes had given me on the Duke and Duchess of Devonshire.

The Duke was said to be a rather shy man, simple in his wants and inherently lacking in ambition. As a member of parliament, his chief contribution seemed to be to doze and snore his way through sessions in the House of Lords, though he was vehemently opposed to Irish Home Rule.

His wife the Duchess, however, was another matter altogether. Born Louisa von Alten, daughter of a German count, she had married not one, but two Dukes of the British peerage. Her first marriage to the Duke of Manchester had ended in his death, whereupon she had married Lord Hartington, the Duke of Devonshire.

She was said to be strong-willed, rigid, and extremely ambitious, her life's greatest disappointment the fact that neither of her husbands had ever been appointed prime minister.

Captain Stayley bowed his head and murmured—in the tone of someone with a good deal of practice at coming up with tactful responses—"Her grace is greatly looking forward to the success of the evening's entertainments and hopes to provide a memorable experience for her guests."

Mary opened her mouth again, but I took pity on Captain Stayley before she could offer another burst of criticism.

"Mary, why don't you go and have a look outside at the gardens?"

Devonshire House is one of the few London townhomes with a large plot of garden at the back. We had already been told of the plans to use the gardens as a welcome outdoor respite for the throngs who would crowd into the house on the night of the ball.

"The workmen are out there building a marquis and tents for the ball. Why don't you have a look and see whether it might be possible to incorporate a stage?"

Mary's lips compressed again, but she nodded, turning on her heel and walking off.

I gave Captain Stayley an apologetic smile. "I am sorry. Please excuse her. Her brother … died last week, and she is shocked and grieving."

Captain Stayley looked startled, then shook his head. "How tragic. But you need not apologize for your friend Miss Mulloy. I served with His Grace in the wars in Afghanistan. I know that it is often easier in the first stages of loss to be angry with the world. It provides a temporary insulation from the pain."

"Yes, it does. How are the preparations for the ball coming along?" I asked.

"Well enough."

Something in Captain Stayley's voice made me look at him more closely.

He gave me a brief smile. "I beg your pardon. I ought not to complain. It is just that after working tirelessly dealing with affairs of state, I find I have small patience for trivial things like party planning. Countless thousands of pounds spent on costumes that will be worn only once. Countless young women dragged over from America by their mothers and effectively sold into marriage with our impecunious nobility who have titles and vast estates but a dire need of funds." He glanced at me. "Not that I mean to cast any offense against American ladies, I hope you understand."

"I promise I have no intention of seizing the opportunity of the ball to win over an impoverished duke or marquis."

Captain Stayley's face relaxed in a smile. "Thank God His Grace the Duke is not a wastrel of that variety, but—" He broke off. "Ah, Miss Digby."

Turning, I saw that a young woman had come into the room. She looked to be somewhere about twenty-five, with a head of fiery red hair, small, neat features, and pale blue eyes.

She also looked as though she was contemplating murder— or at the very least, violence. Although she smoothed out the fury in her expression and as she approached.

"Miss James, may I present Miss Eve Digby, who acts as secretary to Mrs. Bellini, who is the housekeeper here at Devonshire House."

Eve Digby gave me a curt nod of acknowledgement and then opened her mouth, but Captain Stayley spoke first. "Are you here to give Miss James the tour?" Without waiting for an answer, Captain Staley turned to me. "Miss Digby will be of more use to you than I would be. She knows all the particulars of the domestic arrangements in place for the night of the ball—food and drink, available rooms, that sort of thing."

He hurried out, leaving Miss Digby to stare after him with a renewed scowl.

"I'm sorry," I told her. "I'm sure you must have far too much to do already."

For a moment, Eve transferred the scowl to me, but then she heaved a sigh, her expression clearing. "It's not your fault. I mean, yes, I'm busy. But I have a few minutes to show you around. Where would you like to begin?"

"Why don't we start in the basement, and then we can work our way up?"

Eve's eyebrows rose slightly. She was probably wondering why on earth the representative of the D'Oyly Carte opera wanted to see the cellars. But with a shrug and a "follow me" tossed over her shoulder, she led the way down the stairs.

Eve stood silently by the steps while I looked around the basement, which had two doors with locks that would be child's play to pick.

But by the time we had reached the kitchen and pantry areas of the house, she had unbent enough to smile once or twice and introduce me to a few of the other staff we encountered there. Devonshire House employed what amounted to an entire army of servants, and more had been brought in from Chatsworth, the Duke's estate in the north, for the occasion of the ball.

As we mounted the grand crystal staircase back to the ballroom and other reception rooms, I glanced at her.

Over the past weeks, I had read so many of Holmes's miscellaneous files on the subject of Ireland and the Fenian acts of rebellion that it was all in danger of becoming a confused jumble in my mind. But Eve's name—as well as her light trace of an accent—had tugged on something in my memory.

"Digby," I said. "Your name … you wouldn't be—"

Eve sighed again, looking more resigned than offended. "If you're wondering whether I'm related to the Digbys of the Irish peerage, the answer is yes. My grandfather was Lord Digby, of Geashill in the King's County. My father was a younger son, and he made the mistake of falling in love with a commoner and alienating his entire family. Well, that was his first mistake. His second was gambling away all his money, taking to drink, and driving himself into an early grave." Her lips twisted briefly. "Or maybe I mean second, third, and fourth mistakes? At any rate, my mother was left almost penniless, with four of us to support. So here I am, a housekeeper's secretary in the Duke of Devonshire's household." She shrugged. "It's not a bad sort of life, actually. Well, on average it's not."

"On average?"

Eve pressed her lips together, giving me a quick, sidelong glance as she led the way into the grand saloon, where refreshments would be served on the night of the ball.

Her employers probably discouraged gossip. But if I had judged Eve Digby right, she was also eager for a chance to unburden herself. Most people are; it's amazing how much you can learn simply by providing a willing, listening ear.

I smiled at her. "It's all right. I promise not to tell."

I was right; it didn't take much to make Eve want to talk.

She lowered her voice. "Her grace has decided it's not enough that she and all the guests be in costume. Now all the servants—*all* of them—have to be outfitted with specially made costumes for the night of the ball, too. Elizabethan maids for the women, eighteenth-century livery for the men. And guess who gets the job of organizing all of *that*, ever since Maud took it into her head to run off without a word."

My skin prickled. "Maud?"

"Mrs. Bellini's other secretary. Maud Jones."

I barely even noticed the splendors of the saloon, which were characteristically opulent, the walls lined with paintings that looked like the work of Italian masters.

I kept my expression carefully calm. "What happened to Maud Jones?"

Eve snorted. "If God knows that, He's not letting any of us in on the secret." Her Irish accent was a little stronger. "I imagine she took it into her head to run off with a man."

Or maybe she confided her worries in a Catholic priest within the secrecy of the confessional, prompting him to write her an urgent letter, and then—

What?

I didn't yet know, but I had a heavy, leaden feeling that the ending to the story of Maud Jones's disappearance wouldn't be a happy one.

"Can I see her room?"

Eve looked startled.

I added hastily, "If she's gone off, her room must be empty, yes? It might do as a dressing room for some of our principal singers."

Eve's face cleared. "Oh, I see. All right, come along. It's in the service wing."

LUCY

27. HIDDEN AFFECTION

Maud's room was small and plainly furnished with a narrow
bed, a chair, a small wardrobe, and nothing else. It was on an
upper floor and would probably be stiflingly hot come summer.
But there was a square of dull brown carpet on the floor and
a small coal stove in the corner that would have stopped her
from freezing over the winter.

I stood in the doorway. Eve's presence beside me meant that
I couldn't just walk in and start rooting through drawers and
overturning the bed's thin mattress. But something on top of
the dresser caught my eye.

"Was Maud a Catholic?" I gestured to the string of amber-
colored rosary beads that I had spotted.

Eve nodded. "So she said. Mrs. Bellini didn't care, as long as
Maud agreed to come to church with the rest of us at St. James,
the Anglican Church down the street. The whole household is
expected to put in an appearance; it's important to the Duke and
Duchess. So Maud would go to mass on Saturday night and
then come to St. James on Sundays."

"I see." I glanced at Eve, wondering how far I could push her for information before she realized that there was more to my interest in Maud than idle curiosity. A bit farther, probably; she was still enjoying having someone to talk to.

In addition to the rosary, there was a scattering of face powder on the surface of the dresser, and the wardrobe door was slightly ajar. Inside, I could see several dark skirts and plain white shirtwaist blouses, as well as the skirt of a dress that the missing girl had probably worn on her days out: It was made of bright, shiny blue satin—showy, but of cheap quality.

"Didn't she take her clothes with her?" I asked. "I mean, if she ran off to be with a man, you would think she would want to bring her clothing along."

Eve looked startled, as though she hadn't thought of that, but then shrugged. "Maybe he promised to buy her new clothes."

"How long has she been missing?"

"Since last Sunday. No, wait, I'm wrong. She was here on Sunday night. I remember because she told Mrs. Bellini she had a toothache, and Mrs. Bellini gave her some oil of cloves and told her to go to bed early. It was last Monday that she was gone. She didn't come down to breakfast, and when Mrs. Bellini sent me up here to look for her, she was nowhere to be found."

"How extraordinary." A dozen questions crowded onto the tip of my tongue; I selected the one that seemed least likely to arouse any suspicion.

"Did she have a toothache? I mean, maybe she went off to see the dentist and had an accident of some kind—something that stopped her from coming home."

"Toothache?" Eve snorted again. "Not likely. Crying her eyes out over her man, whoever he was, is more like it. My room is the next one to this, and I could hear her, night after night, for these last weeks on end."

"So you think her love affair had gone wrong, then?"

Eve nodded. "These last weeks, she was upset—snappish, even. Forgetting half the things Mrs. Bellini asked her to do. I thought maybe she'd got herself into trouble and he was refusing to make an honest woman of her."

"But if she's run away to be with him now ..."

Eve shrugged again. "Maybe she got him to marry her after all."

"Do you think she was seeing someone in the house here or one of the neighboring houses?"

Eve shook her head. "No. Well, I doubt it. I never saw her with anyone. Jerry—he's one of the footmen—liked her, but she wouldn't give him the time of day. And Bob who drives His Grace's carriage was always making eyes at her, but she put him in his place, too. Maud always had grand ideas. She was always putting on airs and thinking she was too good for any of the other servants."

I sighed. Of course her lover—if one existed—couldn't be anyone in the household. It would be too easy if we could narrow it down from every man between twenty and forty living in the city of London.

"Then how do you know she was upset on account of a man?"

Eve gave me a sidelong look, her expression suddenly wary, with a flicker that might have been guilt or at least consciousness.

She wasn't malicious, nor did she seem to me the type to be naturally nosy or to go snooping through someone else's private belongings. But she *was* bored here—bored, and a little lonely, as well, I would guess.

Her station of birth meant that she wasn't really on a level with the other servants—a fact that they were probably just as aware of as she was and likely shunned her for it. But just as assuredly, she wasn't part of the gentry.

Having attended an exclusive American boarding school as a child of unknown parentage, I knew something of what it was like to be trapped between worlds, not really belonging to either.

"Have you searched her room yet?" I asked. "Maybe we should do it now, just in case there's some clue as to where she may have gone off to. You were her friend. You must be dreadfully worried and wanting to make sure that she's all right."

Eve's expression changed to one of relief. "Yes, exactly." She leaned forward confidentially. "I *did* go through her room. I wanted to see whether she might have left a note or something. There wasn't anything like that, but—well, here, I'll show you."

Eve stepped quickly towards the small stove in the corner of the room. "We aren't allowed to have fires in our rooms after the first of April. But when I came in on Monday to look around, I saw that the grate was open."

Eve extracted a sheet of paper from the grate. "I didn't know what else to do with it, so I just left it there, but look, you can see for yourself."

She handed the sheet of paper over to me, and I took it gingerly between two fingers. Charred to crumbling blackness around the edges, only a paragraph towards the bottom of the page was still legible.

Doubt thou the stars are fire, Doubt that the sun doth move, Doubt truth to be a liar, But never doubt I love.

LUCY

28. A WALK IN THE PARK

"There!" Mary clutched at my arm. "Look at that man over there. I'm *sure* that he's following us."

It was midafternoon, the rehearsal at Devonshire House was over, and we were taking a shortcut back to Exeter Street by walking through Hyde Park.

This was also no less than the fourth pedestrian whom Mary had suspected of ill intent.

I studied the man she had pointed out: a weedy-looking, fair-haired young man in a top hat and gaiters, ogling the world through the lens of a monocle. If he was an enemy agent, I would resign all claim to thinking of myself as an investigator.

But then—unfortunately for both of us—the danger wasn't only in Mary's mind.

She had been jumpy and fearful ever since leaving Devonshire House, although she couldn't—or wouldn't—articulate why, only saying with an edge of hysteria that the men who had done away with her brother might be coming for her next and that she felt certain we were being watched.

But Mary thought only that her brother might have fallen foul of some vengeful Fenian sympathizers. I knew the reality was so much worse.

Keenan Mulloy was dead; Maud Jones, the woman he was writing to around the time of his death, was missing. And I had a scar on my arm from the graze of a bullet which proved our unknown enemies wouldn't hesitate to commit murder.

Besides which, at this hour and at this time of year, Hyde Park was thronged with pedestrians.

We were just passing along the tree-lined path that led along the Serpentine, the park's artificial lake—which happened to be one of the most fashionable promenades in London. Members of high society gathered here, morning and afternoon, to parade about in their expensive clothes.

Today, crowds of London's most elite were taking advantage of the balmy spring weather to see each other and be seen. Ladies with lace parasols to shield their complexion walked arm in arm while men swaggered by with silver walking sticks or rode on horseback.

Just offhand, I could count five gentlemen within sight of us whose frock coats could potentially conceal a pistol or other weapon. There were the ladies, too, with their huge floppy hats that gave convenient shadow for their faces.

I drew Mary off the main track and onto a narrow side path that led through some blossoming azalea bushes. We passed by one courting couple, their heads bent closely together. But apart from them, the path was empty.

I started to relax, then froze. About ten feet up ahead of us, a man had just stepped out from beneath the spreading shade of an oak tree. Medium height, medium weight, brown hair, swarthy complexion—and an extremely ugly look in his brown eyes.

I spun and found a second man closing in on us from behind.

Beside me, Mary gave a frightened gasp, clutching my arm. If it came to a fight, she would be no help at all, which meant that it was their two against my one.

Not ideal. So, so far from ideal.

The man up ahead of us was closer. I stooped, caught up a rock off the ground, and straightened, taking aim.

I would only get one chance at this; I had to make it count.

I let the rock fly, throwing it as hard as I could, baseball-fashion. In addition to sneaking out to see vaudeville shows, I had also spent a significant amount of my time at Miss Porter's boarding school for young ladies ducking out to play ball with the less wealthy neighborhood children.

I held my breath as I watched the rock sail towards the dark-haired man.

It struck him, square in the middle of his forehead.

He toppled over backwards, his eyes rolling back in his head. *One down.*

I spun around to face the second man, who on seeing his associate fall, had quickened his pace to a run. He was built like a giant: six feet tall and correspondingly broad.

My heart rate quickened, hammering in my ears.

Part of knowing how to fight is knowing your own limitations. That wasn't—so far as I knew—one of my father's observations, but it was still true: There were no methods of combat, not even the esoteric, little-known martial arts my father practiced, that would compensate for my being less than half an attacker's size.

What I *did* have on my side, though, was the element of surprise. Very few men expected a girl to be able to hit back and make it count.

"Stay behind me," I ordered Mary.

The big man's stride faltered for a second, confusion crossing his face as though he were wondering why I hadn't turned around and tried to run.

He was middle aged, with an unshaven, small-eyed face and a dirty neckerchief around his throat.

I stood motionless, waiting. With a click, he flicked out a switchblade knife and swung at me.

Perfect.

I caught hold of his knife hand, pivoted, and yanked his arm down and across his body. He jerked forward, losing his balance, which brought his face within my range.

I smashed my elbow as hard as I could into his throat, then kicked his right leg out from under him while he was still choking and wheezing. He flailed wildly with the knife, and I felt it graze with stinging pain across my forearm. But then he collapsed onto the ground.

I aimed another kick. Not at his temple; the skull was fragile there, and despite the fact that he had just tried to murder me, I didn't particularly want his death on my conscience.

I caught him in the jaw, under his chin, with enough force to snap his head back. His eyes rolled up and he went limp.

I crouched down, pulling up one of his eyelids. The pupil remained fixed, unresponsive.

Mary was standing exactly where I had left her, staring at me with her mouth open.

"How ... what ... what are you ..."

"I'm checking to be sure that he's not just faking." I straightened up. The man I had hit with a rock hadn't moved by so much as a twitch when I laid out his confederate, so I felt safe in assuming that his unconsciousness was genuine as well.

"We need to get away from here."

Mary was still staring at me, blank-faced. "Away from here," she repeated, in the tone of a sleepwalker.

"Never mind, just come with me." I took her arm, debated momentarily, then hurried onwards, continuing in the same direction we'd been heading before the attackers appeared.

We were still skirting the edge of the Serpentine; I could catch glimpses of it between the rhododendrons that lined the path. Rented pleasure boats filled with young people floated to and fro across the lake, their shouts and laughter occasionally carrying to us across the water, like something from an entirely different world.

Mary stumbled on beside me. After we had been walking a short distance, she said, in a shaky voice, "You're bleeding."

I looked down, barely suppressing a curse word.

The big man's knife had slashed a rent in the sleeve of my blouse. A wet red bloodstain soaked the white muslin, as garish and eye-catching as a splash of paint.

I took out my handkerchief, winding it as best I could around the cut. But it didn't entirely cover the blood.

"Quick, lend me your jacket." In addition to her white lace blouse, Mary was also wearing a green bolero-style jacket with huge leg-of-mutton sleeves.

Mary looked at me with incomprehension. "My jacket? What?"

"*Mary!*" I resisted the urge to shake her. "We can't afford to attract any undue attention. There may be more men like those two back there looking for us. Things like bloodstains tend to make it harder to avoid notice."

Mary swallowed, but took off the jacket without another word and handed it to me. I slipped it on. The shoulders were a little loose on me, the sleeves a little too long, and the color was a much better match for Mary's green skirt than my dark navy one. But at least it covered the blood.

"Good."

The high, frantic yapping of a dog coming from somewhere up ahead almost made me jump. But as we rounded a bend in the path, I could see there were no other people. Just the animal: a white, furry snowball of the breed I was fairly sure was called a Maltese.

His leash was tied to the trunk of a tree.

I glanced to the right and left. No owner in sight, though whoever he belonged to was clearly wealthy. The leash was of high quality red leather, and the dog was wearing a ridiculous little coat of tartan plaid.

Probably the dog's master or mistress had gone off on one of the pleasure boats on the lake, leaving the animal tied up here.

I knelt down, crouching at the dog's side and murmuring soothingly. "Good boy, who's a good boy, then?"

The dog jumped, trying to lick my face.

Working quickly, I untied his leash from around the trunk of the tree and slipped it over my own wrist. "All right, we can keep going now."

Mary looked from me to the dog and back again. "Lucy, what on earth?"

"In addition to bloodstains, people also notice dogs. Anyone looking for us will be searching for two young women alone, not two girls taking a pampered pet out for a walk."

The dog wouldn't help if anyone got near enough to see our faces. But if searchers caught a glimpse of us from a distance or from behind, I hoped that they would pass on automatically, without bothering to look too closely.

"Now *hurry*," I told Mary. "Don't run—that will attract notice, too. But walk quickly and try and keep your head down."

Even with the little Maltese capering and yapping short, happy barks around our feet, I still felt as conspicuous as a lighthouse beacon. But at last we emerged onto Park Lane and into the usual tangle of London traffic: handsome cabs and fashionable carriages, delivery carts and pedestrians, jamming the streets in all directions.

I turned left, and Mary clutched at my arm. Her voice wavered. "But aren't we—Exeter Street—surely you want to go home—" she gestured to the right, which would lead us back towards the flat.

I shook my head. "If they found us in the park, they probably also know where we live. Someone could be waiting."

There was a small boy with a boot polishing stand a short distance up from the park entrance. I approached, digging out a half sovereign coin from my bag.

"Would you like to earn an easy day's wages?" I didn't wait for the boy to answer, just handed both the coin and the dog's leash over to him. "Take this dog into the park and let him go."

The boy gave me a look of deep distrust from under the brim of his tattered cloth cap. He wasn't one of Holmes's irregulars, unfortunately. I would have paid triple if I could make Flynn or one of the others magically appear.

"What's the catch?" the boy demanded.

"No catch."

Judging by the boy's expression, he thought I was either lying or insane, but he started off, pulling the dog along.

Set free in the park, the dog would surely find its owner again, though I wasn't entirely sure that whoever had dressed him in that coat deserved to have him.

Beside me, Mary was trembling, shivering so hard that her whole body shook.

I took her arm again, starting towards the row of hansom cabs that were drawn up along the edge of the park, awaiting fares.

My step faltered as I thought of the cab driver who had started this all with the attempt to abduct Uncle John and Holmes. But it couldn't be helped. I passed by the first four cabs in the line, then approached the fifth: a battered, older vehicle, splattered with mud and looking decidedly down-at-heel. The driver was a match: a grizzled, gray-haired man with a face like old boot leather, who sat atop the driver's box as though he had taken root there.

I looked him over, making doubly sure that his wrinkled complexion was genuine and not out of a bottle. Then I climbed onto the passenger's seat, pulling Mary with me.

She was still trembling with fright and shock, but she was also staring at me as though she had never seen me before.

"Who ... who *are* you?"

"Never mind that. What we need to know is who paid those two thugs to attack us."

Then I saw the hurt look on her face. I sighed. I could almost see the idea of keeping my identity a secret exploding, raining down in tiny fragments, and settling all around us on the ground.

"I'll explain later, I promise," I told her. I would have to give Mary some version of the truth—just as soon as I could decide exactly what that version was going to be. "But for right now, you just need to trust me if you want to stay alive."

LUCY

29. STRATEGIC RETREAT

Our cab driver barely even glanced at us as we settled ourselves on the cracked leather seats. Apparently fate had decided that we were due for a stroke of luck.

I did take the precaution of changing my American accent for an English one. It wasn't likely that our driver would be questioned by an agent of our enemies, but if he were, I didn't want him to be able to share any details as to where he had taken his young American fare.

He grunted and nodded in response to my explanation that my cousin was visiting from the country and wished to be driven around to some of the most famous London sights.

Sighing, I leaned back, letting the roof of the carriage shadow my face. In addition to being old and dirty, the cab was missing one of the doors that ought to have closed over our legs, shielding us from dirt thrown up by the horse's hooves. But I didn't care.

We drove past Trafalgar Square, with its columned monument to Lord Nelson. We saw Buckingham Palace, Kensington, and the Tower Bridge, as well as the Parliament and Charing Cross Station.

Mary sat beside me without saying a word, her arms locked tightly around her middle and her face tense and set.

I couldn't honestly claim to be enjoying the London sights any more than she was. But the comprehensive tour did accomplish two important purposes: First, it gave me time to think. Second, it gave me the chance to watch the traffic behind us and be certain that we were not being followed.

Finally, I turned around in my seat, rapping on the roof to tell the driver to stop.

Only when I had given him the address where I wished him to take us next did the cabbie show his first signs of doubt.

"You sure about that, miss?" His shaggy eyebrows were elevated nearly to his hairline.

"Quite sure." For the sake of the cab driver's conscience, I added, "My cousin here is interested in doing charity work. We have some friends who run a soup kitchen in St. Giles."

I wasn't sure whether the cab driver believed me or not, but he shrugged. "Just as you like, miss."

I could almost hear him silently adding, *It's your funeral.*

The address I had given him was certainly nowhere that respectable young women would venture. A good part of St. Giles was given over to what was known in slang terms as a rookery: a conglomeration of tumbled-down buildings and cheap lodging houses, all clumped together like a honeycomb and connected by blind alleys and cul-de-sacs.

The rookery of St. Giles was also where criminals of all types banded together: pickpockets, smash-and-grab men, and prostitutes and their procurers.

Mary gave a small squeak of fright as we climbed down out of the carriage and I handed over the driver's payment.

"What *is* this place?"

"Somewhere no one will think to look for us. I hope."

The driver gave us a last, dubious look before rattling off.

The houses that lined the street looked as though a single push would send them falling over, their broken windows patched with rags and wadded-up clumps of dirty paper.

Mary wrinkled up her face, pressing her hand over her nose and mouth.

Night was falling, but there was still light enough to show the crowds of filthy, barefoot boys and girls who played and squabbled and fought in the street.

One girl who looked older—maybe fourteen or fifteen—walked by us, wearing practically nothing at all but a man's overcoat. Men and women, their clothing not much more adequate, lounged in doorways, drinking and smoking.

"It gets better a few streets over, I just didn't want to give the cab driver the address where we're really going."

With any luck, we would also reach our intended destination without my having to hit anyone else.

Mary looked far more frightened than she had during the attack in Hyde Park. But either by miracle or because I took care to keep to the deepest areas of shadow, we reached a street that was less wretched and filthy than the rest of St. Giles.

"This way."

I led the way towards the corner house in a group of buildings set around a central paved square, approached a door on the first floor, and knocked.

There was a moment's silence, and I imagined us being scrutinized from inside. After Jack's false arrest over the winter, he had agreed for Becky's safety to let Sherlock Holmes's workmen install certain security measures in the rented lodgings, including a peep-hole in the front door and a wide variety of locks and bolts on the windows and doors. The Kellys now had a telephone line, as well, thanks to Mycroft and his high-up connections.

The whole operation had been carried out at night, in secret, under cover of darkness. Telephones in St. Giles were not just a rarity, they were unheard of, and spreading the idea that Jack could afford a luxury like this would be tantamount to hanging a sign over the door inviting thieves to break in. But it meant that Becky could now call for help if there was trouble any night that Jack was on duty.

After a second or two, there was the click of a bolt being unfastened, the rattle of a chain being drawn back, and then Becky threw the door open.

"Lucy—and *Miss Mulloy?*" Becky had met Mary during our music lessons at my flat and now looked at her with startled eyes. "What's wrong?"

"Everything is all right."

I looked past Becky to where Prince stood in the middle of the room, wagging his tail in an ecstasy of greeting.

"But where is your brother? Isn't he home?"

It was Monday night, which was usually Jack's night off; that was the entire reason I had brought Mary here.

"No, he had to go on duty." Becky bit her lip. "One of the other constables was sick, and Jack got called in to take his place. He has to be on duty tomorrow, too, so he won't be home until tomorrow night. He said he would have to catch an hour or two of sleep down at the station house if he had time."

"Oh." I stared at Becky blankly for a second, trying to ignore the way my heart sank at that piece of news. Until this second, I hadn't realized just how much I had wanted to see Jack tonight.

"Can we come in?" I asked Becky.

"Oh—yes." Becky stepped back quickly, letting us inside. "What do you need?"

"Food, maybe?" Mary looked close to fainting, and I was hungry as well. I glanced down at my arm. The cut seemed to still be bleeding; a thin red stain had seeped through onto the sleeve of Mary's jacket. "And some sticking plasters, if you have any."

30. A MESSAGE FROM MYCROFT

"What happened? Did you fight someone? Did you have to knock anyone's head in?"

I smiled at Becky. I still had a lump of ice in the pit of my stomach, but her eager curiosity was infectious.

"Only slightly."

I had washed the cut on my arm. It was long, but not terribly deep, and now I was fixing a square of sticking plaster across it.

Mary was sitting slumped on the Kellys' sofa, staring into the middle distance. I kept listening for any sounds of alarm or signs of anyone creeping around the house. But Prince was stretched out across the floor at Becky's feet, snoring, and I didn't doubt that he would be up in an instant if there were any danger.

"There. I think that's done it."

I handed back the roll of extra plasters and the bottle of witch hazel that Becky had brought out. "Thank you."

Becky took everything back inside the second room, the one she used for a bedroom.

"*Lucy,*" Mary whispered to me, as soon as she was gone.

She gestured to the bowl filled with boiled potatoes that Becky had given her, along with sausages on a plate. "What am I supposed to *do* with this?"

"That's up to you."

The Kellys didn't go hungry, but Jack's twenty-six-shillings-a-week salary didn't exactly stretch to four-course dinners, either. And my patience with Mary was beginning to slip.

"I personally would eat it, since it's the only supper that we're likely to get. Also, Becky's feelings would be hurt if you didn't. But it's your choice."

Mary looked across to where Becky was just coming back into the room and, to my surprise, her face softened a little. "She's a sweet girl."

"Yes, she is."

Mary seemed to make more of an effort as we ate, thanking Becky for the meal and even telling her a few stories about the theater.

I listened with half an ear, trying to think.

"Can I use the telephone, Becky?" I asked, when we had finished.

Becky nodded. "Of course."

I stepped over to the box on the wall, lifted the receiver, gave instructions to the switchboard operator, and then waited through the inevitable series of clicks and static buzzes.

Finally, Mycroft's voice came on the line. "Lucy, my dear? Is that you?"

He sounded slightly out of breath, and I pictured him as having just heaved his immense bulk up out of his favorite over-stuffed armchair to answer the telephone.

"Are you in trouble of some kind?"

"No—" I stopped. If I stumbled nearly every time over what to call my father, I had absolutely no idea how to address Mycroft Holmes.

Uncle John came out easily whenever I spoke to Dr. Watson. But though Mycroft might be my father's brother, it was practically impossible to imagine ever calling him *Uncle Mycroft*.

"—Mr. Holmes. I had some trouble earlier, but nothing that I couldn't manage. I believe that I could use reinforcements now, though."

Mycroft Holmes's body might be slow and heavy, but his mind was every bit as nimble as my father's. He said, without losing a beat, "What sort of reinforcements?"

"Nothing too obvious. I don't want to risk attracting attention. If I asked you to send Flynn to us, could you get in touch with him?"

There was a brief pause, and then Mycroft rumbled, "I believe so, yes. But you said, 'send him to *us*,'" he went on. "Is there someone with you, then?"

Also like my father, Mycroft missed nothing. "Yes. Mary Mulloy, my flat mate. If you could ask Flynn to please bring us two complete changes of clothing, of the kind that very poor beggar-women would wear. Oh, and a cart? The sort of thing that a fruit or flower vendor might use for pushing her wares around town?"

"Clothes and a cart," Mycroft repeated briskly. "Very well. Give me your current location?"

I gave him Jack and Becky's address.

There was no pause; Mycroft Holmes had no need of things like pencils and paper to remember a street name.

"Flynn will be with you before morning."

A click in my ear announced that he had ended the call. I hung up as well, feeling marginally lighter.

Flynn, despite his youth, would be able to navigate St. Giles in safety. He would blend in so well with the other street Arabs that no one would give him a second glance.

I turned back to Becky and Mary to find that Becky had brought out her stack of Uncle John's printed stories, taken from copies of the Strand magazine.

Mary had warmed enough to be actually smiling as Becky gave her a spirited account of the "Adventure of the Speckled Band," as Uncle John had called it.

"It's a shame." Mary touched the artist Sidney Paget's drawing of my father's face, which in fact resembled the real man very little. "Such a shame that he didn't survive the Reichenbach Falls. I remember the whole of England mourning when Dr. Watson published 'The Final Problem.' "

Becky looked startled. "Oh, but he—"

She stopped, clapping a hand across her mouth. But Mary had already sat up straight, looking first at Becky and then at me. "You *know* something. You know—" She stopped. "Wait a moment. You said *Mr. Holmes* when you were on the telephone just now. Is he alive?"

Had I? I *had*. I swore inwardly. That had been stupid—beyond careless, even if it had been just bad luck that Mary had put the pieces together so quickly.

But since the secret was already out, there seemed little point in lying. "Yes, but I wasn't speaking to him. That was Holmes's brother, Mycroft."

Mary's eyes widened, then narrowed as she looked at me closely again. "But you do know where Sherlock Holmes is?"

"Yes."

"And you are … are you an agent of his, or something like that?"

"Something like that." It was as good an explanation as any.

Mary seemed to ponder that, absorbing it for a moment. Then she said, with sudden decision, "I want to see him."

"What?"

"Sherlock *Holmes*!" Mary made a quick, impatient gesture. "I want to see him."

Of all the possible outcomes for tonight, this one had honestly never occurred to me. I looked at Mary, at something of a loss. "Well …"

Mary interrupted, her hands clenching hard on the edge of the table. "I *need* to see him, don't you understand?" Her voice was shaking again. "Someone tried to kill me today. We can't even go home. He can keep me safe, I know he can."

"Well …" I sat back down at the table, trying to think. "Mr. Holmes isn't in London right now," I said slowly.

"But he is somewhere in England?"

"Yes." There seemed no harm in telling Mary that much.

"Then that's even better," Mary said. "We can go to him. It will get us out of London, away from anyone who might be searching."

That was true enough. However it had come about, this might actually be the answer to the problem of what our next move was to be. Or at least what *Mary's* next move was to be.

"I have to stay here in London," I said. I had Maud Jones, who had vanished from her post at the Duchess of Devonshire's and needed to be found—if she were still alive. Regardless, there were secrets in that house from which I couldn't just walk away.

"But what I *could* do is see that you get safely on a train to where Mr. Holmes and Dr. Watson are staying," I told Mary. "If we can get to King's Cross Station in the morning, you'll be with them by late afternoon."

"Would you?" Mary sounded almost pathetically grateful. "Would you really do that for me? Thank you, Lucy, I can't tell you how much safer I would feel."

This was Mary's first introduction into Holmes's and my world. All in all, she was handling it better than I would have expected, and I could understand her wanting to clutch onto a legend like Holmes as a lifeline.

"We'll leave before dawn. But that still gives us a few hours before we have to go. We should all try to get some sleep."

Already I could see Becky stifling yawns.

"Mary and I can sleep out here," I told her. "If you have a spare blanket or two?"

Becky nodded, and I went to help her fetch the extra bedding from the other room.

"I'm so sorry," Becky whispered, as she handed me the folded stack of woolen blankets. Her blue eyes were wide with regret. "I didn't mean to give the secret about Mr. Holmes away. I just thought she must already know, because she lives with you, and—"

"It's all right. It wasn't your fault; it was mine for using Mycroft's last name. And anyway, I would have had to tell Mary the truth eventually." I hugged Becky. "Thank you for everything."

Becky returned the hug, her arms tight around my waist. "Lucy? Are you going to tell me what's going on?" Before I could answer, she added, "It's something to do with what happened over the winter, isn't it? Jack being arrested and almost blamed for that police inspector's murder and all the rest?"

I sighed. I might wish that Becky were not quite so perceptive, but she deserved better than to have me lie.

"It seems very likely that it is all connected. *Oh.*" I remembered something. "There is one thing you could do for me. A girl has gone missing. She's probably somewhere around my age, fair hair, light complexion, and probably blue eyes."

Asking Eve to give me a detailed physical description of Maud Jones would have been carrying my supposedly innocent curiosity one step too far.

But the face powder on Maud's dressing table had been a very pale shade, and the blue dress in the wardrobe almost certainly would only have been chosen by a girl with blonde coloring.

"Can you ask Jack to look into whether anyone of that description has turned up anywhere—in a hospital or a charity house?"

It was—just barely—possible that Maud had suffered some sort of accident that had prevented her from returning to the Duke and Duchess's employ, though it was more likely that she was dead.

Since I was passing the message on through Becky, I couldn't include a request that Jack look into police reports on the unidentified bodies that had turned up in London over the course of the past week or so. But I didn't doubt that Jack would understand anyway and take a request for morgue reports as implied.

Becky looked down at the floor, then up at me. "Is it dangerous, the case that you're working on? I mean, someone tried to *hurt* you today."

She gestured to my bandaged arm, her face pale and frightened looking now, all her earlier enthusiasm gone.

"Yes. But I'm very good at staying safe. So is Jack."

"I know."

I waited for more questions, but Becky was silent, her head bowed.

Looking down at her, I wished more than anything that I could promise her that there was nothing to worry about, that everything was going to be all right. But I couldn't foist that lie on her, either.

So instead I hugged her again. "We may have to leave before you're awake in the morning, but I'll come back as soon as I know it's safe. I *promise*."

LUCY

31. DEPARTURE AT DAWN

A light tap at the door jolted me out of sleep. Prince had woken, too. He was already on his feet and growling, though he quieted when I put a hand on his neck.

"Shhh, Prince, it's all right."

I opened the door, and a small boy slipped noiselessly inside. I hadn't wanted to risk leaving a lamp burning, but the light from the banked fire in the grate showed me his face.

Flynn—if he had a second name, I had never heard it—was invariably filthy every time I saw him, dressed in tattered clothes that were several sizes too big for his skinny frame, his face and the rims of his fingernails equally grimy with all the dirt and soot that could be picked up on a London street.

Wherever he lived, he probably didn't have access to water for bathing, but the dirt served as camouflage as well. Dressed this way, Flynn might be cursed at by the odd carriage driver or shoed away by fine ladies. But no one would bother to look at him very closely. That was the reasoning behind my father's employment of the irregulars as spies and messengers: Practically no one in London cared about street urchins like Flynn.

Blue eyed and with a mop of untidy blond curls, Flynn looked as though he couldn't possibly be older than ten, but I knew that he had already been in my father's employ for at least the past two years.

"Thank you for coming," I murmured after I had shut the door behind him.

"No trouble, miss. I got what you asked for." Flynn thrust a bulky parcel into my arms.

"And the cart?"

"Parked just outside." He jerked his thumb.

"Perfect."

Mary was still asleep, draped across the sofa. Since I hadn't wanted to sleep deeply anyway, I'd let her have the more comfortable bed while I made do with a blanket on the floor.

She was snoring lightly, but came awake when I touched her shoulder, looking up at me in groggy confusion.

"Lucy, what—"

"Shhh. We need to leave now. Here, put these on over your own clothes."

I separated out the bundle that Flynn had given me into two piles: a ragged, threadbare skirt for each of us, a dirty apron and an old-fashioned poke bonnet for me, and a worn-looking woolen shawl for Mary. Flynn had done well; the bonnet would largely conceal my face without looking as though it were meant to be a disguise. For Mary, the clothes were largely a precaution, since with any luck she wouldn't be seen. But still, in an emergency, she could pull the shawl up over her head and shoulders and become just another of the anonymous poor on the London streets.

I glanced at Flynn. "You didn't steal these, did you?"

Flynn gave me a virtuously wounded look. "Nah, of course not. I bought 'em off a rag shop over in Limehouse." He grinned. "They just don't know it yet. They'll find the money I left when they open up shop in the morning. Can't swear that the clothes don't have fleas, though."

"That's all right." At the moment, I was in no mood to be particular.

I hadn't even unlaced my boots when I lay down to sleep. A minute to button the skirt over my own and pull on the bonnet, and I was ready. Mary grimaced and wrinkled her nose at the smell of the clothes I'd given her, but put them on.

"One other thing." I turned to Flynn. I'd done absolutely everything I could to ensure that we weren't followed here, but no plan was completely without risk or room for error. "Can you stay here for the rest of the night? There's a girl in the bedroom, sleeping. She's about your age. If anyone comes to the door, don't answer it, just get her out the back. She'll show you the way."

As well as the locks on the front door, Holmes had also installed a hidden back exit to the Kellys' lodgings, crafted by the same discreet firm of builders who had constructed his bolt-holes.

Flynn nodded. "Got it."

Becky had a set of clothes almost identical to Flynn's; she'd worn them and passed for a boy before. If trouble came knocking, she could blend into the underbelly of London just as well as Flynn, though I hoped it wouldn't come to that.

"Thank you."

"Good luck, miss." Flynn tipped his hat.

Just as he had promised, the handcart was waiting outside: a rickety wooden affair that, judging from the stains, had been used to sell oranges or some other squashy fruit in the recent past.

"Get in," I whispered to Mary.

The houses that lined the court were all dark and quiet, but nowhere in London is ever entirely asleep, even at four o'clock in the morning. From the street nearby, I could hear the occasional tramp of boots, the odd snatch of voices arguing or raised in drunken song.

"What?" Mary looked at the cart in horror. "You want me to *ride* in that thing?"

"They'll be looking for two of us," I said, as patiently as I could manage. "So we're going to make sure that there's only one of us to be seen. You'll get in, and I'll cover you with this canvas." I held out the square of folded material that Flynn had included. "Anyone watching will just see a tired fruit-vendor, pushing her wares to the early morning markets."

Mary still looked doubtful, but took a deep breath and climbed into the cart. "Fine. I just hope you know what you're doing."

LUCY

32. THE MULLOY FAMILY TRAGEDY

"One ticket to Newcastle, please."

The gray-haired ticket seller behind the window barely glanced at me as he made to comply with the request. There was no reason for him to notice me particularly. I had abandoned the poor fruit-vendor's costume and was now back in my own clothes, my hair covered by a wide-brimmed straw hat that I had bought at a street market as we made our way across London. I had also picked up a shawl that I could wear instead of Mary's eye-catching green jacket to cover the bandage on my arm.

The railway assistant pushed my ticket to me from under the bars of the window, and I made my way back outside.

Even at this hour of the morning, King's Cross Station was a busy place. There were families surrounded by piles of luggage and hat boxes, looking as though they might be on their way to summer holidays. Businessmen in dark suits hurried along to their platforms. Ladies from the country were up for a day's shopping in London, with servants trailing along behind to carry their parcels.

The air rang with a cacophony of raised voices, the clatter of train wheels, and the hiss of steam engines.

Mary was where I had left her, sitting on a bench on Euston Road, outside the station. She, too, was transformed out of the clothes that Flynn had given us. I had rolled everything up into a bundle and left it inside the cart, parked in a nearby alley where we could still find it if we had to make a hasty retreat.

Mary looked up as I approached. "You've been a terribly long time."

"I have your ticket."

Mary was fine, and none of the pedestrians hurrying past us gave a second glance or raised any of my internal alarm bells. But a prickling uneasiness still crawled its way up my spine, even before I consciously identified the cause: there was a scattering of crumbs across the lap of Mary's skirt and a dusting of powdered sugar on her fingers.

"Did you go and get something to eat while I was gone?" I demanded.

Mary looked taken aback. "I was hungry! I only went into that bake shop over there and bought a sweet roll." She gestured to a store with a striped pink and white awning a few doors down. "Why? Did I do something wrong?"

I ground my teeth together to stop an impatient reply. Maybe it was too much to expect that Mary would be aware of every possible danger, although I could have wished that some of her terror from last night could have carried over to today and kept her on the bench, too afraid to move.

"If anyone comes here asking questions, you want as few people as possible to have seen your face."

"Oh." Mary looked chastened. "But I doubt anyone will remember me. There was a crowd of other customers, and the shop girl was almost rushed off her feet trying to keep up with everyone's orders."

Maybe I was letting paranoia cloud my judgment. It was unlikely, after all, that in a city the size of London anyone would make enquiries at this particular bakery here.

Unlikely, but not impossible.

After our escape yesterday, a logical thing for our enemies to do would be to start canvassing railway stations, on the theory that fear would drive us to flee London.

"Let's just get you on your train," I told Mary.

We were at the platform a few minutes before Mary's train was to depart. Without luggage, we had no need of a porter. I climbed aboard with Mary and walked along the train's corridor until we came to a compartment that was occupied by a mother with three young boys.

Mary made a face as she peered in at them through the doorway. "Can't we find somewhere else?" She looked at the boys, who were energetically clambering over the seats and trying to stuff themselves and each other through the train windows. "I'm sure I won't have a moment's peace the whole journey."

"Maybe not, but it's also extremely unlikely that any of the boys or their mother will try to murder you."

"Oh." Mary sighed "Very well. Thank you," she added, as an afterthought.

A blast sounded from the train's whistle. Two minutes, until departure time.

"Will you tell me something?" I asked. "Who was it you knew that was mixed up with the Fenians? Was it your other brother—the younger one?"

Mary's eyes widened fractionally. Then her face hardened. "Yes."

She pressed her lips together, and for a second, I thought she wasn't going to say anything more. But then the words seemed to burst out of her.

"The English—" She stopped and laughed shortly. "Well, you already know—or maybe you don't—how the English soldiers stationed over in Ireland treat us. Rape ... robbery ... beatings ... even murder. I'd seen it all before I was your little Becky Kelly's age. My brother Michael was eighteen, and the girl he planned to marry—" She stopped, squeezing her eyes shut and shaking her head. "Never mind. But he had reason to hate the English right enough. The Fenians, though." She stopped again, her mouth twisting as though she had bitten into something rancid. "The lot of them got boys like Michael—angry, outraged boys—all worked up, promising them that they could make a difference. Letting them think that maybe things could actually *change*." She laughed shortly, bitter and mirthless. "The only change Michael made was to himself. He went from being eighteen with his whole life ahead of him to dying in a hangman's noose." She almost spat the last word.

I drew in a quick breath.

Mary kept going. "Our father was already dead, but the shock and grief of it killed our mother. She died within three months of Michael. Keenan and I were all that was left, and—" Her voice cracked, wavering between pain and anger. "And now he's gone, too. The Fenians took him from me, just like they took Michael."

The train whistle blew again, short and sharp. There wasn't time for more, but I took Mary's hand and squeezed. "Sherlock Holmes may be a little abrupt in his manner at times, but you can trust him absolutely," I said. "And Doctor Watson is the kindest of men. They'll keep you safe."

Mary exhaled and gave a shaky nod. "Thank you."

I watched as Mary settled herself on a seat across from the young mother. Then I made my way back along the corridor and jumped down to the platform, just as the train was starting to move.

I had done everything I could to keep Mary from harm, so why did I still feel sick to my stomach?

I shook my head, gathering my shawl more tightly around me as I hurried away. I needed to send a telegram to Holmes, warning him to expect Mary's arrival.

And I had to hope that my father would forgive me for putting Mary onto the train to become his trouble instead of mine.

WATSON

33. A VISITOR AT CRAGSIDE

A note from Mycroft arrived when I was at breakfast the morning of June 16.

Nearly a week had elapsed since my arrival at Cragside. The horrific impact of the artillery shell had shaken my nerve momentarily. But somehow the destruction merged with the human suffering that I had seen in Afghanistan, and my soul rebelled against the shock. I felt a burning determination to prevent the same thing from happening at the Jubilee. I could not stop men from going to war, but I could at least do my best to keep war's atrocities away from my country and my Queen.

Holmes's instructions had kept me very busy. Each day I had risen early, traveling to the munitions works and the shipyards, seeing what I could of each in the time allotted until I had to take one of Sir Robert's carriages back to Cragside. I had examined and re-examined ledgers and files of correspondence and production records and reports. I had located the Japanese letter of complaint. It appeared to be perfectly genuine, although the envelope bore the name and address of the Japan Society of

London, which I thought odd since the gun had been ordered by the Japanese government. I made a note to tell Holmes.

However, other than this minor discrepancy, I had found no evidence of any missing weaponry, whether a big naval gun or a smaller field artillery weapon.

As Holmes had instructed, I had also kept a watchful eye for persons who might be following me or making inquiries about my progress. So far there had been no sign that I was under observation by anyone other than those whose ordinary curiosity would cause them to take notice of an outsider newly arrived within the confines of a private enterprise.

Sir Robert was away from Cragside. I did not know where he had gone or when he would return. Nor had I known when to expect Holmes. I had received no word from Mycroft, or from Holmes, or from Lucy. I had been on my own. Each morning I watched the post for what I hoped would be some word of his arrival. Less than one week remained until the Queen's Jubilee parade.

I was alone in the breakfast room, finishing my eggs and bacon, when one of the maids appeared at my side with a silver tray. On the tray was an envelope. "Sir, it's addressed to you," she said, holding the tray out for my inspection.

I recognized the handwriting of Mycroft, the letters small and precisely formed with a pen of very fine nib. Dropping a curtsey, the maid left me.

The note read, "Whitehall, 13 June. Expect Lansdowne and his assistant on 16 June. They wish to learn what you have discovered, if anything. M.H."

And this was June 16, the very morning noted by Mycroft! With Lord Lansdowne's return, there would of course be questions. I wished that I had more time to prepare and assemble my thoughts. I had taken notes of each day's investigation, of course, but they were merely chronological lists, hardly the kind of synthesis expected by a man so busy as Lord Lansdowne. I was about to call for the maid to ask whether the household had had other notice of the arrival of Lord Lansdowne and whether something might have delayed the delivery of the note that Mycroft had sent to me.

But then I heard a commotion on the gravel path outside. The sound of hoof beats, carriage wheels, nickering horses, and bustling footmen. Then voices in respectful greeting. Then a second carriage. And a woman's voice. The words were high-pitched and indistinct, though I thought I heard my own name among them.

The butler appeared a few moments later. "Your guests are here, Dr. Watson. Lord Lansdowne and Mr. Greco. And also a young lady. She says she is expected."

I was about to tell the butler that I was not expecting any young lady. But then at the entrance to the breakfast room I saw the tall, aristocratic figure of Lord Lansdowne and beside him his assistant, Mr. Greco.

I stood in greeting. "Lord Lansdowne," I began. "I have only just now received—"

From behind Lansdowne came the cry of a woman. "I will *not* wait here! I demand to be taken to Dr. Watson and Sherlock Holmes at once!"

All heads turned to identify the owner of the much-agitated voice. Moments later she herself was in the room, pressing awkwardly but determinedly past Lord Lansdowne and his assistant to stand before me. She was a dark-haired young woman in a prim grey dress. Her complexion was pale, her features swollen and without a well-defined structure, from poor diet or weeping. Or so I thought. Eyes flashing, she stopped just in front of my table.

"Oh, Doctor Watson—you are Dr. Watson, of course? I was sure of it. Lucy says you are the kindest of men. I implore you to allow me to stay here and to keep me safe, for I am in great need of protection."

"And you are—"

"I am Mary Mulloy. My brother, the priest Keenan Mulloy, was murdered a week ago. I know who killed him and why, and I am being hunted to ensure my silence. I must tell someone. Where is Mr. Holmes?"

We stared. Even Lansdowne looked taken aback.

Mary's face flushed. "And I haven't any cab fare. The nice man is waiting in his cab outside. I'm frightfully embarrassed."

I stood up and handed a half crown to the butler. "Please see that the cabman is paid."

"Then I can stay here?"

The butler was looking at me as if for guidance. I realized that since Sir Robert had departed, I was the principal guest at the moment and that Lansdowne and Greco did not feel it was their place to give direction in another man's house. The trifling nature of the social niceties involved was irritating to all concerned. I knew, however, that Lord Armstrong was not the sort of man to stick at trifles.

"Let us get you settled in a room upstairs," I said. "Then you can come back here and tell us all your information about your brother. You will be perfectly safe."

"We have some questions for you, Doctor," said Greco.

"They are urgent," added Lansdowne.

"And confidential," added Greco.

"I've had a very long journey and I haven't eaten a thing for nearly a whole day," Mary said.

I said to the butler, "Perhaps you would be so good as to escort Mary to a room near mine and possibly arrange for her to have some tea and scones? You might ask the housekeeper to accompany you and remain with her for"—I looked at Lansdowne—"half an hour?"

Then I turned to Mary, trying to conceal my impatience beneath an avuncular tone. "Now, Mary, I know you must be tired from your journey, but would you please give us a moment to speak? Then you can come down and tell us all you know after you have had your refreshments."

After a long, sulking look, Mary followed the butler.

I was alone with Lansdowne and his assistant, Greco, who gave a brief smile from across the table. "Please forgive our impatience. The Secretary is not accustomed to waiting. Have you heard from Holmes?"

"I have not," I said.

"What have you learned about the missing weapon?"

"In my room I have a journal with my notes on the records I have examined over the past five days. I have made and recorded observations at the gun works—two days—the shipyard—two days—and the shipping dock from which the products are dispatched. The long and short of it is that I found no evidence of a missing artillery weapon. Nor did I find anything regarding its production, shipping, or invoicing."

"Did you find the notice of complaint from the Japanese?"

"I did. I compared it with two previous acknowledgements of delivery. It appeared quite genuine and had been sent to the Foreign Office in accordance with the treaty of commerce and navigation."

"How did you know that?"

"The letter itself made reference to the treaty. All three letters mentioned the treaty and the means of delivery, as a matter of fact." I added, "However, the envelope of the letter came from the Japan Society in London."

"Was that the same as the envelopes for the other two letters?"

"I could not tell. Those envelopes were not in the file."

Greco shrugged. "Likely of no consequence." He glanced at Lansdowne as if for permission to proceed and then went on. "Why do you suppose Lord Armstrong wanted to divert our attention to the smaller field artillery?"

"I took what he said at face value. The smaller weapons are more available, and so are far more likely to be used in any attempt to attack the Jubilee."

"Yet impossible to track and therefore futile for us to focus on as a threat."

"A formidable threat, though." I was not about to yield the point that Armstrong's logic about the big gun was, to my view, quite sound. "I saw personally what the smaller weapons did to our troops in Afghanistan. And I attended the demonstration last Thursday morning, the day you left."

"Armstrong wants to sell us his latest creation."

"The gun I saw was a new variety, and so was the shell. But the accuracy and power were most impressive."

"Were they, now?"

I was put off by his suspicious tone, but merely nodded.

"And you are certain you do not know where Holmes has gone?" Greco held my gaze for a long moment.

I said nothing.

"To Rome, for instance?" Greco went on, his tone suggestive, "You do not think he may have gone there? Ah, you look surprised, Dr. Watson. You are surprised that we know?"

I felt the flush of indignation. "If you already know something about Rome and Sherlock Holmes, I am surprised that you asked."

"Can you tell us any reason why he may have gone to Rome?"

I immediately thought of Lucy's mother. And once again I remembered Holmes's words. *It is better that you do not know.*

But of course I could not say anything about Zoe, for to do so would be to reveal far more of Holmes's personal life than he would wish to be known. I tried to think of another reason.

Then I remembered.

I said, "We were met at the first railway stop after we left London by von Bulow, the German diplomat."

"I know von Bulow," said Lansdowne.

"What did he want?" asked Greco.

"He wanted to know the whereabouts of his two thugs, Dietrich and Richter."

"What did you tell him?"

"The truth. That I did not know where they were."

"You knew we had sent them to the Andaman Islands, along with Arkwright."

"But I have no knowledge of where they are now."

"Did von Bulow ask after Arkwright?"

"He had heard Arkwright had died. I believe he wanted to understand what Holmes knew of the matter."

"Was that all?"

"I felt that he wanted to intimidate us, by making it clear that his men were following us and knew our whereabouts—in particular, the train we were on, after we had been accosted at King's Cross Station. Holmes thought von Bulow wanted to keep us focused on Elswick and the threat of the Japanese gun. Which we now know is negligible."

"Why did you mention von Bulow just now, when we were asking why Holmes would have gone to Rome?"

"I knew von Bulow had previously served as Wilhelm's ambassador to Italy. He was stationed in Rome. That may be the connection that Holmes made. However, Holmes did not even hint at that when he took his leave of me. He simply said that I was to continue to Cragside and the Armstrong works and that he must take a different path."

Greco looked inquiringly at Lansdowne.

Lansdowne looked at me for a long moment.

Greco said, "May I see those notes of yours—the ones in your room?"

"Certainly."

Lansdowne stood. "We must be getting back to London. We have fewer than six days remaining until the Jubilee."

Greco shrugged and stood up beside Lansdowne. "Please cable me immediately if you find anything suggestive."

Then his eye flickered up in the direction of the doorway and the staircase beyond. Moving like a cat and more quickly than I would have expected, he took a few rapid strides. There was a woman's high-pitched shriek.

He returned with Mary Mulloy in tow. "Caught her behind the door. She was listening on the staircase."

"I wasn't!" Mary squealed. "I wasn't listening at all! I was just waiting for you to get through with your—whatever it was you all were talking about—so that then I could come in and tell you what I know about my brother."

LUCY

34. AN EXCHANGE OF BANKNOTES

I would have expected the butler in a household like the Duke and Duchess of Devonshire's to be a stately, silver-haired personage with a name like Worthington or Cogswell. Someone stiffly dignified and proper, who fairly oozed upper crust respectability from every pore.

The actual Devonshire House butler, however, was the opposite of that mental picture in nearly every regard.

Mr. Bellini, husband to Mrs. Bellini, the housekeeper, looked rather like an Italian version of St. Nicholas from a Christmas card illustration. Only an inch or two taller than I, he had a plump, round frame and an equally round, jolly-looking face, with a pair of humorous dark eyes and wisps of curly black hair circling the edges of his otherwise balding head.

He was energetically polishing the silver when I came into the butler's pantry to speak with him, but he was happy to talk to me as he worked, especially after he had studied my face and then declared, "Ah, you've Italian blood in your veins, or I'm a Dutchman."

He spoke English well, but with a strong accent.

I smiled. "Yes, my mother. My grandfather still lives in Rome."

It still gave me a slight jolt of surprise to say as much. For my entire life, I'd had no idea who my parents, much less grandparents, might be. But Mr. Bellini beamed at me. "I knew it!"

It took me only a few moments to turn the subject from the meals to be provided for the D'Oyly Carte players—my ostensible reason for the visit—to the subject of Maud Jones.

"Ah." Bellini shook his head, the smile momentarily slipping from his face. "Poor unhappy girl. Her work was no good, no good at all. My wife spoke several times to her about it. Mrs. Bellini had made up her mind to recommend that the girl be dismissed from service if she did not improve."

A day had passed since I had put Mary on the northbound train. So far, I had had no outraged telegrams from Holmes, which I took to be a hopeful sign. Granted, I had not been back to the Exeter Street flat. I had spent yesterday in rehearsals for the Duchess's ball and then slept last night in an unused dressing room at the Savoy.

But if my father had wished to communicate with me, I did not doubt that he would have found a way.

"Maud was going to be let go?" I asked Mr. Bellini.

Bellini dipped his head, working the edge of his polishing rag into the elaborate swirls on the handle of a serving spoon. He wore a heavy gold signet ring on his left hand—another detail that did not at all fit my picture of the perfect butler—and it caught the light as he worked.

"My wife had as good as told the girl herself." He leaned forward a little. "We think that was why she chose to leave—to spare herself the shame of having been let go."

A footstep sounded in the passageway behind me.

Bellini glanced up, looking past me, and the change in his expression was so sudden that I blinked, all his jollity freezing into a look of barely concealed dislike.

"Mr. Hardcastle." Bellini's voice, too, was frosty. "What do you want?"

Turning, I found myself face to face with a tall man of about forty-five or fifty. His face was long and slightly horsey, and his gray hair was so smoothly combed back from his forehead that it had an almost mirror-like sheen.

"Ah yes, Mr. Bellini." Mr. Hardcastle's voice was slightly high for a man, with an exaggerated, public-school drawl. Ignoring me completely, he drew out a leather-bound notebook and pen. "I wished merely to confirm that you secured the locks on the windows and doors last night?"

Bellini's upper lip trembled, barely on the edge of a sneer. "Last night. The night before that." He waved his hands. "I locked up just as I've done all the nights for the last fifteen years."

Mr. Hardcastle nodded, ignoring the butler's tone. "Excellent. And the new locks I ordered for the wine and liquor cabinets have been installed?"

Bellini only snorted for an answer, giving the spoon he was working on a few furious digs with his polishing cloth.

Mr. Hardcastle made a notation in his book and started to turn away.

"Is His Grace the Duke concerned about security?" I asked.

Mr. Hardcastle turned, giving me a look of mild surprise, as though he were shocked to find that I had followed the subject of the conversation.

"A man in His Grace's position must naturally ensure that his home and estates are adequately safeguarded."

"But has something happened to make His Grace particularly concerned?"

Mr. Hardcastle's face creased in a tolerant smile. "Certainly nothing a charming young lady such as yourself need worry about."

I half expected him to pat me on the head, but he turned to the butler with a dismissive nod. "Very well, then, Bellini, that will be all."

Bellini barely waited until Mr. Hardcastle had made his way out of sight down the passage before muttering *"coglione"* under his breath.

I bit my lip in an effort not to laugh, and Bellini gave me an unwilling smile—probably remembering belatedly that I understood Italian.

"Pardone, miss, but the man is an idiot. A security expert, supposedly. He is the head of security for the Waterloo and City Railway Company, or so he claims. And *porca miseria*, what does he do? Wanders around scribbling notes in that little book of his and asking me whether I've locked the doors!" Bellini snorted in disgust.

"Does Mr. Hardcastle know about Maud's disappearance?"

Bellini gave another sound of derision. "You want to know what Mr. Hardcastle said?" He drew himself up and stretched his face into an obvious imitation of Mr. Hardcastle's smooth, aloof expression. "I was hired to keep miscreants *out* of Devonshire House, not to keep inefficient young women *in*."

"He didn't like Maud?"

"I—" Bellini stopped again, his attention once more caught by something behind me in the doorway.

"Ah, the extra silver polish that I sent for. Thank you, boy. You may leave it here and go."

Turning, I was just in time to see a small boy almost throw a wrapped-up paper parcel onto the floor, duck his head, then whirl around and vanish down the passageway.

The butler made a *tsk*-ing sound under his breath. "We have so much added work, you understand, with the upcoming ball that we have taken on a few temporary errand boys. Willing boys, most of them, and bright, but with no sense of the proprieties. Still—"

I scarcely heard him. I was staring down the passageway in the direction the boy had vanished, a horrible suspicion blossoming in my mind.

"Excuse me."

I ducked out of the pantry and followed, emerging into the kitchen. Antoine, the household's French chef, was bellowing orders at a pair of hapless kitchen maids, but I didn't see—

The chain lock on the kitchen door was still swaying, slightly, as though the door had just been closed. Looking out the kitchen window, I was just in time to see a boy's figure vanishing around the side of the house.

I caught him just as he was about to reach the garden.

"You wouldn't be running away, would you?"

The boy spun around, fast enough to knock off the cap he was wearing. A pair of blond braids slithered down to hang over his—*her*—shoulders.

"Becky!"

Becky Kelly looked up at me with large, guilty blue eyes.

I stared back at her, momentarily at a loss for words. "What are you *doing*—"

I broke off, yanking Becky behind a clump of ornamental flowering bushes at the sound of a door opening somewhere not far away.

Then I pressed my eyes shut and resisted the urge to kick myself. I had acted on instinct. But apparently my instincts were sometimes completely half-witted. As one of the performers for the ball, I had a perfect right to be in the garden. I was far more likely to arouse suspicions if I was caught skulking amongst the shrubbery.

Looking out from behind the bush, though, I was just in time to see Mr. Hardcastle standing at one of the French doors that led out into the garden. He was speaking to someone inside the house, someone standing just inside the doorway. But it was bright sunlight outside and dim inside, and all I could make out of the second figure was a vague shadowy form.

Mr. Hardcastle said something, too low for me to make out the words, then turned away, shutting the door behind him. His head was bent, examining the contents of an envelope; otherwise he would probably have seen Becky and me as he passed within fifteen feet of our shrub.

He didn't look up. But I managed to catch sight of the envelope's contents and suppressed a sharp intake of breath. The envelope was filled—*stuffed*—with Bank of England notes.

Becky was already standing motionless beside me, but I put my hand on her arm, warning her to complete silence.

Mr. Hardcastle vanished around the side of the house.

"Is he someone bad?" Becky whispered.

"I don't know. He's not entirely who he wishes to appear to be, at any rate."

Being an actress meant that I had made a study of all sorts of accents. I was good at imitating them and good at differentiating true patterns of speech from assumed ones.

Mr. Hardcastle's plummy, Oxford-educated drawl was very well done, but not effortless, in the way a genuine scion of the upper classes would be. He was trying just a bit too hard.

Of course, that didn't make him a criminal, only one of many men who aspired to a social station higher than the one they had been born into.

The money I had just seen him counting was far more suggestive. It might be Mr. Hardcastle's salary, but if that were the case, I had to agree with Bellini that he was being overpaid for putting extra locks on liquor cabinet doors.

I shook my head. Mr. Hardcastle didn't matter right now.

"That still doesn't answer the question of what you're doing here," I told Becky.

Becky scuffed her toe into the ground.

"I only wanted to help," she said in a very small voice. "Because I accidentally let Miss Mulloy know about Mr. Holmes. I thought maybe I could help you discover an important clue to make up for it." Her eyes dropped. "And I wanted to make sure nothing happened to you. My mother died. I would hate it if you died, too."

I wasn't sure whether it was warming or terrifying to know that I had so large a piece of Becky's small heart.

I put my arm around her shoulders. "How did you even know where to find me?"

I'd been careful—*very* careful—not to let Becky know any details of the investigation, out of fear that she would do exactly what she had.

"That boy of Mr. Holmes's—Flynn—told me." Glancing up at me, Becky added, quickly, "It wasn't his fault, though! First I challenged him to an arm-wrestling match, and then I beat him. Boys hate that. Then I said that I bet he didn't even know where you were investigating, and he wanted to prove that he *did* know. So he told me that you were here at Devonshire House."

I tried and failed to smother a smile. "You're too smart for your own good, Miss Becky Kelly, you know that?"

This was my fault as much as anyone's—first for bringing Mary to St. Giles the other night and then for thinking it was a good idea to leave Flynn and Becky together. I might have known the combination of the two of them would be like mixing nitrous oxide and glycerin and then hitting it with a meat mallet.

"But Becky." I crouched down, putting my hands on her shoulders. "As much as I appreciate your offer to help, this is dangerous. I don't want anything to happen to you, either. And think of your brother, how he would feel if you put yourself into harm's way. Jack probably doesn't even know where you are right now, does he?"

"No." Becky's shoulders slumped. "He's on duty. I thought I could be back before he came home." She added in the same small voice, "Please don't tell him?"

It was actually an appealing thought.

I shook my head. "Becky, I can't keep this a secret from him!"

Becky slumped even further, heaving a sigh that seemed to come all the way up from the soles of her boots. "He's going to be furious."

"I know." My voice sounded as doom-laden as Becky's.

"Not that he'll do anything," Becky said in the same gloomy tone. "He's too nice to ever punish me. He'll just get quiet and disappointed, and that's even worse."

"I know."

Actually, I thought there was a good chance that I was in for more than just quiet disappointment when facing Jack. Jack kept his temper under firm control, but it was still there—and in this case, scowling, shouting, or swearing were all possible responses that in fairness I would have to classify as justified.

I looked around. Miraculously, there didn't seem to be anyone within range of sight, although someone could always be looking down at us from one of the upper-story windows.

"I'm going to give you some money, just in case anyone is watching us," I told Becky in an undertone. I fished in my bag for a coin. "If anyone asks, say that I asked you to run to the nearest pharmacy for some throat pastilles. Then come back and run your last errands for Mr. Bellini. It will look strange if you just disappear in the middle of the workday, and we don't want to attract anyone's notice."

I tugged Becky's cap back on, tucking in her braids and adjusting the brim. "But then wait for me on the corner of Curzon Street. I'll meet you after rehearsal is finished, and we can go back to St. Giles together. We may as well tell your brother everything and get it over with."

35. A TALE FROM MISS MULLOY

Mary Mulloy appeared to have been correct, as I saw the matter now. Lansdowne had gone. Greco had gone with him. Eager to return to London, they had departed without waiting to learn what she thought were the circumstances connected with her brother's death. However, they had asked the Armstrong Company for the assistance of the robust Mr. Crenshaw, the former army officer who had been my guide for the artillery demonstration. He was assigned to listen to my interview of Mary Mulloy and report developments and then escort Miss Mulloy to a house in London where she would be safe.

Crenshaw sat quietly alert on a sofa at the edge of the great library. Mary and I each sat in upholstered chairs opposite one another.

"Now, Miss Mulloy," I began.

"Who were those men?" Mary asked.

"The taller gentleman who was here is a member of the British Cabinet," I said.

"What's that?"

"He is a high government official. He is very much preoccupied at the moment."

"He paid attention to you, didn't he? Because you know Sherlock Holmes. And Sherlock Holmes is alive. I know that from someone who knows. Just like you, Dr. Watson."

"And who may that be?"

"Why, Miss Lucy James. She sent me here. And she told you. She sent a telegram."

"I received no telegram."

"Are you telling me that Lucy James lied? Or are you calling me a liar?"

It was difficult not to be swept up in her acrimonious presumptions. "There may be another explanation, Miss Mulloy. Do you think that might be possible?"

Reluctantly she nodded.

"Now, what brought you here?"

"I was afraid for my own safety. Some men were following Lucy and me. She said that it would be best if I came to where Mr. Holmes was staying, so that he could help me learn who killed my brother."

"I shall do everything in my power to assist you. If I see Sherlock Holmes, I shall do everything in my power to get him to take the case," I said.

A long moment went by. She gave me a long, sullen stare, her puffy eyes even redder and more swollen than when she had first arrived.

"My brother told me never to become involved with a peer or with anyone above my station."

"Your brother."

"Yes."

"When did he tell you this?"

"February. I had received a number of very nice Valentine's cards from several gentlemen. My brother became quite agitated when he saw them."

"Why do you think that was?"

"He said that social climbing was the ruin of many a girl like me and that I mustn't *ever*, under *any* circumstances, no matter *what*, become involved with *any* man above my station because I might learn something that might get me killed."

"What did you say?"

"I told him I would never stop trying to better myself, that I had come to London and now I had to rise up in the world or go back to Dublin and submit to daily beatings at the whim of our drunken father in exchange for my food and shelter."

"What did he say to that?"

"He asked if there was any man of high position who had showed any interest in me."

"And was there?"

"I told him there wasn't."

"What happened?"

"He looked relieved. Then he said he didn't want to stand in my way, but he wanted me to promise not to get close to any man of high station just yet. He wanted me to wait until after the Jubilee."

"If there is a man in high position who has paid you his attentions," I said, "Mr. Holmes will want to know who he is. His identity may have bearing on what happened to your brother."

She only pressed her lips together and glared at me.

LUCY

36. A MURDER IN WHITECHAPEL

"I'm so sorry," I finished. "I would never, ever have gotten Becky involved in any of this willingly. But it's still completely my fault that she was at Devonshire House today."

Jack sat unmoving, his elbows resting on the table, his hands braced against the space between his eyes. We were sitting at the Kellys' small wooden dining table, and so far Jack hadn't spoken throughout my entire account of Becky's exploits.

I edged my chair slightly back.

Jack looked up at me, one eyebrow raised. "What?"

"I'm just wondering whether I should duck and cover my head before the explosion."

Jack smiled briefly, but then rubbed his eyes again. He looked tired—understandably, considering how many shifts of duty he had worked in a row these past days.

"I'm not mad. Not at you, anyway. I've been trying to keep my sister out of trouble for two years now. Trust me when I say it can't be done."

Jack's mother had abandoned him on the London streets when he was even younger than Becky, leaving him without a backward glance so that she could run off with a man. Then a little over two years ago, she had turned up with Becky in tow, found Jack, and more or less dumped the responsibility for Becky onto him before dying of consumption.

"Will you be terrified if I tell you that she reminds me a good deal of myself when I was her age?"

"Terrified." Jack was smiling at me, though. Our eyes caught and held, and for a moment everything—the room, the rattle of carriage wheels, and London street noises from outside— seemed to take a step back.

Becky's voice came from inside the bedroom. She had gone into the other room, ostensibly to change her clothes—more likely to hide—while I spoke to her brother. "Have you decided how much trouble I'm in? Can I come out now?"

* * *

Not long afterward, supper was over. Jack and I had washed and dried the dishes. Prince was sprawled out, asleep at the hearth, and Becky was dozing on the sofa. She had been fighting sleep for the past half hour, vehemently declaring that she wasn't even a little bit tired. But a few minutes ago, she had lost the battle and was now curled up with her head pillowed on her folded hands.

"How's your arm?" Jack asked. "Becky said you'd been hurt."

We were back at the table, sitting across from each other.

"It's fine. It was just a deep scratch, really."

Jack nodded.

"Have you had a chance to look into any cases of missing women?" I asked. I kept my voice low so as not to wake Becky. "Anyone who might answer to Maud Jones's description?"

Jack glanced over at Becky as though checking how deeply asleep she was, then stood up. "Yeah, there was one." He reached for a file that sat on the top of an upper shelf. "I asked around and got this from a Detective Constable I know who works in H division."

"H division ... that's Whitechapel, isn't it?"

Whitechapel was most famous for being the locale of the Jack the Ripper murders ten years before. The rates of prostitution and other crime there made even St. Giles look like a seaside health resort.

Jack nodded. "Anonymous dead girls turning up on the streets around there—it's not exactly unheard of. But this one caught DC Graves's attention. She was clean and well fed, for one thing. Hadn't been living on the streets or in flop houses."

I felt a cold lurch in the pit of my stomach. I hadn't really been expecting to find Maud alive and unharmed, but this still wasn't the answer that I had hoped for.

"Is that the autopsy report?"

Jack nodded, pushing the file across the table towards me. "There are a couple of photographs. Would you recognize her?"

"No, unfortunately I've never met Maud or even seen a picture of her. But I can see whether this girl answers the general description."

I set one hand on the manila folder, then stopped, frowning at Jack.

"What is it?"

"You're not going to tell me that the photographs are ugly and that I should brace myself?"

Jack looked mildly surprised. "You already know they're ugly. That's why we're sitting here, trying to figure out what happened to her, right? Besides." One side of his mouth tipped up in a quick, crooked smile. "I figured anyone who brought up words like *delicate sensibilities* and *no sight for a lady* with you would get pretty much the same treatment you gave the mug who pulled a knife on you."

"Possibly a modified version." Still, I couldn't help but be impressed. I had been fighting against notions of what girls could and couldn't do for almost as long as I could remember—long enough to be aware that there were very few men who didn't harbor at least *some* deep-down misgivings about a woman's place in what were popularly considered men's affairs.

Uncle John had the highest respect and affection for me, but he wouldn't be able to show me photographs of a murder victim without wincing, bless his chivalrous heart.

I opened the folder and scanned quickly through the words of the coroner's official report. *Female ... age estimated to be about twenty-five ... found under a rubbish heap in Brick Lane ...*

I looked up at Jack. "She was found in a rubbish heap? That makes it sound as though she were killed elsewhere and then her body was dumped in Brick Lane."

"Sounds like."

I kept reading. *Cause of death strangulation ... no other signs of abuse or injury ...*

I turned the page and found the mortuary photographs Jack had mentioned.

They *were* ugly. No uglier than many other sights I had seen and less violent than many, but the cold, clinical tone of the pictures was almost worse, in a way, than seeing the on-site aftermath of a violent crime.

The dead girl lay on a coroner's slab. She was plump, with a frizz of curly blonde hair around her face, and might have been on the pretty side in life. But death had flattened her features into soft, flabby anonymity. Her mouth was a little open, her eyes closed.

The bruised marks on her neck from where she'd been killed were plain. Finger marks, from large, capable hands. No rope had done this.

"It could be Maud Jones," I said. "We'll have to find a way for someone to show these pictures around at Devonshire House."

Jack nodded. "I can pass a word on to Detective Constable Graves that he should make inquiries there. We can call it an anonymous tip-off."

"I'm sure the Duke and Duchess are going to love—"

I broke off as Becky woke up suddenly with a frightened cry. "Jack?"

"I'm here. It's all right, Beck, I'm right here." Jack crossed to his sister, and I quickly flipped the autopsy report shut, sliding it out of sight back onto the upper shelf.

Becky clung to her brother, burying her face against his shoulder.

"It's all right. You were just having a bad dream. Come on." Jack picked her up. "You should be in bed."

He carried Becky into the bedroom. Prince trotted after them, settling himself with a sigh at the foot of Becky's narrow painted bed.

"Jack, wait." Becky caught hold of her brother's hand as he started to turn away. "Will you tell me a story first?"

"Now you're just milking this." Jack tugged on one of Becky's braids. "But fine. Which one do you want?"

"Tell me the one about the burglar who locked himself inside the house he was trying to rob."

It was possibly an odd choice for a bedtime story. But then, at Becky's age, I had wanted more exciting material than Cinderella or Rumpelstiltskin, too.

Becky sat up, pulling the blankets around her as she listened to Jack's story of being called to a house where a burglar had attempted steal the silver. But stumbling around in the darkened house, instead of *un*locking the door to the butler's pantry where the silver was kept, the would-be thief had managed to lock himself *into* the dining room. Then he had dropped his set of lock picks and been unable to find them again in the pitch dark.

I settled on the couch to listen and realized that this was actually a wise move on Jack's part. Not all the criminals he encountered would be as bumbling as the unfortunate purloiner of silver, but Becky would worry about him significantly less if she thought of them that way.

I watched as she giggled through the end of the story, in which the hapless burglar was found crashing around in the dining room, trying to use one of the chairs to break down the door.

Becky finally consented to lie down, then. Her eyes slowly drifted shut, her breathing deepening.

The fire in the hearth sent up a shower of sparks. Someone shouted in the street outside.

"What are you thinking about?" Jack asked.

I looked up to find that he had come back into the outer room and was watching me.

"I was just thinking how much nicer this is than Devonshire House."

Jack gave me raised eyebrows. I had to admit that on the surface it was a strange thing to say. Devonshire House was palatial in every sense, and Jack and Becky lived in two-room's worth of rented lodgings, with bare floorboards and windows that rattled every time the wind blew.

Still, I shook my head. "I mean it! Everything in places like Devonshire House is so ... so *polished*. And yet almost nothing is real or true. I grew up visiting places just like that. Nearly all the girls I went to school with came from those sorts of backgrounds. Families with more money than they knew what to do with, and then they spent their entire lives doing nothing, accomplishing nothing except to be slaves to their own fame and fortune. Everything had to be done just so—everyone had to *act* just so—to keep up appearances and make sure that they were spending money just as ostentatiously as their neighbors. The husbands and wives were nearly all trapped in these loveless marriages, marriages just for show, made so that their already rich families could get even richer. I knew long before I left school that I was never going to belong anywhere in that world."

I stopped speaking. Jack was looking at me with the strangest expression on his face.

"You could stay here," Jack said.

"What?"

Jack cleared his throat. "I mean, I'm due back at the station house at eleven. But if you're worried about going back to Exeter Street and need somewhere to sleep for tonight, you can have the couch."

"Thank you."

I wasn't going to think about the way my heart had jumped for the instant I thought Jack had meant ... something else by that offer.

"Becky will be glad if you're here when she wakes up," Jack said.

"Of course I'll stay with her."

If I had inadvertently put Becky in danger, the least I could do was make sure that she was protected tonight.

I curled up on the couch, tucking my feet under me and watching the glow of the fire. Jack took down his blue uniform coat from where it hung by the door and slid it on, fastening up the buttons. He took down his police truncheon—the heavy wooden club all members of the force carried—and slid it into the buckle on his belt.

I sat bolt upright. "Butler's pantry!"

Jack looked at me. "Don't tell me I have to tell that story for you to go to sleep, too."

I shook my head. "It just reminded me of something. Today at Devonshire House, I was talking to Bellini, the butler, and he was polishing the silver in the butler's pantry. He was wearing a ring—a big gold signet ring—on his left hand. Now look at this."

I jumped up, reaching for the autopsy report that I had hidden up out of sight. I flipped to the photographs, the ones showing the closest images of the marks on the dead girl's throat.

"Assuming that this really is Maud Jones, look at that bruise, here." I pointed to a circular discoloration on the skin.

Jack came over to stand beside me, studying the picture for himself. "It could be. You'd have to get the actual ring and compare. But you're right. Whoever did this was wearing some kind of a ring. On the left hand, too."

"I need to send a telegram to Holmes," I said. "He has to know of this. Except—" I shook my head, frowning down at the picture.

It was easier to think of the dead girl as an image in a photograph, a collection of clues to be interpreted. But at the moment, I needed to remember the living, breathing human she had been.

"Except?" Jack repeated.

"Except it makes no sense to think that Mr. Bellini killed her. He's plump, middle aged, and jolly and looks like a garden gnome. Which isn't proof of innocence, I know; plenty of jolly men are murderers at heart. But according to Eve, Mrs. Bellini's other secretary, Maud was romantically involved with someone. And while Mr. Bellini might be a murderer, I absolutely cannot imagine him being the object of anyone's secret romantic pining."

Jack frowned. "Maybe Eve was wrong about there being someone in Maud's life?"

"I don't think so. Look at this."

Yesterday at rehearsal, I had slipped back into Maud's room when no one was watching and taken the sheet of half-burned paper that Eve had found in the grate. I still had it in my bag, carefully sandwiched between sheets of music.

I took it out, laying it down on the table next to the photographs.

"Doubt thou the stars are fire; Doubt that the sun doth move; Doubt truth to be a liar; But never doubt I love," I read.

Jack and I were standing so close that our shoulders were almost touching. When I turned to glance at him, our eyes met. The space between us felt suddenly charged, electric, like the air before a thunderstorm.

I looked quickly back down at the burned page. "Which proves nothing except that Maud's lover wasn't terribly original. That's Shakespeare—Hamlet—and probably the most commonly quoted passage in the history of sloppily sentimental love letters. Never mind that things didn't exactly turn out well for Hamlet and Ophelia."

Jack was still frowning. "All right. So maybe this Bellini character killed her, but he wasn't this man she was seeing. Maybe whoever she was involved with had nothing to do with her death at all."

"It's possible, of course." I shook my head. I hadn't any tangible proof that Maud's unhappy love affair and her murder were linked. Yet I felt somewhere, deep in my bones, that they had to be. "I don't know, though. She was very secretive about this man, whoever he was. She didn't tell Eve anything about him. She didn't even hint about being involved with anyone, and that's unusual for girls in their position."

I had been the recipient of enough confidences from the other girls in the opera company to know that most young women were *dying* to tell someone about their affairs of the heart.

"Maybe he was someone different, someone who didn't belong in her world," Jack said. His voice was quiet. "Maybe he was poor, uneducated."

I turned quickly to look at him again.

Jack cleared his throat. "Maybe he'd never met anyone like her before and he couldn't believe he'd ever deserve her."

The firelight highlighted the hard planes and angles of his face, picking out the scar that bisected one of his brows.

We were so close that I could see the points of his dark lashes and my own image reflected in his eyes. My heartbeat echoed in my ears.

"Maybe he was wrong." My voice came out almost as a whisper.

A knock sounded on the front door. I jumped. Jack was already across the room, moving to answer it.

A small boy stood outside. He thrust an envelope at Jack, ducked his head, and then sped off without a word.

One of my father's irregulars—he had to be.

"I take it this is for you." Jack handed the envelope over to me.

The address—just a single word: *Lucy*—was written in Mycroft's crabbed, spidery hand, as was the cover note inside.

Lucy, my dear, this arrived tonight from our mutual friend, and I judged it best to send it on to you without delay.

Of course Mycroft had known exactly where I was to be found.

"It's from Holmes," I said. Enclosed with Mycroft's note was a yellow telegram form.

I read it out loud. "Kindly ascertain any Italian speakers in Devonshire House."

Jack's eyebrows went up in surprise.

I dropped the telegram onto the table. "Two hundred years ago, he would have been burned at the stake for being a warlock."

"So what's our next move?" Jack asked.

"The police need to show these photographs around Devonshire House, obviously, and try to get a positive identification of the dead girl as Maud." I frowned. "But I'd also like to see the area where her body was dumped. I know the H division police constables have probably made enquiries, but no one in Whitechapel ever admits to seeing anything when it's a policeman doing the asking. There might be someone who saw the girl's body being left and who would be willing to talk to me."

Jack didn't say anything, but I could almost hear him biting off words inside his head.

I shook my head. "It's all right. I may not like being treated like a fragile flower, but I'm not suicidal. It would be inviting trouble for me to walk around Brick Lane on my own, asking a lot of thieves and cut throats if they could please tell me about a girl's murder. If you would be willing to come with me tomorrow—except looking less like a policeman than you do right now—I would be willing to accept your company."

Jack grinned. "How can I pass up an offer like that?"

LUCY

37. TO THE SCENE OF THE CRIME

Jack the Ripper hadn't only stalked the fallen women of London's East End. His murders also had the unintended effect of shining a spotlight of public attention on Spittalfields and Whitechapel. I had been in America at the time of the famous killings, but even I had read of them in the newspapers—and of the abyss of poverty and despair in which the people of those neighborhoods lived.

Since then, missionaries had opened so-called ragged schools with the intent of educating the neighborhood children. Temperance guilds campaigned for the closure of beer houses and taverns, and brothels had been pulled down, which typically meant only that the prostitutes had to ply their trade on the streets instead of with the small luxury of a roof over their heads.

The poverty and filth of Whitechapel remained largely unchanged. But on a spring morning, it was at least partly masked by the fierce hum and rush of life in the streets. Brick Lane was in the heart of the Jewish neighborhoods, where so many Russian immigrants had begun to settle. A former church on the corner had been replaced by a synagogue, and street vendors were pushing carts filled with roasted chickpeas and garlic pickles, calling their wares aloud in Yiddish.

Jack and I had brought Becky along with us, since—as Jack said—she would probably get into worse trouble if we tried to leave her behind. She skipped a few paces ahead of us, holding on to Prince's leash.

As I watched, she hopped with both feet over a muddy puddle, dragging Prince with her and laughing as they both landed on the other side.

"How do you stand it?" I hadn't meant to ask the question, but the words just seemed to come out on their own. "How do you manage to live with caring for another person, always having to worry about her, keep her safe?"

Jack loved his sister, I knew that. I loved her, too, but I still had no idea how he survived the weight of responsibility.

Jack raised a shoulder. "It's not like I—"

A small boy racing along the side of the street suddenly veered, nearly crashing into us.

Jack caught him, steadying him with a hand on his shoulder. "Careful there."

The boy was probably eight or nine, but tough looking, with dirty, swarthy features and straight dark brows. He glowered at Jack. "Let go of me."

"Yeah, I'll do that. Just as soon as you give back the money you just stole from me."

The boy's scowl deepened. Jack didn't say anything or utter any threats, but the boy seemed to decide that his odds of getting away weren't good.

"Fine." With a grunt of disgust, the boy handed over the coins he must have just taken when he'd pretended to bump into us.

"Thanks." Jack transferred his grip to the back of the boy's tattered jacket, sliding the money back into his own pocket. As per my request, he was out of uniform and wearing plain gray woolen trousers and a white cotton shirt.

The child glared. "I gave you yer rotten money back, now let go, can't you?"

"Maybe you can tell us something." Jack took a half shilling out of his pocket, holding it in two fingers. "Is there anyone around who's usually doing business around here late at night?"

The boy eyed Jack narrowly. "Who wants to know?"

"Someone who'll give you enough money to buy food and a bed for tonight." Jack flipped the coin up, catching it in the air.

The boy looked at it, then jerked his thin shoulders. "Fine. Try old Polly, up the street. Got an orange cart. She's usually around. When she's not too drunk to stand up."

He practically snatched the coin from Jack's hand and was gone the second that Jack released his hold, vanishing with eel-like speed into the crowds.

"What do you think will happen to him?" I asked.

Jack shrugged. "He'll keep stealing until he's caught and sent to jail. Then he'll either die in prison or be back on the streets, stealing until he's caught all over again. In this kind of neighborhood, you've got two choices: steal or starve." Jack was silent, then glanced down at me. "The truth is, I'm lucky Becky did show up in my life. If she hadn't, I'd probably have ended up exactly where that kid is going—either in prison or buried six feet underground."

As a child and then a teenage boy, living alone on the streets, Jack had run with one of the London criminal street gangs. But when his mother died and left him with Becky, he had cut all ties to that life, joining the police force so that he could take care of his sister and give her a stable home.

"Or captured by Sherlock Holmes and his brilliant, crime-solving daughter," I said.

Jack grinned, his expression lightening. "Think you would have caught me?"

"Obviously."

We tried several orange sellers before Becky spotted the one we wanted. We had told her who and what we were looking for, but not why.

"You go ahead," Jack told me. "Becky and I will go look at the bird-seller's place over there." He nodded towards a market stall with dozens of songbirds in small wooden cages. Becky was already gravitating to it as though drawn by a magnet.

"You realize you're dooming yourself to buying her a bird?"

"I'll tell her Prince would only try to eat it."

I approached the orange cart.

"Two oranges, please."

The cart's owner—presumably old Polly—was a bent, wizened figure, so swathed in dirty black shawls that I could see little more of her than her age-seamed face. Her eyes were flatly blue and rheumy, either with age or the drink that our pickpocket friend had mentioned.

"They're thrrrrree for a penny."

Definitely drink. Her words were slurred to the point of being almost unintelligible, and when she opened her mouth, I caught a gust of gin strong enough to make me step back.

"I'll take three, then."

She scrabbled up the fruit with one gnarled, arthritic-looking hand, dropped it into a brown paper bag, and held out her other hand for the money. I took out the coin, but held onto it.

"I was wondering. Were you here two weeks ago last Monday?"

Old Polly peered at me. "Eh?"

"I'm looking for someone who might have seen something that happened on this street at night, two weeks ago, near the corner of Flower and Dean Streets."

Polly's rheumy blue eyes regarded me with profound lack of interest or curiosity. Withdrawing a flask from some inner fold of her shawl, she uncorked it, took a long swig, and then wiped her mouth with the back of her hand. "Eh?"

This was probably pointless. On to the next orange cart.

"I saw."

The voice, coming from underneath the cart, almost made me jump. I crouched down and was confronted by a small girl who looked to be a year or two younger than Becky, with a thin, sharp-featured face and stringy dark hair. She peered out from between the spokes of the orange cart's wheels.

"Hello." I smiled at her. "What's your name?"

"Sarah." She didn't return the smile, but continued to regard me with owlish dark eyes. "Are you talking about the dead girl?"

38. A LETTER

Just before supper on Saturday, the nineteenth of June, three days before the Jubilee parade was to begin, I received this letter from Lucy:

Dear Uncle John,

Please don't worry. I know beginning a letter in that fashion isn't exactly reassuring, but I really am fine. I'm sure Mary will have given you a dramatic account of the way we were attacked in the park by now, and I won't try to claim that it wasn't serious or that we weren't in danger. But the cut on my arm is healing cleanly, and no one has tried to abduct or assault me since.

I think Becky is slightly disappointed by the lack of action or excitement.

I need to bring you—and, through you, Holmes—up to date on what I've learned. A body was found on Brick Lane which answers the description of Maud Jones, who I think must be the "Miss Jones" to whom Keenan Mulloy was writing. She was secretary to the Duke of Devonshire's housekeeper and recently disappeared from his household without a trace. Too many questions about her, and I run the risk of rousing the suspicions of the rest of the Devonshire House staff. But I have learned that she was involved with a lover, whose burned letter was found in the grate of her room after she disappeared. Otherwise, though, I'm afraid I've learned very little about Maud Jones herself.

I do, however, have a significant narrative to tell about the way Maud's body came to be discovered on Brick Lane. I went there myself to find out whether I could find any witnesses—in company with Jack (I told you that you didn't have to worry)—and found a small girl named Sarah, the granddaughter to an orange vendor who parks her cart near the corner where Maud's body was found.

She popped up from beneath her grandmother's cart and asked me whether I was asking questions about "the dead girl."

Since I know that Holmes will glower if he is deprived of any possibly significant details, I will set the rest of the conversation down here, exactly as it happened:

"What dead girl?" I asked.

"The one that was dropped off up the road." Sarah gestured. "Two weeks ago, on a Sunday night."

"How do you know it was a Sunday night?"

Sarah gave me a look that said I was very feeble-witted. "Because Sunday's the best day for doing business. All the rich toffs come out of church with their best pocket watches and 'andkerchiefs in their pockets."

"Ah." I realized belatedly that doing business meant pickpocketing, as opposed to actually selling oranges.

"That Sunday I got three silk 'andkerchiefs," Sarah said. "Enough to buy a pudding with raisins. So I remember."

"And why are you telling me now?"

Sarah gave me another withering look. "You've got money. I figured you'd give me some."

I decided that it would be quicker not to barter. "I will."

I took out ten shillings. "Now will you tell me what you saw two Sundays ago?"

Sarah eyed the money, then gave a brisk nod, in the manner of a businesswoman satisfied by a transaction. "All right. That Sunday night, I was minding the cart. My grandmother was in the pub down that way." Sarah jerked a thumb in the direction of a public house on the corner with The Frying Pan painted on a sign over the door. "All of a sudden, a big black carriage rolled up."

"A carriage? You're sure? Not a cab?"

Sarah shook her head. "Not a cab. I'm telling you. It was big and black and it had some fancy gold pattern on one of the doors. The driver jumps down, opens the door, and takes out a woman. She was all limp, 'er head flopping over onto 'is shoulder. I thought she was just drunk. 'E dumps 'er on top of some rubbish in the alleyway. Then 'e jumps back up onto the driver's box and scarpers. Rides off like 'e's got the devil on 'is tail."

"How did you know the woman was dead?" I asked.

"I didn't. Not then. I thought she was just sleeping it off. But then in the morning, there were a lot of police over there, all makin' a fuss."

"But you didn't tell them anything."

Sarah looked affronted. "I'm no snitch."

"Of course not." I took out another ten shillings, holding it out to her. "Can you tell me about the man? The one who left the woman's body to be found?"

Sarah's eyes shifted, and for the first time she looked a little nervous. "Well, it was dark. I didn't rightly see all that well."

"It's all right. I'd be grateful for anything you can tell me. Did you ever see his face?"

"Well, all right, then, I did see 'im." Sarah's throat contracted as she swallowed again. "But it wasn't a man at all, miss. It was a monster. A monster with a black beard."

That is the story that the child tells. Holmes can make of it what he will.

In addition to the coins, I gave Sarah the 221B Baker Street address and told her to call there if she were ever in need of a job. Holmes will probably glower at that as well—and I'm not even sure that the child will come. But if she does appear, I fully intend to persuade my father that girls can make equally effective additions to his force of irregulars as boys. Take good care, Uncle John, of yourself and of Holmes. I know he depends on you, as do I.

With love,
Lucy

WATSON

39. RETURN

Sunday, the twentieth of June, two days before the Jubilee parade was to begin, I was awakened in my room at Cragside. I heard a respectful knock, followed by the quiet voice of the butler.

"Telegram for you, sir."

The message contained a clear directive.

Return to London. Board carriage 1B on the 2 PM train from Morpeth. Take 3:35 to London from Newcastle. Carriage 1A.

It was signed "S.H."

There was no telegraph office indicated to which I could reply. I puzzled for a few moments over what to do. Holmes had no way of knowing that Mary Mulloy was with me, nor that Lieutenant Crenshaw had been assigned to stay in our presence for protective reasons. Would Holmes want me to bring those two with me? What if seats were not available?

I then decided that, if Holmes had wanted me to come alone, he would have said so.

Accordingly, the three of us boarded both trains as directed by Holmes. Crenshaw had obtained permission from his garrison to make the journey. I noticed that he appeared genuinely protective of Mary. She, however, remained somewhat distant in her manner. It occurred to me that a mere army lieutenant was not the match she had been looking for to better herself.

Dusk was falling over London when our train pulled into King's Cross Station in the middle of a hard rain. Dismounting from our carriage, I could see the area surrounding the platform was more crowded than when we had left. Sprinkled among the ordinary travellers were white Indian turbans, colourful saris, brightly striped African robes, and a variety of military uniforms and helmets. I sensed a note of urgency in their hurried steps and searching glances as they looked for friends or transportation or simply an umbrella to protect them against the downpour that was cascading from the edges of the platform roof. I wondered how many still needed to find lodgings and get settled before tomorrow, when the first events of the Jubilee would begin.

The recollection of our being accosted at the cab line eleven days before was still fresh in my mind. I did not tell either Mary or Crenshaw of the attack, for I saw no point in alarming either of them. But I kept a watchful eye as the attendant piled our luggage onto his cart, and I became even more watchful as we walked ahead of him along the disjointed line of rain-spattered cabs with their wet horses stamping and their passengers loading and unloading. Crenshaw and I walked on either side of Mary, for her protection. It gave me some comfort that there was no omnibus in sight. There were only cabs.

We were nearing the front of the line when a familiar figure in a battered bowler hat and rain-soaked tweed coat suddenly stepped out from between two cabs. I recognized Inspector Lestrade.

His beady little eyes shifted rapidly from me to my two companions. "They are with you?"

I introduced Miss Mulloy as a friend and roommate of Lucy James, and Lieutenant Crenshaw as an officer on special protective duty by order of Secretary Lansdowne. "You'd better all get in, then." He opened the door to the coach immediately ahead of us. I saw an empty interior with room enough for six passengers. From the other side of the coach, two burly constables emerged. Lestrade directed them to help the attendant load our luggage.

Mary and Lieutenant Crenshaw had seated themselves in the coach. I was about to climb up when I realized that the attendant had drawn closer and that I had forgotten to give the man his tip. I was reaching into my pocket for coins when the attendant said quietly, "Am I to receive not even a single word of greeting, Watson?"

It was Holmes, of course. I was about to cry out in surprise, but Holmes pressed a finger to his lips. He indicated that Lestrade—who clearly knew of the disguise—should get into the coach and that I should follow. Before doing likewise, Holmes turned to his luggage cart and picked up a carpetbag that had been resting there with our luggage. He was soon inside the coach, where he quickly donned his own coat and hat and placed his uniform cap and jacket in the carpetbag, handing it over to one of the constables. He seated himself beside me and across from Miss Mulloy and Mr. Crenshaw.

When we were under way, he addressed them both.

He said, "I am Sherlock Holmes. Mr. Crenshaw, I have read your reports to Secretary Lansdowne. Miss Mulloy, I assure you that I appreciate the dangers that you have intuitively grasped following the tragic loss of your brother. I am concerned for your safety. Inspector Lestrade has made arrangements for you to be taken to an anonymous home away from London, where you will not be disturbed. When we have apprehended those responsible, you will be free to resume your activities as before."

I watched Miss Mulloy as Holmes spoke. It was plain to me that Holmes was sincere, masterful, fully competent, and had her best interests at heart. The only rational conclusion she ought to draw from his speech was to consider herself in good hands and act accordingly.

To my surprise, however, she pursed her lips, thrust out her chin in a pouting, defiant way, and shook her head. "I won't," she said. "I decline."

"What is it that you decline to do?"

"Now that I am back in London, I do not wish to leave it again. I'm going home."

"Home?"

"I insist that you take me to my home immediately. I live at Number 12 Exeter Street. It is close to the Savoy Theatre and very near the Strand."

LUCY

40. BELLINI'S RING

Holmes looked up from the letter that I had written to Dr. Watson. "A black-bearded monster," he repeated.

We were together in the sitting room of 221B Baker Street. Outside, the cold rain lashed at the window. A fire burned in the grate, the light picking out the *VR* my father had shot into the wall.

Holmes was seated in his favorite armchair beside the hearth. Uncle John sat in an armchair opposite, looking bleary-eyed but still attentive. I hadn't been surprised to learn that my father's investigations had kept him awake through most of last night, and I knew Uncle John had journeyed on the train back from Newcastle early the previous morning.

A police constable from H division had already visited Devonshire House and confirmed the identity of the dead girl on Brick Lane as Maud Jones. Not that there had ever been any doubt in my mind.

Now Jack was on duty while Becky was downstairs in the kitchen, no doubt being thoroughly spoiled with cakes and biscuits by Mrs. Hudson. And I was perched amidst the piles of newspapers on the sofa, studying my father's expression.

"You don't sound surprised," I said.

"By the child's account? No. The details ally perfectly with what I expected."

"You expected to learn that a monster had murdered Maud Jones and left her body on Brick Lane?"

Holmes gave me a look from under half-lowered eyelids. "You of all people—well versed in the tricks and trade of the theater—should know that appearances can deceive. There are putty and greasepaint, even fully formed masks, which can be used to alter the facial features."

"So you think Maud's body was dumped by someone wearing a monstrous mask?"

Sherlock Holmes steepled his fingers, resting them against his upper lip. "On the contrary, learning as much would surprise me greatly."

I glanced at Uncle John. How he had managed to avoid swearing off my father's company years ago was a complete mystery.

"Mr. Bellini could have worn a false beard." I had already filled my father in on the Devonshire House butler and his Italian heritage. "And the description of the carriage might fit one of the Duke's—big and black with some sort of gold crest on the door. But I'm sure that His Grace has an entire fleet of coachmen and stable boys who keep a close eye on his horses and carriages. And as butler, Bellini would have no excuse whatsoever for taking a carriage out, alone, and at night."

"Precisely." Holmes paused. "So you have already come to the same conclusion that I have done."

"About the bruise on Maud's neck?" At the time, the mark of a signet ring had seemed to point to Bellini as the guilty party. But the more I thought about that particular clue, the more suspiciously convenient it became. "Has anyone tried to match it to Bellini's ring?"

"No. The police, in their infinite wisdom, failed to notice the pattern of the bruising. Although in their defense, they are likely under considerable political pressure *not* to find any link between Maud Jones's death and His Grace's household. A man like the Duke of Devonshire does not welcome having his staff investigated for murder. I believe the current theory is that Miss Jones ran away to be with a man, who then killed her in a jealous rage."

Holmes's tone said clearly what he thought of that idea.

"And you didn't point them in Bellini's direction."

"I did not. For precisely the reason that has occurred to you. To strangle someone, one holds the hands thus." Holmes held out his own hands, miming wrapping them around someone's throat. "Only the palms of the hands come into contact with the victim's skin. The backs of the hands, never."

His tone was as detached and clinical as though he were speaking of the best way to cook chicken for dinner, not cold-blooded and intimate murder. Not that that should have surprised me.

"Bellini's ring could have slipped round on his finger," I said. I tried to match Holmes's calm. "But it's not likely. The ring fits him quite tightly; he must have purchased or been given it when he was a younger, slimmer man. The round part of the seal on it wouldn't turn towards the inside of his palm easily."

"Just so. The logical conclusion is that Maud Jones was murdered not by Bellini, but by someone who purloined his ring and wore it in order to commit the murder. Turning the ring deliberately so that the seal would leave a mark on the victim's skin and thus point the finger of guilt at our Italian friend the butler."

That was exactly the same conclusion that I had reached, but I still suppressed a shiver, hearing Holmes say it out loud.

In my mind's eye, a faceless, nameless figure calmly slipped Bellini's ring onto his own hand, then ... what? Caught Maud alone in her room? Sent her a note, arranging a meeting outside the house?

"It does point to the killer being someone inside His Grace's household, though," I said.

"Indeed."

"You don't think—" I had seen His Grace the Duke of Devonshire only at a distance in this past week of rehearsals at Devonshire House. He seemed a quiet, amiable man.

But we were looking for someone in authority. Someone who could communicate with the German high command, influence and pull strings amongst the London Metropolitan Police Force, orchestrate a Fenian rebellion—

I shook my head. If Maud had contrived to become involved with His Grace the Duke, she would have had good reason indeed for keeping the affair a secret. But men like the Duke of Devonshire didn't carry on secret love affairs inside their own homes, under their wives' very noses.

I had no idea whether His Grace was faithful to his wife, the Duchess of Devonshire. Perhaps he truly was. But if men of his class *did* stray from their marriage vows, they set their mistresses up in expensive flats in the Pall Mall neighborhood, not in tiny, barren attic rooms in the servants' wing.

Holmes interrupted my line of thought. "I think—as I have always done—that it is a capital mistake to theorize in advance of one's data."

"Where is Mary?" I asked. "I hope that she was not too much trouble for you."

Holmes waved that away. "Watson and I returned her to the Exeter Street flat last night. At her insistence, I might add. We saw that she was safely locked inside and gave her strict instructions to on no account open the door to anyone whose voice she did not recognize. Mr. Crenshaw, a former army man who was assigned as Watson's guide in Elswick, accompanied us to London and will remain with her as bodyguard. Lestrade has agreed to double the normal presence of the Metropolitan Police constables in the area. Also Flynn and some of the other lads are taking it in turns to watch the building from outside."

"You think she is still in danger, then?"

Holmes reached for his pipe, struck a match, and inhaled. "There will be crowds near Exeter Street, eager to position themselves for a good view of the Queen's parade passing by on the Strand less than thirty-six hours from now. The crowds will complicate matters. But provided that Miss Mulloy follows her instructions, I believe that the chances of her being attacked again are few. And those chances diminish greatly once the Jubilee parade has concluded."

"Because she will be of little interest to those who would disrupt the Jubilee, after their attempt has either failed or succeeded."

"However, she is a most willful and headstrong young woman, which increases the number of possible outcomes considerably."

I opened my mouth, then snapped it closed. My father had his methods, and as much as I would like to take him by the shoulders and demand that he give me a plain answer, it would accomplish nothing.

Instead, I scrutinized his face. Holmes generally regarded the world with an expression of near-boredom, which hinted practically nothing of the furious inner workings of his brain.

Today, though, I thought he seemed more than usually abstracted, as though he were attending to our conversation with only half his mind.

That made two of us. Ever since I had set foot inside Baker Street, my heart had been racing, my hands clammy with the prospect of telling Holmes what I had done—not in regard to the case, but the secret arrangements I had set into motion weeks before.

Apparently I hadn't conquered my tendency to act first and think later. What had seemed like a good idea at the time now struck me as practically lunatic, especially considering the danger of the upcoming Jubilee.

"Where have you been?" I asked. "And don't say Newcastle. Your skin has clearly been under sunnier skies than the north of England in the past days. *And* you look as though you haven't eaten or slept appreciably in the past week."

Uncle John tended to look drowsy and exhausted after days of Holmes's frenetic schedule. Glancing at him now, I saw that he had finally succumbed and was dozing peacefully, his legs stretched out to the fire.

With Holmes, though, despite all my worrying, physical exhaustion and sleepless nights still seemed to have the opposite effect.

My father would welcome concern from me approximately as much as he would welcome the late Professor Moriarty into his home as a dinner guest. Possibly even less. But over the course of these last five months, I'd had ample opportunities to observe Holmes after weeks on end of little food or rest.

Instead of becoming lethargic, my father's muscles seemed to quiver like the tightly drawn strings of a violin. His usually sallow cheeks burned with color, and his gray eyes took on a fierce, almost feverish light.

Logic said that he could not keep driving himself like this indefinitely without suffering an eventual collapse. But he seemed determined to prove logic wrong.

Holmes's brows lifted. "I was not planning to insult your intelligence by claiming otherwise. However, I believe that you have an appointment that must be kept at Victoria Station this afternoon."

I felt my jaw drop open. I had always thought the word *dumbstruck* an exaggerated figure of speech, but in this case, I could think of absolutely nothing to say.

"How—"

Holmes made a quick, impatient gesture with his pipe. "A traveler from Rome takes the train from Rome to Paris and then Calais, the ferry from Calais to Dover, and finally the train from Dover to London's Victoria Station. It is quite elementary."

I stared at him a moment longer before finding my voice. "Will you come with me? If you already know of her arrival—"

Holmes' expression didn't change. "I think not. There are several important matters demanding my attention this afternoon."

I nodded slowly. Glancing at Uncle John, I wished briefly that he would wake up. But then, I hadn't told him of my plans, either.

"I'll be in touch later, then," I said.

Holmes was already hunkered down in his chair, his head sunk on his breast and his gaze lost in that particular mixture of intense focus and distraction that meant his mind was following some complicated inner track. He might be ignoring me or, knowing him, I might have been entirely forgotten.

I went out through the kitchen so that I could say goodbye to Becky on my way out. She was swathed in one of Mrs. Hudson's aprons, helping to roll out dough for biscuits.

"Do you have to leave?" Becky asked.

I nodded. "Yes. I have to meet my mother at Victoria Station." Since Holmes already knew of her arrival, there seemed little point in keeping it secret from anyone else.

"Your mother? The violin lady in the picture?" Becky's eyes widened. "Really?"

I nodded. "She'll be staying with me at my flat in Exeter Street. Maybe tomorrow you can come over and meet her."

At least my mother would have someone besides me in London who was happy to see her.

41. ᴛHE BANK OF ENGLAND

Holmes and I rode in a cab that had been sent by Mycroft, who had telephoned to our Baker Street rooms to provide us the number of the cab and the description of the driver. It was just past noon. In the cab, Holmes was monitoring our progress through the side window. The rain had cleared, leaving the streets wet and shining; from time to time, the overhead sun broke through the departing clouds.

Holmes had been questioning me regarding the notes I had taken during my visit to Elswick. He had been particularly interested in the artillery demonstration that I had witnessed on my first morning at Cragside.

"What did you think of Crenshaw?" Holmes asked.

"Sturdy chap. Reliable. Mary is in good hands, I would expect."

"Why do you suppose Lord Armstrong wanted to demonstrate the field artillery weapon?"

"For business purposes, I thought."

"Was he attempting to direct attention away from the missing naval weapon? It would have been in his interest to do so."

"I did not get that impression. And as you saw from my notes, I could find no evidence of any missing naval gun."

"Let us review the facts regarding the smaller weapon." Holmes spoke quickly, ticking off the points on his fingers. "Lord Armstrong is a man of method. He had invited Lansdowne and his assistant, Greco, to Cragside to discuss the merger with Whitworth, his former rival. Presumably they would also discuss future business our military might have with the larger company. There are impending wars on the African and Asian continents, in which many field guns will be required. Both Lansdowne and Greco are in a position to influence a decision as to whether our government will purchase an Armstrong gun or whether some other competitor's weapon will be selected. All correct so far?"

"Yes, quite correct."

"But Lansdowne and Greco did not want to see a demonstration."

"They said they had urgent business in London."

"Yet Lord Armstrong carried on with the demonstration, with you as the audience."

"Possibly as a matter of politeness. Lansdowne suggested that I attend."

"And you never gave him the impression that you were in a position to influence business matters."

"Certainly not. I had the impression that he wanted our investigation to succeed. Armstrong had already given his opinion that field artillery weapons were a far more likely threat to the Jubilee than naval guns. I believe he thought I might observe something from a demonstration that would be useful."

Holmes nodded. "Now, concerning the weapon that was demonstrated that morning, Armstrong had shown it to someone of business influence in the government before, I believe you said?"

"Crenshaw said that he had, yes. But Crenshaw did not remember the name."

"Nevertheless, that is an extremely suggestive fact. It may be a point of absolutely vital importance." Holmes considered, closing his eyes for a moment. "Or it may not."

"I do not follow."

Holmes shrugged. "What did you think of Mr. Greco?"

"Energetic. Officious. Jealously guards his master."

"Loyal?"

"He gave me that impression."

"Mycroft thinks the same. Yet Greco pressed you to find out why I had travelled to Rome."

"He assumed that I would know." I paused, then added pointedly, "I still do not know, Holmes. Nor do I know why we are going to the Bank of England."

"You will be satisfied on both points very soon, old friend."

So saying, he withdrew into that shell of silence that my years with Holmes had made so maddeningly familiar.

Our carriage drew to a stop not long afterwards. We were at the rear of the bank. "Close as I can come," said our driver as we stepped down. "Bit of a shambles round the front."

"We shall walk," said Holmes. He then directed the man to return at half past one. The man agreed, with a smile at the coins Holmes had handed up to him.

We walked between high granite walls down the narrow road and soon reached Threadneedle Street. Ahead of us about a dozen construction workmen in their shirtsleeves and muddy clothing were taking their noonday meal. "The signs of progress," Holmes said. "The Waterloo underground line is being extended."

"One day we may visit the bank by train without having to seek out a cab."

"Not I," said Holmes. "I decline to arrive for a meeting at any bank when enveloped in the sooty residue that now clings to all passengers who have the misfortune to ride on the present underground line."

"There is talk of electrical power for the engines," I said, recalling a recent newspaper piece. "The Americans have already electrified a railway line in one of their cities."

"Chicago," Holmes said. "And you are correct, Watson. That would remove my objection. But now here we are at the entrance to the bank. Prepare to meet for a second time Sir Michael Hicks Beach, Chancellor of the Exchequer."

We waited for the Chancellor inside the bank. Perhaps ten minutes passed, five minutes past the time of our appointment. Finally we saw him, his unmistakable craggy features wearing a glum expression that was not obscured one bit by his heavy black beard and was, in fact, intensified by his large, thick, and downturned black moustache.

Without a moment's pause for a greeting, Sir Michael cut his eyes towards a hallway to the right of the entrance, indicating that we should follow. A few doors down the corridor we passed the large room I recalled from our previous visit, where gold crowns are weighed on precise scales. A few doors past that room, the Chancellor stopped, opened the door, and ushered us into a small, unoccupied room containing a table and half a dozen chairs. We sat. He closed the door and joined us at the table.

As he sat, his manner became instantly less circumspect.

"Now, Mr. Holmes and Doctor Watson. It is good to see you. Forgive my disregard of you in public just now. Mycroft Holmes has told me that this meeting ought not to be made known to anyone other than ourselves."

"Quite understood," Holmes replied.

"Now, how may I be of assistance? And have you brought another million pounds in bearer bonds for Her Majesty's treasury?"

Holmes smiled. I knew the Chancellor was referring to a morning two Novembers ago, when we had prevented the delivery of that enormous sum to the German Embassy. The funds were being held by a banker named Kent and were to be paid to the surviving brother of Professor Moriarty for the assassination of the Prime Minister and many of his cabinet, not to mention several American industrial magnates. After Holmes had foiled the attempt, Kent had appeared at the German Embassy, where we had intercepted him and taken the funds. Kent had fled, but was later found murdered. The German government had denied any knowledge of the affair.

"In this instance, Sir Michael, I hope to be of equal value," said Holmes affably, "though in a different way. I have two requests for you. Both are for information of a highly confidential nature. And I beg of you that you take pains to conceal however you acquire the information. It is essential that it not be thought by anyone at the bank that Her Majesty's government has any interest other than a routine, humdrum need for record-keeping or some other form of bureaucratic nonsense."

"May I ask why?"

"You recall the unfortunate banker Perkins, who was in league with the remnants of the Moriarty gang and was killed by them."

"I do."

"It is quite possible that Mr. Perkins may have had an associate at the bank, someone who knew both him and the equally unfortunate banker named Kent, from whom we took the bearer bonds that you referred to a moment ago. I will admit that it is also possible that Mr. Perkins acted of his own initiative. However, that is a chance we cannot afford to take."

"Very well," the Chancellor replied. "What are your two requests?"

"I need two lists of transactions conducted by the bank. First, I need the details of any sale of foreign promissory notes or bonds since January 1 of this year that resulted in a cash distribution of more than one thousand pounds."

"That will be fairly voluminous, but I can readily obtain it. I can say that Her Majesty's government wishes to ascertain the nations with which the bank does the highest volume of business. And the second?"

"The second list should supply details of all shipments of gold that have been brought in for storage in the vaults the bank and credited to a foreign account. Also since January 1 of this year."

"When do you need this information?"

"As soon as possible, Chancellor. It may be vital to the security of the Queen's Jubilee parade."

"But the parade is tomorrow, Mr. Holmes. The Queen will leave Buckingham Palace in less than"—he looked at his watch—"twenty hours."

LUCY

42. A DISCOVERY
ON EXETER STREET

My mother was absolutely nothing like Sherlock Holmes. That might seem an obvious statement—*elementary*, Holmes probably would have called it—but it struck me every time I thought of my parents: Zoe Rosario and Sherlock Holmes were so unlike one another that it was astonishing they had ever come together, even for a short while.

Not that it was surprising that any man should have fallen in love with my mother. There, I had to disagree with Becky, because my mother was more beautiful by far than I ever would be. She had dark hair and brilliant green eyes, and her pale, oval-shaped face would have looked at home in a portrait by a Renaissance master artist.

What was surprising—to me, at least—was that Sherlock Holmes should have ever noticed her charms. My mother was a brilliant violinist, so they did at least have that in common. But she was also warm and open-hearted, vivacious and affectionate. Even Uncle John, arguably his best friend in the world, would never use any of those words to describe Holmes.

As though she had picked up my thoughts, my mother turned away from the carriage window and glanced at me. "And how is your ... father?"

We were in a hansom cab, riding from Victoria Station back to Exeter Street, though at the moment, our carriage was caught in a snarl of traffic involving a greengrocer's cart, a butcher, and a pack of beggar dogs. Howls, barks, and angry shouts occasionally filtered back to us from up ahead.

I had already told my mother about the upcoming performance at Devonshire House and filled her in on news of the theater, though she knew most of it already from the letters we wrote back and forth.

Impulsively, I took my mother's hand. "I'm glad that you're here."

She smiled, squeezing back. I saw her blink away a sheen of tears. "I am, too."

I knew that my mother felt guilty for having given me up twenty-two years ago, even though it hadn't been her fault.

Our time together always felt a little as though both of us were *trying* very hard—she to make up for lost years, and I to make sure she knew that I didn't blame her for those same years when I had thought myself alone in the world.

Still, I was glad—very glad—to see her again.

"And Holmes is ... Holmes," I said. "Determined to prove that he is beyond the limitations of ordinary mortals."

"There have been no new developments in the case?"

"None except what I've already told you." I had filled my mother in, as well, on Maud Jones's murder, leaving out only the attack on Mary and me and in the park. I didn't want to frighten her. "I'm worried about him, about what will become of him if this case isn't solved."

My mother started to speak, but I kept going.

"This isn't one of Uncle John's stories, with everything wrapped up at the end and tied off in a nice, neat bow. There is no guarantee that whoever is behind these attacks will ever be caught."

My mother nodded slowly, a frown etched between her brows. "I do understand. I'm just not sure that I can help."

"I know. But there is—there must be—a part of Sherlock Holmes that *is* human. However hard he tries to keep it hidden from the rest of the world, *you* must once have reached that part of him. I'm hoping that you can do it again. At least convince him that he doesn't have to carry all his burdens alone. Uncle John—Dr. Watson—and I are right here, willing and ready to help, if only he would let us."

My mother smiled at me again. "It seems to me that he has already let *you* get far nearer to him than I ever did. But I will try."

* * *

Flynn was lounging in a doorway a few houses down when the cab drew up outside our flat. He didn't look at me as we climbed down from the carriage, but he raised one hand, pushing the brim of his cap back, then rubbed his nose.

Everything quiet, the first gesture meant. Rubbing his nose meant that Mary was still inside.

"You haven't met my flat mate, Mary," I said, as my mother and I started up the stairs to the second floor.

We had made arrangements for my mother's luggage to be sent on by the railway porters, so all there was to carry was her small hand valise, which I had.

I had let my mother go first, but as we reached the landing, the back of my neck prickled.

"Wait a moment."

Holmes had said there would be little danger, provided that Mary followed instructions. Flynn hadn't seen any sign of trouble from outside. And there was nothing out of place in the stairwell. Above us, I could see the door to my flat, closed, just as it should be. Yet cold needles of uneasiness were dancing across my skin.

I scanned the stairwell again and saw a tiny smudge of red on the wooden bannister, as though the hand of whoever had grasped the railing was—

I took the remainder of the steps two at a time. My heart was pounding, my hands shaking so that it was hard to get the key into the lock, but finally the latch clicked. I pushed the door open, then instantly spun back around to my mother.

"Don't come up any further!"

My mother didn't obey. In fairness, I likely wouldn't have either. She came up the steps and then stood with me in the doorway, her hand pressed over her mouth.

The window was open. Scarlet footprints traced a path across the sitting room and onto the windowsill.

Two bodies lay sprawled on the floor.

The one nearest us was lying on his back: a stocky, red-bearded man of perhaps thirty-five. His neck was twisted to one side. A bullet had entered his forehead and blown away the back of his head.

The body nearer the window was Mary's. She lay face down in a pool of blood.

43. A CLUE TO THE MURDERER

We left the bank and returned to Baker Street, but immediately upon our arrival Mrs. Hudson gave us a telephone message from Inspector Lestrade. We were to come immediately to Lucy's flat. When we arrived, Lucy and Zoe were standing in the hallway at the top of the stairs. From that vantage point I could see into the sitting room. There was blood on the sitting room floor, pooled around and near the two bodies that Lestrade's message had told us to expect. Still, as I recognized Mary and Crenshaw, my heart pounded and my emotions surged hot, as though someone had struck me in the face.

Holmes paused for only a moment to take in the scene. "Zoe," he said, "I regret that you had to witness this atrocity. Would you please go with Lucy to Baker Street. I have arranged a police coach, and it is waiting outside. Lucy, before you escort your mother, would you please tell me what you know."

"I saw blood on the stair rail. Inside, there is blood between Mary's body and the window. There are footprints leading to the window, made from a woman's shoe. None outside.

Crenshaw was shot, and Mary's throat was cut. She had also been garrotted."

"The time of death?"

"Flynn said Crenshaw and Mary had both shown themselves at the window at noon as agreed. We arrived at two fifteen."

"And during those two hours—"

"Flynn saw no one enter or leave other than Mrs. Travers, who always does her grocery shopping at noon. She went out at the usual time and returned with her usual shopping bags. Then she went out again."

"Carrying—?"

"She had one of the shopping bags with her. Flynn thought she might be returning something."

"Do you know Mrs. Travers?"

Lucy replied without hesitation. "White haired, grandmotherly, stooped. Wears a shawl."

Zoe added, "She is very sweet. I have taken tea with her in her rooms, and vice versa."

"Which flat does she occupy?"

"She lives one floor below," Zoe said. "It would be across the hall, if we were on that floor."

"Where did Mary keep her personal items?"

Lucy said, "In a wardrobe just outside my bedroom." Then she added, "It's been ransacked. Along with my own wardrobe and everything else in the flat. As one would expect."

"I am sorry. Where did Mrs. Travers do her shopping?"

Lucy shrugged.

Zoe said, "At Plumbridge's, in Covent Garden."

"Thank you both. When you reach Baker Street, please wait for me. I shall be there within the hour. Lucy, please telephone

Mycroft to meet us there this evening as soon as he can. Watson, please see that Lucy and Zoe are safely put on board the police carriage. Then return here."

I did as Holmes had requested.

Climbing the stairs once more, I met Lestrade. His face was chalk white as he passed me, going in the opposite direction.

His voice came in a weary rasp. "Holmes says there'll be another body. Between here and Plumbridge's. An old woman."

WATSON
44. RECONSTRUCT THE CRIME

It was nearly six o'clock when Holmes and I returned once more to Baker Street. Two constables on guard at our front door recognized Holmes and stepped aside to let us pass. Upstairs, Mrs. Hudson was replenishing tea for Mycroft, Lucy, and Zoe. We had no sooner settled ourselves than Inspector Lestrade also appeared.

His grim features foretold his report. "We found the body of Mrs. Travers behind a row of dustbins in an alley off Tavistock Street. Her shawl was missing, as was her skirt. Her neck was broken."

"At least she died quickly," said Zoe. "That is a small mercy."

"We found her shawl and skirt down the Strand, in another alley off"—Lestrade paused to consult his notebook—"Burleigh Street. They were stuffed into a dustbin, wrapped around a white wig and a bloody knife."

"He kept the garrotte and the gun," said Holmes.

Mycroft asked, "Did anyone on the street remember seeing the killer remove his disguise?"

"The Strand is a right madhouse tonight, closed off as it is with the parade preparations and the fences and the bunting and the flags." Lestrade made a discouraged face and then went on. "My men have all they can do now, and that's nothing compared with what they'll have to contend with tomorrow when the Queen and her parade come marching through."

Lucy said, "So the murderer has been watching the flat and knows when Mrs. Travers does her shopping. He follows her to Plumbridge's. He waits for her to come out. He kills her, puts on his white wig, and cloaks himself in her shawl and skirt. He walks like a stooped old woman, bent over, carrying the shopping bags and hiding his face as he passes Flynn. He enters the building. He mounts the stairs to my flat and knocks at the door."

"Where the civilian Crenshaw was on guard," said Lestrade.

"Crenshaw would have opened the door," Lucy said. "He may have seen through the disguise, but by then the door is far enough open to allow the killer to shoot at point blank range. The killer then takes Mary alive. He applies the garrotte as an incentive to interrogation."

"I agree," Holmes said. "Please continue, Lucy."

"When he has learned what he came to learn or found what he has come to find—or given up the attempt—he kills her with his knife."

Lucy paused, but only for a moment. "He uses her shoes to lay a false trail to the window and throws out a knotted sheet to make it appear that this was his means of escape. He wipes the shoes on her skirt and replaces them on her feet. After donning his wig and the shawl he leaves the building the same way he entered, carrying his own shoes and coat in the shopping bag.

His only mistake is to leave a small smudge of blood on the stair rail."

Lestrade said, "I would think that is an accurate description of the events."

"Accurate it may be," said Mycroft, "but if we assume the murder was done to prevent Miss Mulloy from telling us the details of a threat to the Jubilee, then the murderer has succeeded." He paused and looked searchingly at Lestrade. "Unless there were other clues left behind at the flat?"

"Her clothing was searched. No hidden papers or notebooks or keys."

Holmes persisted. "Anything missing from the flat?"

"How could we tell that?" Lestrade asked in an injured tone. "We didn't know what was there in the first place."

Lucy said, "Did you find a silver music box? Very ornate, very expensive."

Lestrade shook his head. "Don't think so."

"She kept it in her wardrobe. I think it must have been a gift, since she could never have afforded it on what she earned at the Savoy. But she didn't tell me who had given it to her."

"The murderer might have pinched it," said Lestrade. "A bonus of sorts."

"There I disagree," said Holmes. "He would not waste his time on matters outside whatever mission it was that brought him to Exeter Street."

"So if the music box is no longer there—"

"It means he was told to find it," said Lucy. "And to remove it, so as to remove any connection between Miss Mulloy and the donor of the music box, or to conceal what was in it."

"We can check on that," said Lestrade. "I've left two men watching the flat. But I can't keep them there after tonight."

Holmes stood, crossed to our table, and picked up a large map of London. He spread it over the table where we all could see it. I thought it identical to one we had seen at the Diogenes Club. "Lestrade, you will need every one of your men to cover the Jubilee parade, which begins at eleven-fifteen tomorrow morning."

"Just so."

On his knees, Holmes pointed to where St. Paul's Cathedral was shown on the map.

"There may be a thousand points of attack upon Her Majesty's parade," he said, "but I propose that we keep our attention on the facts that we know and reason from those as best as we are able. Now. First, we have Miss Mulloy's brother, the priest who came to us last February. Why did he come to us?"

I said, "He was concerned about Fenians. A threat to the Jubilee."

"Quite right, Watson. But you mistake my meaning. Why did he come to *us*?"

Lucy said, "Because I arranged the appointment."

Holmes drummed his fingertips on the map.

"Oh," said Lucy after a moment, "you are asking how Father Mulloy came to *me*? Well, he was in my flat, visiting Mary. I came home late from rehearsal. I interrupted them."

"What were they doing?" Holmes asked.

"They were sitting on the couch, in conversation."

"Was there anything to indicate what they were discussing? Letters, papers—"

"Now that I recall, that music box of Mary's was on the coffee table." Lucy turned to Zoe. "On top of all those copies of *The Strand Magazine* that you collected, Mother. I still have them, of course. The music box wasn't playing, though. At least I didn't hear it."

"Can you please describe their attitudes—their evident feelings at the time. Happy, sad—"

"Mary seemed grumpy. Irritable. She kept looking at the music box. I remember thinking that the music box may have been the subject of the dispute. Her brother disapproved of her accepting presents. Disapproved of her being on the stage at all, as a matter of fact."

"And her brother's attitude at the time?" Holmes asked.

"That's what was puzzling. He kept looking at the music box as well, but in a furtive, guilty way, as though he didn't want me to notice. That wasn't like him at all."

"No?"

"I'd been there for other discussions about Mary spoiling her reputation. Her brother was very open and forthright and indignant. But on this occasion he was none of those things. As I said, he seemed to feel guilty about something."

Holmes was gazing intently at the map. "What did you do?"

"I waited until he said goodnight to Mary, and then I walked with him to the hallway stairs. I told him it was obvious something was bothering him and that I wondered what it was. He said that he needed to discuss something that could involve great peril to the Empire with someone knowledgeable about such things. That's when I recommended that he speak with you."

"So let us review the facts of the case." Holmes began to tick off the points on his fingertips. "After your recommendation last February, Father Mulloy comes to me. But he will tell me nothing on which I can take action. He describes shadowy Fenian figures who were at his church. But the Fenians are no longer there. He tells of clandestine meetings with the Commissioner of Police. But the Commissioner himself denies even knowing of Father Mulloy's existence. Then two weeks ago, after four months of inactivity, Father Mulloy is abducted. He is taken to the rooftop of St. Paul's and thrown off, with his wrists bound in order to give the appearance that he is in prayer and to lead us to the conclusion that he had gone mad and committed suicide. To further discredit him, scrawled written materials are left in his room that are patently the ravings and rantings of an unreliable mind. Also that day, an attempt is made to abduct Watson and me. The attempt fails."

Holmes tapped the map on the location of St. Paul's and drew an invisible wide circle with his fingertip.

"The next morning," he continued, "Watson and I begin a journey to Elswick, following a clue from Arkwright's interrogation, to continue an investigation into the theft of a large artillery weapon that might be placed anywhere within this circle and fired upon the ceremony of thanksgiving that is to be the highlight, the very centrepiece, of the Queen's Jubilee celebration. On the train we are met by von Bulow, an emissary from the highest levels of the German government."

"Indicating that the Germans had knowledge of your plans," said Lucy.

"So I change my plans. I ask Watson to continue on to Elswick. But I proceed to Rome, where von Bulow had formerly been stationed. I learn some information in Rome that I continue to hope will prove useful. During the same period, thugs attack Mary Mulloy and Lucy. Lucy sends Mary to Elswick for her safety. This protective measure succeeds, until Mary returns to London and insists on staying at the flat on Exeter Street. Have I omitted anything that is material?"

A long silence ensued. I looked at my boots. My gaze happened to stray in the direction of our fireplace, often the scene of Holmes's brilliant discourses. Now it was dark, as it had been since the weather had turned warm. The black coals and cold grey ashes seemed somehow to reflect my inner state.

Mycroft said, "The bank."

Lestrade had been leaning forward, his hands on his knees. Now his head popped up, like a rat suddenly scenting his next meal. "What bank?"

"The Bank of England," Holmes said. "Eighteen months ago, you, Lestrade, were instrumental in preventing a dynamite attack there. You discovered the dynamite, accompanied by young Flynn."

"And you think there could be a similar attack during the Jubilee?" Lestrade rubbed his hands together in satisfaction. "Well, we at the Yard had the same idea. We've searched every single spot in the area where dynamite could be stored."

"Including the construction area for the underground train?"

"Including that, yes, sir. Indeed. That search has been conducted. Officially."

"Very reassuring. Now, Mycroft what was it you wanted to say about the bank?"

"I had word from Chancellor Hicks-Beach. The information you requested will be delivered to my rooms this evening."

"What information?" asked Lestrade.

"I asked for a record of transactions in foreign notes redeemed for cash," Holmes said. "I reasoned that, if a foreign government is funding an attempt to attack the Jubilee, that government will need to pay the attackers."

"Very reasonable," said Lestrade.

"I also asked for a record of shipments of foreign gold bullion in and out of the vault."

A crafty look appeared on Lestrade's ferret-like features. "I see what you're up to there as well," he said. "If foreigners know the bank is to be attacked, they'll want to get their gold out in time. But as I said, we've searched the area and we don't believe—"

"I quite understand." Holmes stood up. "Now, Mycroft, I should like to accompany you to your rooms and await the information from the Chancellor. Inspector Lestrade, may we have the use of your police coach and driver? I shall send it back directly. I plan to return here before midnight."

LUCY

45. MISSING

I picked up the telephone receiver, looked at it, and then jumped
and put it back down again when the clock on the mantle started
its twelve midnight chimes.

I was in the sitting room of 221A Baker Street, downstairs
from the rooms my father shared with Dr. Watson. My own
flat having been abruptly turned into a crime scene, my mother
and I had been in need of somewhere to stay, and with its police
guards front and back, the Baker Street residence was more
secure than any hotel.

I had no idea how my father felt about my mother being
installed in the flat just below his own. His attention today had
been all for investigating the scene of Mary's murder, with little
to spare for anyone else. And I didn't seem to have space in my
head to worry about Sherlock Holmes's feelings on that subject
right now.

I was too taken up with guilt for having brought my mother
all the way to London and landing her in the middle of all this.
And Mary—

I squeezed my eyes tight shut. I hadn't cried over Mary's death. In a way, I wished I could, but it seemed dishonest, somehow, when I hadn't even really liked her.

I looked down, realizing that I seemed to have picked up the telephone receiver again.

My mother was asleep in the adjoining bedroom, thankfully too worn out by her travels to stay awake. I had told her that I would be happy to sleep on the couch. But so far, I hadn't even tried to lie down.

Instead, I seemed to be making a hobby out of picking up the telephone and then putting it back down again.

I looked at the clock, which now read five minutes after midnight.

Jack would be at home. He had come off duty yesterday at two o'clock, and had picked Becky up from here afterwards. He had arrived at Baker Street while my mother and I were still on our way to the Exeter Street flat, so he knew nothing yet of Mary's murder.

If nothing else, he needed to be told what had happened.

Before I could change my mind, I waited for the signal, then asked the exchange operator for Jack's number.

There was the usual series of clicks and buzzes, and then Jack's voice came on the line.

"Hello?"

His voice sounded a little husky, and I realized belatedly that he'd had so many nights on duty lately that he had probably been sleeping tonight while he had the rare chance.

"I'm sorry, did I wake you?"

"Hey there, Trouble." There was a slight rustle, and I pictured Jack shifting position, maybe running a hand through his hair.

I would have sworn that my voice was steady—and all I had said in any case was six words.

But the next thing Jack said was, "What's wrong?"

"Mary Mulloy is dead." I hadn't intended to tell him so abruptly, but the words just seem to spill out.

"What?" Jack's voice was fully alert now. "Where are you? Do you need me to come—"

"No, no. I mean, I'm fine." I took a breath. "It happened this afternoon. I was bringing my mother back to my flat, and we ... found her. Them. Mary and the guard my father had assigned to protect her."

I stopped, swallowing, trying to blink away images that I would remember for the rest of my life. I hadn't even known Crenshaw. I had barely been acquainted with Mrs. Travers, either. And now both of them were dead, along with Mary.

My hands were shaking again. Uncle John had probably thought me very nearly as unemotional as Sherlock Holmes this afternoon. Which wasn't entirely untrue. In a moment of crisis, I *could* force myself to be calm.

I had examined the bloodied footprints across my floor and studied the marks on Mary's body and never once screamed or broken down or even flinched. But now reaction was hitting me like the recoil of a tightly stretched India-rubber band.

"Do you know what happened?" Jack asked.

"No. I mean, it must have to do with Keenan Mulloy's murder, but ... she'd been garroted first." I swallowed again, thankful that I hadn't been able to even think about eating dinner. "The killer slashed her throat afterwards, probably trying to cover up the marks, but they were still visible."

"So it was a professional job, then." Jack's voice sounded grim.

"Yes, or at least an accomplished killer."

I was still trying to keep my voice steady. But Jack said, quietly, "You know this wasn't your fault, right?"

I squeezed my eyes shut. "I wish I could believe that."

Holmes blamed himself, as well. I knew he did. I had rarely seen my father in a towering rage, but his expression as he had stalked around my flat this afternoon had been terrible.

He had believed Mary would be safe. He had left her with a guard inside the flat and with watchmen outside. And yet she had been murdered, brutally and efficiently so, in the home she shared with his daughter. And I wondered if this had been the mistake I had feared Holmes would make due to his overwork and fatigue, though I could not bring myself to even hint at that possibility.

"Do you ever get ... just *sick* of it?" I asked Jack. "Even if we do catch Mary's killer, there'll always be another one. Another murderer, another traitor, another thief. No matter how many cases we solve, there'll still be evil people doing evil things."

"Maybe. But it's not winning the fight that matters; it's the fight itself."

"What?"

Jack was quiet for a second, and then he said, "It wasn't just because of Becky that I joined the police force. It was because I wanted my life to ... I don't know ... count for something. Because I wanted to be able to stand up every day and know that I'd fought for something that mattered, even if it wasn't a fight that has a clear-cut winner or even any end in sight." He stopped. "Well, that and I'd always wanted to whack people with a big wooden club."

I laughed. It didn't entirely lessen the weight that sat on my heart like a lump of cold rock, but it helped. "Thank you."

"No other news?" Jack asked.

"No. I probably should have waited until the morning to call instead of dragging you out of bed. I'm sorry." I knew I should let Jack go, let him get back to catching whatever sleep he could before his next shift of duty started in the morning. But somehow instead I heard myself say, "I think I mostly just wanted to hear your voice."

There was a second's pause on the other end of the line. I shut my eyes, wondering whether I had just surprised Jack as much as I had surprised myself.

Jack's voice changed, softening. "I could come over to Baker Street, if you need me to. Becky's already asleep, and she'll be all right on her own for a couple of hours. She's got Prince, and she knows I have to leave early, anyway."

My reply formed itself instantly in my mind. Twenty-one years of being on my own in the world might have taught me to solve my own problems and face fears without relying on anyone but myself, but right now, I wanted to tell Jack that I would *love* not to be alone tonight.

Then I heard rapid footfalls coming down the stairs. The sitting room door burst open, revealing Uncle John.

"Lucy." He was out of breath, his usually steady, and reliable soldier's countenance now visibly agitated. "Lucy, it's Holmes— he's gone!"

WATSON

46. DIRECTION FROM WHITEHALL

The rooms of Mycroft Holmes were in Whitehall, an upstairs flat directly across the street from the Diogenes Club. Lucy and I had visited him there only once before, on a November night in 1895. I remember our feelings of anxiety and dread at that time. On this occasion, the same feelings were magnified by my discovery of the sudden disappearance of Holmes.

Lucy and I were perched on the edge of Mycroft's leather couch. Mycroft sat across from us on his leather club chair. It was nearly four o'clock in the morning. The first reddish glow of the sunrise shone between a crack in the heavy curtains that covered Mycroft's window. Today, I remembered, was the summer solstice, the longest day of the year. I hoped it would not also prove to be the worst day of the year. But the facts remained. Eight hours from now the Queen's parade would be at St. Paul's Cathedral, and we had no notion of what wickedness was in store or how to stop it. We did not even know where Holmes was now.

"Did he say where he was going?" Lucy asked.

"He did not. But he repeated that he would return to Baker Street before midnight, and then we would organize our response. Those were his exact words. I waited until midnight and then I telephoned. Your line was busy, so I called Mrs. Hudson."

"What happened when Holmes was here?"

"The report from the Bank of England arrived. Holmes read it over once and then stuffed it into his pocket."

"Did he comment on the report?"

"Not a word. But he did not appear dissatisfied. So it likely did contain some information of value."

"Well, he certainly wasn't going to the bank at this hour."

"Nor at any time until Wednesday. Today is a bank holiday."

"We must try to imagine ourselves in his place," I said.

"When we were in Baker Street he seemed to make up his mind about something," Lucy said. "He was asking me why Keenan Mulloy first came to him. At the very beginning of the case."

"The music box," said Mycroft.

"The music box that may be missing," I said.

Lucy said, "At Exeter Street."

WATSON

47. EXETER STREET REVISITED

At that hour there were no cabs to be had in Whitehall. Mycroft stayed in his rooms so as to be available by telephone. He also promised to call Scotland Yard and report the missing police coach and to have another police coach sent to pick us up when we reached Lucy's flat.

We walked along Pall Mall, passing the monument to King George and then onto the Strand. Now we were walking directly on the route that the Queen and her parade of thousands would employ. In less than seven hours the street and sidewalks would be thronged with crowds desiring to see the Queen and to be seen in the Royal presence so that one day they might tell their children and grandchildren about the great event. Already those who would claim a position with a good view had arrived and were in various postures along the edge of the pavement, some crouching, some lying down, some huddled together. I recognized no one.

There was a constable on guard outside Lucy's building on Exeter Street. We introduced ourselves. "Oh, yes, sir.

Mr. Holmes was here. He left strict instructions that you two and only you two were to be admitted."

"When did he leave?"

"I was on duty and made a note of the time. Ten forty-seven."

"Where was he going?"

"He said you would ask that. He said you would know, after you had been inside."

"We had better go inside, then," said Lucy. "Was he carrying anything with him?"

"He said you would ask that as well. He said he was 'only carrying papers from Mycroft's.' Those were his exact words. He said to tell you."

" 'Only papers from Mycroft's.' " Lucy repeated the words as we entered the flat.

The electric lights had been left on. The floor and the windowsill had been cleaned of blood, but the sharp coppery tang of it remained in the air.

"I don't want to come back here again," Lucy said.

The music box was not in Mary's wardrobe, nor was it on any of the shelves where Mary's clothes had been. Those were still in untidy piles on the floor, undisturbed from where they had been found that afternoon.

"He doesn't have the music box with him," I said.

"He is only carrying papers from Mycroft's."

"The report from the Bank of England."

"But we will find something here that will tell us where he has gone." Lucy's brow knotted in vexation. "We *will* find something."

"Something the murderer did not find. Something the police did not find."

"Because we know something that they did not."

"And Holmes knows that we know that something."

"He knew it as well."

"Because he found it. And he expected us to find it."

"Because we told him."

Lucy paced to and fro for a few moments. Then she stopped.

"Because *I* told him," she said.

She took a few steps back and stood at the entry to the flat.

"Sit down on the couch."

I sat.

"Imagine yourself to be Father Mulloy. You are talking with your sister. I open the door. You see me. When I look at you, you appear guilty and furtive."

"Am I looking at the music box?"

"You were then. At least I thought you were then. But maybe you weren't. So if you weren't looking at the music box, what were you looking at?"

I understood. "Father Mulloy was looking at the two stacks of magazines that are before me now. They were here the last time I was in this room, two Novembers ago."

"My mother's collection of *The Strand* magazines. Your tales of Holmes."

Now Lucy was at my side, picking up the topmost magazine. Riffling through the pages. Then picking up the next. As she did so she spoke. "Ask yourself. What did Father Mulloy have to look furtive about? What made him look distressed and guilty when we were in his presence in his rooms?"

"Our reference to what one of his parishioners might have told him during a confessional."

"And we found his partially written note to Miss Jones, one of his parishioners." Lucy continued as she examined the next magazine, holding it by the spine and turning it upside down and shaking it. "A servant at Devonshire House went missing this month. Her name was Maud Jones. She was murdered in Whitechapel, two days before Father Mulloy was murdered."

Lucy's search had reached the third magazine down in the stack on my left-hand side. She opened that magazine, spread the pages, and—with a look of triumph and relief—extracted a folded piece of drawing paper.

She turned to me, her green eyes flashing. "Let us try to understand what has happened to this paper before we examine what it contains. Assume that Maud Jones had stolen this paper from Devonshire House. She was afraid she would be discovered with it in her possession. She gave it to Father Mulloy. He had it with him in February, the day he told me that he knew of a grave threat to the Empire. He knew he was being followed. He wanted to leave the paper where he could get at it, but not somewhere directly connected with him. He was about to ask Mary to keep it for him when I opened the door."

"So he hid it in the nearest place."

"He tucked it into this magazine. Not the top one, because that would be more likely to be opened by a casual visitor. A few hours ago, Holmes found it, using the same chain of reasoning. Then he left it for us to find. That is why he told the constable he was carrying *only* papers from Mycroft's."

"From Mycroft's," I repeated mechanically, understanding what had happened, and at the same time feeling baffled as to what would come next and what we could do about it in Holmes's absence. But I was also unable to stifle the apprehension that Holmes was in mortal danger and needed us to help him.

Lucy unfolded the paper. It was a pencil tracing of an architectural drawing. It looked like the floor of a very long building with irregular but symmetrical sides. Within what must have represented the walls, there was a large X mark, in black ink, at one end, and three smaller X marks at the other end.

There were also numbers.

Below the three X marks on the right was written *8X4*.

Below the X mark on the left was the number *120*.

"What does this mean?" I asked.

"Something important enough for Father Mulloy to hide and for Mary's murderer to torture her in hopes of making her reveal its location. I've seen this outline before. I remember it from my last year at Miss Porter's school. It was in my art history textbook." She tapped the sketch. "Notice that the outline forms the shape of an elongated cross." Then she folded the paper and tucked it into her jacket pocket. "This is the floor plan of St. Paul's Cathedral."

WATSON

48. CONFRONTATION

Lucy telephoned Mycroft, letting him know what we had found and that we were on our way to St. Paul's.

Outside the building the constable was still on guard, but there was still no sign of the police coach Mycroft had promised. I told the man that we would walk.

"Probably just as well, sir. They're closing down the Strand right now for the parade. Fleet Street will be next. Bound to be crowds."

It was just before seven a.m. according to my watch when we set out, with about one mile separating us from our destination. It being June, the air was warm and relatively clear of coal smoke. A moist breeze came from along the river. Along the Strand people were milling about everywhere, waiting to position themselves for the parade or simply watching the preparations. Bunting had been draped from windows. From several rooftops, what appeared to be ordinary bed sheets had been hung up, with the words GOD SAVE THE QUEEN painted across the white fabric. There was an unusual silence due to the lack of horses or cabs or other traffic, but there was also a murmur of expectancy as people talked among themselves.

"Did Mycroft say anything?" I asked.

"He said the Commissioner would be there. Mycroft was in a hurry to call Scotland Yard and try to get word to him so that we could get through the protective ring and mount a search for Holmes. I now wish I'd told him about the new danger that the drawing represents."

"What new danger?"

"All the protective measures were based on the ceremony being held outside on the western steps and on Father Mulloy's falling from the roof and landing outside the cathedral. The police thought the man who threw him off had been signalling to someone. With the artillery weapon missing—" I remembered Holmes tracing the radius around St. Paul's on the map. "The police were expecting an attack from outside the cathedral."

Lucy tapped her jacket pocket. "But the drawing marks two locations. Both are *inside*."

* * *

The closer we came to our destination, the slower our rate of progress became. People in their best clothing were all around us, jostling each other in the excitement of the great moment that was to come. It appeared that of the fifty thousand souls who were expected to join in the thanksgiving ceremony, at least twenty thousand had already arrived, and more and more were coming every moment. We moved among them as quickly as we could, though I could not see what we were going to do when we reached the cathedral.

Up ahead I could see the sun's rays glinting above the great dome. The soot-dark columns soared like blackened towers over the crowds of onlookers and participants gathering at their base and on the stands that were now fully constructed above the steps to the western entrance. White robes and black surplices mingled with red uniforms, as if a living tapestry was trying to form itself into some yet-unknown design. Mounted policemen and army cavalry on their proud horses paced along the edges of the multitudes, herding them like cattle.

Fortune was with us, for in the crowd of men at the base of the stands I saw Commissioner Bradford. He was in full ceremonial uniform, with gold braid and medals. He was talking to a smaller man also in military dress and also appearing to be in his mid-sixties, with white side-whiskers and a round face. The smaller man was gesturing energetically up towards the clock on the western tower.

The clock began to chime. The hands on its great dial proclaimed the hour of ten o'clock.

Lucy approached one of the guards ringing the plaza. "Do you see that man in uniform, with his left sleeve empty?" she asked. "That is Commissioner Bradford. This man here with me is Dr. John Watson, and I am Lucy James. We are both associates of Mr. Sherlock Holmes. The Commissioner is expecting us."

The guard responded with a look of extreme scepticism. After a few minutes and several similar conversations, however, we found ourselves in the company of Commissioner Bradford.

The Commissioner welcomed us. "Dr. Watson, Miss James. Indeed. I had a message from Mycroft that you'd be coming. Didn't say what it was all about, only that it was crucial. May I introduce my counterpart, Colonel Henry Smith, Commissioner of the City Police. This is his jurisdiction."

Colonel Smith shook my hand vigorously and gave Lucy a formal bow.

"Bit of an anomaly, this crowd, isn't it? Never seen anything like it. Last Jubilee was indoors but now—well, can't be helped. So. I understand you've come about the security arrangements."

"Whatever you can tell us would be appreciated," I said.

"We have men all around this side of the cathedral now. Four thousand army men will arrive here at eleven o'clock, coming from St. James Park. When the Queen and her retinue set out from Buckingham Palace at eleven-fifteen, the protective ring will be three deep. The Strand and Fleet Street and Ludgate Hill will all be cleared for her passage. When the ceremony starts at noon, we will have men with binoculars on the pediments watching the crowd. Sharpshooters will be at every corner of the building, with their weapons concealed, of course. We have searched every building within a one-mile radius. And of course there will be thousands of armed soldiers in the parade itself, and sixteen carriages, each with their military escorts, coming before the Queen's carriage. Hers is the seventeenth."

Lucy smiled and nodded. "Might we see the inside of the cathedral?"

"The choirs and orchestra are gathering in the narthex. The nave and the chapels are closed off."

"Naturally they would be. Since the ceremony is outside." Lucy smiled again. "But might we see inside anyway?"

The Commissioner said, "I take your meaning. We ought to leave no stone unturned."

"I'll have one of our best men escort you," said Colonel Smith.

Arrangements were made, and soon we had gone through the narthex and were inside the vast expanse of the cathedral, with a tall City Police constable. Lucy and I recognized him as Griffin, the man who had witnessed and reported the death of Keenan Mulloy two weeks earlier.

"I've already been round the interior with my electric torch," Griffin said. "Before the sun was up. Not much light in here then, but you can see well now. Look at that light, streaming in those east windows."

We walked up and down the aisles, from the western door to the high altar. We looked behind every pew. We listened for other footsteps, possibly scurrying to get out of a hiding place. We heard only the sound of our own shoes on the hard polished marble floor tiles and the wavering notes of orchestral instruments being tuned outside. We circled the altar. We looked into the entrances of the great high ornamental wall behind the altar. Above us the colours of the stained glass became more subdued as the sun rose higher and the rays became less direct. Perhaps forty-five minutes went by. We found nothing and no one.

"Well that's it, then," said Griffin. "Unless you'll want to go up the stairs? Or maybe down to the crypt and storage areas? Like the other fellow did?"

Lucy's head snapped up. "What other fellow?"

"Why, Mr. Holmes, of course. You were with him two weeks ago. Thought you'd know. He came just as I was coming on duty. Just before midnight. Perimeter guard was just getting into formation. Sergeant said to show him anything he wanted. Just like you. Same orders. Only I had to use my electric torch, as I said before."

"Where is he now?"

"No idea, miss. He went down the steps with me. I opened the door to the main crypt for him and turned on the lights and left him to it."

"What happened?"

"Well, nothing much happened. I stood there in the hallway and waited. After a minute or two he comes right out. Now he wants to go back upstairs, says he needs to get out onto the street right away. So we came back up and I let him out the south entrance. Right over there. It was dark then, and I didn't see which direction he took."

"You better show us where he went downstairs," Lucy said.

We entered a passageway at the north aisle and descended some narrow stone steps that curved in a spiral. There were no windows below the ground level. Only a dim electric light burned at the doorway through which we had entered, and another at the bottom of the staircase ahead of us. A tall, unornamented wooden door stood just beyond. It was shut, barring further passage. The air was musty. Grime coated the stones of the stairway walls.

"The door leads through to the main crypt," the constable said. "That's where Mr. Holmes went." He thumped the bare surface of the heavy wood with his open palm. "Built to last, you can tell that much. I'll wait here for you, if you like."

Then, as if by its own accord, the door swung open.

A man stepped from behind the door, blocking our path. I saw a familiar, wolfish face.

It was the false cabdriver Owens.

By reflex, I turned around to get help from Griffin.

The constable now had a pistol in his hand and was pointing it at Lucy's head.

Patches of dim light shone on Owens's feral features, twisted in an evil leer beneath his scraggly beard. "Well, well, and if it isn't my old chum Dr. Watson. Your friend is waiting for you." He gestured towards a man who lay bound and gagged on the dirt floor, up against the bricks and stones. Even in the shadows I could recognize Holmes. He was apparently unconscious.

"You slipped through our fingers twice before," Owens was saying. "Seems as though the third time's the charm."

PART FOUR

WHAT THE FALSE HEART DOTH KNOW

WATSON

49. DEATH IN THE CRYPT

Griffin roughly pushed us inside and closed the door behind us. The electric light illuminated the immediate area, highlighting the shadowy columns and curved archways that formed the high ceiling. But beyond was only darkness.

Lucy recovered her balance. "So, Constable Griffin from St. Paul's. Was it you who threw Keenan Mulloy over the edge?"

The constable shrugged.

"He may have had a bit of help from me," said Owens.

"Was Father Mulloy in the cab when you stole it?"

Owen's accent now took on an Irish lilt. "I had just enough time to drive to your flat after the tragedy occurred."

"What have you done to Holmes?"

Owens gestured magnanimously. "Don't worry, Doctor. Your friend is still breathing. We haven't even roughed him up. We just gave him a wee injection, same as we gave that unfortunate priest. It'll be wearin' off soon, though. We'll have to give him another. Same as we'll give you. You'll have a nice little sleep."

Owens jerked the revolver towards Lucy. "Now, missy. About that reticule of yours. Why don't you just let it drop to the floor, nice and easy. Or I shoot your friend."

Lucy did as she was told. Owens kicked the reticule away. It slid into the shadows.

"Now, Mr. Griffin. Have you a pair of handcuffs with you? Two pair? That is excellent, my man."

Lucy extended her wrists. She and I were soon handcuffed, our hands in our laps, sitting on the cold stone floor. Outside the small circle of light cast by the electric bulb, there was only darkness.

Owens looked at his watch. "It's eleven-fifteen. The Queen will be leaving her palace. The thanksgiving service starts at noon. All those nice clergymen and choirboys are gathering out there on the steps. After we deal with them, we'll be moving you."

"Moving us where?"

"Somewhere safe. Man who's paying us wants you very safe and completely healthy. We don't get half as much if we deliver you"—he bit his upper lip and raised his eyebrows in an expression of mock concern—"the other way."

"Why?"

Owens shrugged. "I'm guessing a bit, but knowin' the nature of the fella who's to take charge of you, I think he wants to be sure you fully appreciate everything he has in mind for your future conditions."

"You mean we're to be tortured."

Owens only shrugged.

"And you think we'll just go along with this."

"You'll be injected." He pointed to a stack of olive-drab canvas stretchers. "You won't be able to move. And you'll have plenty of company."

"We know what you're up to here," Lucy said.

Owens shrugged. "Then you know more than I. My orders are only to keep this gentleman safe. And now you two."

"Who's to attend to matters upstairs?"

Owens's eyes flickered. Griffin was standing behind me, so I could not see his reaction. He said nothing.

"We have the paper," Lucy said.

"What paper?"

"The plan showing where your little implements of destruction are located. I believe you call them your 'unholy trinity.' "

Griffin stepped around me and came face to face with Lucy. Placing the muzzle of his revolver beneath her chin, he said, "Do not try to trick me. You have no paper. You only have heard two words somewhere and you think they mean something."

"I do have the paper and I have shown it to the Commissioner this morning. When you go back upstairs you will find that your plans have—shall we say—mis*fired*?"

"I was with you all the time you searched the cathedral. You found nothing. You did not even know what you were looking for."

"On the contrary. I knew precisely. The intention of that search was to test your loyalty, City Constable Griffin. And you failed the test. You brought us down here."

"Rubbish. You have no paper."

"You keep saying that. But you are quite wrong."

Owens said, "In her handbag, I suppose." He turned away, looking at the floor. The reticule lay about three feet from where I sat, where Lucy had kicked it.

"No, I have it on my person, in fact," Lucy said. "It is in my inside jacket pocket. If you are a gentleman you will remove these handcuffs from my wrists so that I can take out the paper and show it to you to prove that it exists."

"I am not a gentleman," Griffin said with an evil leer.

Still grinning, he set down his gun and crouched down before Lucy, grasping her coat by the lapels, one in each hand. He pulled the lapels apart in a sudden jerking movement, hard enough to tear the fabric and burst off the buttons. But at the same moment, Lucy rolled back and brought her knees up, delivering a sharp blow under his chin. Griffin recoiled at the impact, and she lashed out with the heels of her boots, kicking him in the face.

With a groan, he slumped to the ground, unconscious.

Owens was by my side, reaching for the reticule, but he turned away to look at the fallen constable. I saw my chance. I scrambled to my knees and lunged at him, reaching up and outward, coming down on him with both my hands and the metal handcuffs. The blow landed at the back of Owens's dirty neck with all my weight behind it.

Lucy was crouching beside Griffin. She looked inquiringly at me.

I pressed my fingertips beneath Owens's right ear. There was no pulse.

I shook my head.

Lucy took the constable's key from his belt. Her handcuffs made a clanging noise when they hit the stone floor.

A moment or two later, my hands were free as well. Then we turned to Holmes.

WATSON
50. ACTS OF CONCEALMENT

"Hold on," Lucy said, bending over Holmes where he lay. She drew a knife from the top of her boot, slid the blade under the dirty rag that had been bound across Holmes's mouth, and sliced the gag away.

Holmes cleared his throat and then eyed her warily as she turned to the ropes that bound his wrists. I couldn't entirely blame him; her hands were not entirely steady as she sawed at his bonds.

"Do take care." His voice was slightly hoarse, but very nearly back to normal. "It would be ironic in the extreme if I were to survive the events of the past twenty-four hours only to perish due to blood loss from a spouting arterial wound."

Lucy spoke through clenched teeth as she went on with her task. "Thank you, Lucy and Watson, for your brilliant and speedy intervention that prevented not only my death, but the death of thousands. I believe that is what you intended to say, is it not?"

The rope around Holmes's wrists dropped to the floor, and to my surprise, Holmes coughed, flexed his arms to restore circulation, and then laid a hand on her shoulder.

"Indeed. That is precisely what I intended to say."

Lucy blinked hard, turning to sever the ropes that bound Holmes's ankles. To my even greater surprise, she appeared to be on the verge of tears. But she said nothing as, with a final swipe, she cut through the rope.

She flung the rope away. I moved forward, extending a hand to help Holmes to his feet.

Holmes rose stiffly but his grip was firm, his thin lips compressing to hold back his obvious pain. "Now let us attend to these two."

He bent over Owens and turned him onto his back.

"Watson, would you please help me slide Mr. Owens beneath the constable."

Constable Griffin groaned faintly, but did not stir as we shifted him. Moments later, his body lay sprawled across Owens's.

"It will appear that the two men fought, struck one another unconscious, and that Owens was killed when Griffin collapsed on top of him," Holmes said. "Now we must climb the stairs to the sanctuary. We were never down here."

I took one last glance at the motionless bodies. I felt Lucy's hand resting briefly on my arm. "You didn't have any choice, Uncle John," she said. "He would have killed all of us. I would have done the same, if I'd had the chance."

We left the crypt and climbed the stairs. In the sanctuary, sunlight streamed through the south windows.

Holmes lifted the embroidered cloth that covered the high altar. There was plenty of light to see the three brass cannons beneath it. All three were aimed at the western doors.

Three braided leather lanyards lay coiled on the floor, one at the base of each weapon.

"Lucy, your knife," Holmes said.

She cut each of the three lanyards where they were tied to the trigger mechanism and pulled them away, handing each in turn over to me.

Carefully, Holmes unscrewed the breech mechanism from the first gun. Then he gently lifted the barrel and extracted from the breech a shiny brass-covered object that looked like an enormous bullet. He handed the object over to me. It was heavy, and I had seen many others like it during my stay at Cragside.

"An exploding shell," he said. "It would have detonated as it passed through the door and rained death and destruction over Queen Victoria and those thousands of people outside on the steps and in the plaza. They would have been flayed alive."

Holmes continued to methodically extract the other two shells. He handed the second to Lucy and kept the other in his possession.

Holmes led us to the baptismal font. Carefully setting down his shell, he slid back the heavy ornamental cover. There was water inside. "Perhaps it will be of some effect," he said, placing his shell, and then each of ours in turn, gently into the water. He repositioned the heavy cover so that the font appeared undisturbed.

"What time is it?" he asked.

"Eleven-forty-five," I said, glancing at my watch. "We are safe, and we can notify the Commissioner of the location of these weapons. We can tell Lestrade we heard a disturbance downstairs in the crypt. The Queen can arrive as planned, and the ceremony can proceed in safety. No one need ever know how close England came to a horrific apocalypse."

"I very much fear, Watson," Holmes said, "that the worst is yet to come."

LUCY

51. ACTS OF MERCY

I stared at Holmes.

"There is a bomb planted somewhere under the Bank of England," he said. "Go, now. Find the Commissioner. I shall follow as quickly as I may."

For all his stiffness, Holmes had recovered with almost superhuman speed. Not that it should have surprised me by now. Maybe someday Uncle John would have to write a monograph of his own: *the medicinal effects of shag tobacco, sleeplessness, irregular eating habits, and the occasional use of cocaine.*

Holmes was only a few paces behind us as we burst out onto the steps on the western side of Saint Paul's. My heart was pounding nearly hard enough to blur my vision, but I could see that the crowds of spectators had only increased in the time we'd been inside. Throngs of people wound through the streets like a multi-colored crocodile. The air filled with the din of thousands of voices.

Fifteen minutes until the Queen's carriage arrived. But what if we had missed something at the cathedral? If another attack was planned—

Or if an accomplice was waiting to provide cover for the escape of Owens and the constable—

"Sherlock!" A single voice rose above the din of the crowd, making me spin in place.

My mother had caught sight of us and was trying to push her way towards us through the crowds. Jack was beside her. He looked up, too, smiled at me, then froze, his attention caught by something to our left.

Gun.

I saw Jack's lips shape the word, though the sound of his voice was drowned out by the roar of blood in my ears.

About ten feet away, a man in a dark gray Burberry coat, with a hat pulled down low over his eyes was just drawing a heavy, double-barreled revolver from his pocket.

I whirled, shoving Uncle John as hard as I could towards Holmes. "Get down!"

Then I spun back, ready to kick anyone between me and the gunman out of my way.

Jack was already there, though. As the gunman raised his hand and pulled the trigger, Jack threw himself forward, into the path of the bullet that I didn't doubt was intended for Holmes.

"No!"

It was like a nightmare: one of those dreams where as hard as you try to run, you can't move a muscle. I saw Jack's body jerk as he was hit. Even so, he managed to grab hold of the man in the Burberry, dragging him to the ground.

Someone screamed, the crowds shifting as people turned, looking for the source of the confusion. Another shot rang out, then a third. I heard someone nearby say, "Must be letting off fireworks."

But I couldn't see what was happening. I couldn't see anything with so many people in the way.

"Uncle John!" I spun around, finding him just behind me in the crowd. "Jack's been hit—he needs you."

I stamped hard on the foot of the man nearest to me, earning myself an angry look, but I was long beyond caring. Pushing and shoving, I elbowed my way to the spot where I had seen Jack and the gunman go down.

Jack and the nameless assassin were on the ground. A small ring of spectators had gathered around them, though fewer than I would have thought.

With the other noise and the crowds and the spectacle, most of the people on the steps hadn't even noticed that anything had happened.

"He had a gun," I heard someone say in a low, shocked tone. "That policeman stopped him."

I was still trapped in the nightmare, the nightmare where my whole body was stuck in quick-hardening cement and I couldn't move.

The man in the Burberry lay on the ground. Dead. His hand was still wrapped around the revolver, but half his head was gone. Having failed in his attempt to kill my father, he had obviously turned the gun on himself.

Beside him—

The paralysis locking my muscles finally let go, and I dropped down to kneel by Jack's side. There was patch of blood on his shoulder, just under his collar bone, and a spreading pool of blood on the ground under his leg. Two shots: one in the shoulder and one in the thigh. Somewhere, underneath shock and terror, a part of my mind ticked off the details.

The leg wound was the more serious. The bullet must have struck near one of the arteries. Jack's body was losing blood with every single beat of his heart.

My own heart hammering in my chest, I put my hands over the wound.

Apply direct pressure. I had heard Uncle John say that, months ago, when Holmes was shot. But I couldn't remember any more, and Watson must have gotten caught somewhere in the crowd ...

Jack's eyes were closed, but they fluttered open at my touch.

"Lucy." His voice was weak, so weak.

"It's all right." I pushed down harder against the leg wound. "You're going to be fine."

Finally, Uncle John's legs and feet moved into my field of view. He crouched down, his movements brisk, assured.

"Knife."

It took me a moment to process the request, but then I drew my knife from my boot, for the third time that morning.

Uncle John took it, neatly sliced off a length of fabric from the lining of his coat, and wrapped it around Jack's thigh above the wound, pulling the makeshift tourniquet tight.

Uncle John almost never spoke of his experiences as an army doctor in Afghanistan. It was easy to forget all the blood and death he must have seen—as well as all the lives he must have saved on the field of battle. But right now, experience and competence were visible in his every movement, even in every line of his grim expression.

He turned, crisply rapping out words to Holmes. "Get Lestrade. He can organize a carriage to convey Constable Kelly back to my surgery. I've slowed the bleeding, but he needs a surgeon now—at once."

For once, Holmes seemed willing to obey someone else's orders. He lowered his head and pressed forward to make his way through the crowd.

I sat motionless, counting Jack's raggedly indrawn breaths until men in police uniforms appeared, carrying a stretcher. Jack coughed as Uncle John and the other men lifted him, his eyes fluttering open. "Lucy?"

"I'm right here."

His hand moved as though he were trying to reach for me, but then fell back. "Lucy, I wish ... more time." He coughed again. "Tell Becky ..."

"No!" My eyes were hot, burning. I shook my head furiously, wrapping my hands around Jack's. "No, stop, you do *not* get to say your goodbyes. You are not going to die, do you hear me?"

I wasn't sure Jack did hear me. His eyes slid shut, and his hand went limp in mine.

The other police officers hoisted the stretcher, and I stepped automatically to follow.

Uncle John turned to me. There was a shadow in his gaze: pity mixed with sorrow, mixed with something almost like an appeal.

"Lucy, my dear—"

I squeezed my eyes shut. "The bank."

I spun to Holmes. "How long until the parade reaches the Bank of England?"

"Approximately half an hour." Holmes cleared his throat. "Lucy, you do not have to come—"

"Yes, I do."

I took one more look at Jack, lying motionless on the stretcher as his fellow officers worked to clear a path through the crowd.

I would have sworn I felt something ripping inside me, sharp and painful. But I drew in a breath and faced Holmes. "Jack needs a surgeon. I can't help him now. But I can go with you to the Bank of England and save other lives."

"Lucy—"

I interrupted. "I'm coming with you. If there really is a bomb, it's likely to be well guarded. You can't go alone."

Uncle John was just preparing to follow the stretcher down the steps. I touched his arm. "You're going to do everything in your power to save him."

It wasn't an order, just a statement—a promise to myself. I *knew* Uncle John would do his utmost to keep Jack alive.

Uncle John nodded, reaching to clasp my hand, and I saw an echo of the same promise in his eyes that he must have seen in mine.

"Just as you will do all in your power to guard Holmes."

WATSON

52. ACTS OF NECESSITY

I should very much like to forget what occurred after we emerged onto the steps of St. Paul's. To preserve an accurate record of our case, however, it must be set down at this point in my narrative that our adversaries, not content with relying on the artillery weaponry they had positioned inside the cathedral, had also stationed a marksman in the crowd. Constable Jack Kelly, to his great credit, apprehended this man and was critically wounded in the struggle with the would-be assassin. The attacker died at the scene.

Holmes had become aware of another imminent catastrophe about to occur at the Bank of England. I wanted to go with Holmes and Lucy, but they both urged me to remain with Jack and do what I could to save Jack's life.

I complied with their request. I still recall the desperation that overtook me as I rode in the police wagon with the unconscious Constable Kelly, struggling to keep pressure on his wounds while at the same time struggling to keep my thoughts from turning to the perils that Holmes and Lucy would be facing without me.

My medical notes as to what I did for the young constable are found among my medical records in Kensington, and I shall not reproduce them here.

LUCY

53. ACTS OF DEFIANCE

My father had occasionally lamented the fame that Uncle John's
stories had brought him, but it did have its advantages, not the
least of which was the instant recognition most people had for
the name of Sherlock Holmes.

Like the street outside Saint Paul's, Threadneedle Street was
a riot of colorful decorations and throngs of eager spectators.
Vendors were moving amongst the crowds, hawking souvenirs:
Jubilee flags, china plates and teacups, and other memorabilia.

Along the parade route, a human fence of red-coated soldiers
armed with bayonets walled off the streets on either side, and
from the windows and balconies all around and above us were
draped Union Jack flags, buntings, and signs proclaiming "God
Save the Queen."

Holmes ascended the steps to the Bank of England two at
a time and had only to introduce himself to the uniformed gatekeeper on duty outside to earn both immediate cooperation and
a look of respect.

"Sherlock Holmes!" The gatekeeper was a cheerful, bearded
man of middle age, with blue eyes and a solid, upright carriage

that made me think he might once have seen military service. "Well, lord love a duck, begging your pardon, sir. But just wait till I tell my missus about this. And here I was thinking this day couldn't get any grander, with the Queen herself due to roll by any minute." He shook his head, his face creasing in a frown. "I don't know what help I can give you, though, sir. No one's come in here today. I give you my word on it. The bank's closed for the holiday, and everything's locked up tight. I wouldn't even need to be on duty but, to be honest, I wanted to see the parade go by."

"There was a delivery of gold—" Holmes began, then broke off with a sudden sharp cry.

The bank gatekeeper looked alarmed, and even I jumped. "What is it?"

"My mental faculties must be growing soft." Holmes gave a quick, furious shake of his head, gesturing to where about a hundred feet away a sign read *London Underground Waterloo Line*, followed by the words *Under Construction*.

* * *

"Why the Bank of England?" I whispered.

The air in the underground tunnel was dank and chill, the only light coming from the glow of the lantern Holmes had found where some workman had left it near the entrance.

The tunnel was still under construction, although work had obviously been suspended for the Jubilee celebration. The torch beam picked out piles of bricks and heaps of earth here and there, as well as the bare wooden framework of beams and supports that still lined the walls and ceiling.

I clamped my jaw shut before I could ask Holmes the added question of whether he was sure the tunnel would not collapse on our heads, burying us under several tons of earth and rubble. Holmes—predictably enough—appeared unaffected. He had also so far avoided mentioning Jack's name, for which I was grateful. I had managed to construct a kind of internal wall, blocking off any thoughts of Jack and the surgery that Uncle John was probably even now performing. But it wouldn't take very much to make the wall come tumbling down.

"An attack on the banking records and the vaults would destabilize the British Empire by striking at the heart of its reputation for financial security. The world would know that the gold deposits had been opened to theft. The deposits would be insecure, in the minds of world financiers, whether or not anything was actually taken. The result would end England's dominance in world banking."

He studied the walls around us, gesturing to a metal tube that ran along the wall. "Here you see the tube used to carry compressed air to the air-lock, which is used to keep water out while digging—"

He broke off. Up ahead of us lay a bend in the tunnel, and around that bend, I could just make out the dim glow of another light.

Holmes raised his eyebrows at me in silent question. I drew in a breath, taking a last look around, trying to fix in my memory the layout of the tunnel in front of us: a heap of bricks maybe ten paces straight ahead and to the left. A wheelbarrow parked near the center of the tunnel about twenty feet after that.

I nodded at Holmes, and he extinguished the torch.

The tunnel was not absolutely black; I could still see the faint ambient light from around the tunnel bend. But it was dark enough that I was glad to have memorized any obstacles in our path.

Together, moving noiselessly, Holmes and I crept around the piles of bricks and builders' tools, finishing up with our backs against the wall directly before the tunnel's curve. There was enough light now that I could see the shadowy outlines of Holmes's features, grim and almost mask-like.

He looked another question at me, and I edged forwards, inching my way closer until I could peer around the corner.

If I was confronted by a man with a gun leveled in my direction, I was going to find it inconveniently difficult to escape being shot in the head.

There was a man, and he *did* have a gun. But his back was to me. He sat on an overturned crate three or four paces away from me, with a lantern—masked, so that only a thin strip of light escaped—at his feet. The gun—a Webley Mark I revolver—rested on his knees.

I bent, picked up a stray brick that lay on the ground, stepped forward, and clubbed the man over the head. He collapsed with a faint moan and lay unconscious.

"Impulsive, but nevertheless efficient," Holmes murmured behind me, his voice all but noiseless. "Perhaps his weapon might be of use—"

"I had the same thought."

I retrieved the Webley, checked to see that it was loaded, and then kept it at the ready as together Holmes and I stepped past the unconscious man, moving further down the tunnel.

This must be nearing the area that was still being dug out. The air felt damper, permeated by the smell of wet earth, and carts full of muddy clay stood at intervals, clearly in the process of being hauled back to the surface.

Holmes gestured to the ground beneath us.

I frowned. "What is it?"

"The color of the mud precisely matches the mud on the man Owens's boots."

He stopped speaking as we neared what had at first glance appeared to be a plate of metal reinforcing the wall between two of the wooden support beams. The plate stood slightly askew, though, revealing a dark gap behind.

"Another tunnel?" I raised my eyebrows. "Am I imagining, or does that tunnel lead—"

"Directly towards the bank," Holmes finished for me. "And unless I am much mistaken, directly into the vault. It would perhaps be more prudent to extinguish this." He put out the lantern's flame.

In the darkness that followed, I could see faint light seeping out around the edges of the metal plate.

Holmes's near-soundless murmur came from the blackness to my right. "On three?"

At the count of three, we heaved the metal plate aside. It fell with a crash that felt like a physical force, pounding against my eardrums.

Inside the second tunnel, a man whipped around.

A wave of shock pulsed through me, moving inch by inch down my spine.

We were face to face with Adrian Arkwright, the assassin who had been reported killed in the Andaman Islands.

Nearly nine months had gone by since a bullet had torn into Adrian Arkwright's face at the corner of his mouth and then upward, to break off the edge of his right cheekbone before it exited. Now his face was fallen on that side, the skin sagging almost like a stroke victim's, but was also swollen and distorted by the bone fragments still lodged under the skin. Jagged scars, still pink and angry-looking, marked both the entrance and exit wounds, neither of which was entirely covered by the obviously false black beard that covered the lower half of his face.

This tunnel was narrower than the first and only recently finished: pickaxes and shovels lay scattered near the entrance on the ground.

The only light came from the small, hand-held lantern that sat on the ground, but it was bright enough for me to see that the man facing us held an arrangement of switches and wires—one that even to my untrained eye was clearly the detonation device for a bomb.

"Ah, Mr. Arkwright." Holmes sounded as though he were meeting a casual acquaintance on the street. "Reports of your death were exaggerated, I see."

Adrian Arkwright's lip curled back. He held up the detonator. "Take one step closer and we're all dead." His voice, too, was changed; it had grown husky, the words blurred by the damage to his mouth.

"I think not." Holmes' voice was still calm. "You are not a martyr, Mr. Arkwright. You are a great deal too angry with the world to sacrifice yourself for a noble cause—a great deal too certain that the world owes you some sort of reparation for the harm that you have brought on your own head. You will, I feel sure, have built in both an escape route and the time to use it after you pull that switch."

"Quiet!" Arkwright's hands shook on the device in his grasp. The muscles of his jaw stood out. "You just can't stand to admit that you've lost, Mr. High-and-Mighty Holmes. This bomb is going off, and there's nothing you can do to stop it."

I hefted the Webley revolver. "Try it." The shock had worn off, leaving behind anger that hissed through my every nerve. For an instant, I could still see Jack's motionless, bloodied body as I leveled the gun at Arkwright. "Right now, I would love an excuse to shoot you where you stand. Please, give me a reason."

Arkwright's gaze flicked in my direction. "I can set off the bomb before you get off a shot."

I didn't move, except to angle the gun upwards from being aimed at Arkwright's torso to just between his eyes. "Shall we try it and see?"

"Ah." Holmes had been studying the tunnel around us. "I see that you have utilized the system for carrying compressed air into the tunnels to house the wires which will detonate the dynamite—which I take it is stored somewhere up ahead?"

He peered past Arkwright into the darkness that shrouded the tunnel beyond.

"An ingenious system," Holmes went on. "Ingenious, but hardly invulnerable."

Holmes acted so quickly that his movements were almost a blur. Seizing up one of the pickaxes from the pile by the doorway, he swung it in a whistling arc, smashing it through the tubes that carried the compressed air. The metal split and caved in, revealing a tangle of broken wires that Holmes wrenched out with one hand.

In the same moment, I heard a voice, weirdly distorted and echoing, coming from somewhere near the underground tunnel's entrance.

"This is the police!"

Arkwright gaped at him for a moment. Then, in a movement almost as lightning-quick as Holmes's, he acted. I was braced for an attack. Instead, Arkwright kicked over the lantern at his feet.

Darkness so absolute that it was an almost physical force slapped against my face. Somewhere nearby, I heard Holmes cursing.

I heard running footsteps, a metallic clang, and then light flared. Holmes had managed to locate the lantern—not Arkwright's, which was broken, but ours—and get it lighted again.

Arkwright was gone.

I swore, then glanced at Holmes. Ladies of his generation did not typically employ such language.

However, my father's gaze met mine and he jerked his head in a brief nod. "Indeed."

Holmes took a few steps deeper into the tunnel, holding the lantern up. "At least my theory of an escape route is proven justified."

A section of the tunnel wall had been filled in with bricks, and in the center stood a heavy metal door.

I stepped forward, shifting my grip on the revolver so that I could catch hold of the door handle.

"Don't bother." Holmes's voice was thick with disgust, though still scarcely winded. "If Arkwright has the rudimentary sense for which I give him credit, he will have made sure that the door is—"

"Locked," I finished. "From the other side."

"As you say."

I turned to look at Holmes. "You knew. You knew that Arkwright was still alive, didn't you?"

Holmes twitched his shoulders in the briefest of shrugs. "My own experiences in the line of miraculous resurrections have led me to mistrust any death that is not substantiated by the presence of a corpse."

From the mouth of the tunnel came another shout. "This is the police! Come out with your hands in the air!"

Holmes glanced back. "Before leaving Saint Paul's, I took a moment to alert the police as to the possible danger here. It appears that they have at last caught up to us."

He looked at me. "Another moment, and they will be with us, at which point, I shall probably be forced to answer a great many tedious questions as to what has just occurred. As will you, particularly if you are still holding that weapon. However, if you were to give it to me—thank you." He took the Webley from me and then slipped it into the pocket of his coat. "I will endeavor to persuade our policeman friends that you were merely a bystander in all of this and have nothing of substance to add."

He likely wouldn't have to try very hard. My gender alone would be enough to persuade a fair number of the male population that I had no value as a witness.

Still, I frowned. "Why?"

Holmes looked at me, and I realized that his gray eyes were touched with sympathy. Which somehow struck me more coldly than anything else today. Even Sherlock Holmes was sorry for me right now.

"Because questions and police interviews take time. And I imagine that you will wish to proceed to Watson's surgery without delay."

LUCY

54. ACTS OF COURAGE

The sky outside the windows of Uncle John's surgery had turned dark, so I assumed that it must be night. But time had lost all meaning. I could have been sitting on the hard, uncomfortable wooden bench in his waiting room for hours, days, or anywhere in between.

Becky was slumped beside me, her golden-blonde head a solid, heavy weight against my arm.

Every nerve in my body was twitching with the wish that I could get up and move ... pace the room ... *anything* to avoid sitting here another second. But after hours of tearful waiting and worrying and watching the surgery door for any sign that Uncle John was coming out again, Becky had finally cried herself to sleep.

I wouldn't risk moving and waking her. Asleep, she wasn't eaten up with fear that her brother was going to die.

I should have been exhausted, too, but my mind refused to shut down. I kept reliving, over and over again, those moments on the steps of Saint Paul's.

I should have been faster—or spotted the gunman myself—done something that would have saved Jack from being shot.

I should have told him how I felt.

I looked down at my hands. I had scrubbed off the blood when we arrived here, but Uncle John didn't keep spare changes of ladies clothing in his surgery, and my skirt and sleeves were still stained.

I leaned my head back, closing my eyes. I'd had a few seconds where Jack was conscious. Why hadn't I said anything then?

Why hadn't I told him how I felt *long* ago?

Except that wasn't the crushing weight that pressed in on me right now proof of exactly how dangerous loving someone could be?

Maybe Sherlock Holmes had the right idea.

Stop.

The surgery door opened, and Uncle John stepped out into the waiting room.

I jumped, and Becky woke up with a gasp. She saw Uncle John and clutched at my hand. I held on tightly.

Uncle John looked exhausted, his face nearly gray with weariness and his eyes red-rimmed. My breath went out as though a giant's fist had just crushed my ribcage.

I didn't want to hear whatever he was going to tell us. It might be cowardly, but I wanted to clamp my hands over my ears and—

"He's alive," Uncle John said. His voice, too, was flat with fatigue, but he came forward and put a hand on Becky's shoulder. "Alive, and I believe that his life may for the time being be considered to be out of danger. I also believe that I have saved his leg, and if we can avoid the danger of the wounds turning septic—"

I lost the entire rest of Uncle John's words in the rush of relief that hit me, making my vision waver and the blood thunder in my ears.

When my hearing cleared and the room stopped spinning around me, Uncle John was still speaking. Something about nerve and muscle damage and the long-term prognosis being uncertain. But I still couldn't seem to process more than a word or two, here and there.

Alive. Jack was still alive.

Only when Uncle John stopped did I realize what he had just said.

Becky had followed his words much better than I. She looked up at Uncle John, the tracks of her earlier tears still visible on her cheeks. "Do you mean that Jack might not be able to walk again after this?"

Uncle John looked at her, and I could see the desire to spare her warring with his obligation as a man of medicine to give a truthful diagnosis.

Before he could answer, Becky added, her voice small and quiet in the stillness of the waiting room, "Because Jack will hate that."

Uncle John patted her shoulder. "We must wait and see, my dear. Your brother has both strength and health on his side, and we will know more once the wounds begin to heal and the inflammation subsides. For now, you may look in on him. Just for a moment, mind. He is still under sedation and will likely remain so for some days to ensure that his body rests and begins to heal. But you may see him, to set your mind at ease."

Becky and I followed Uncle John through the swinging doors and back along the passage to his surgery, where a uniformed nurse was clearing up bloodied bandages and surgical instruments.

"Just through here," Uncle John said.

A small alcove at the back of the room had been curtained off by hanging white draperies. Jack lay inside on a hospital bed, his face almost as white as the sheet drawn up to cover his chest. His eyes were closed, his breathing so deep and slow that it was a moment before I could detect it at all.

"*Jack.*" Becky's voice caught on a sob, renewed tears rolling down her cheeks.

I hugged her. "It's all right. He's alive, that's all that matters."

Becky wiped her eyes, nodding.

"Come along." Uncle John put an arm around her shoulders. "My nurse has made up a bed for you in the examination room. I thought you would rather stay close to your brother for the remainder of tonight. Come along, now." Gently, Uncle John drew her away. "You can see him again in the morning, but for now, you need rest, and so does he."

Becky allowed herself to be led away.

I blinked hard as I stepped towards Jack's bed.

Uncle John had said his life was out of danger—in front of Becky. But I knew at least enough of medicine to read between the lines. His life wouldn't be in danger *if* he could escape infection … sepsis … hemorrhage … internal bleeding …

"Hello." My voice wavered. Jack's hand lay open on the blanket, and I took hold of it, threading my fingers with his. "Remember what you told me the other night, about the fight being more important than the victory?" My throat threatened to close off. "Well, I need you to fight—and to keep fighting—now."

WATSON

55. PLAN OF ATTACK

The colour of Sherlock Holmes's eyes varied according to his frame of mind. When he was peaceful or contemplative or playing his violin, his eyes were the pale grey of a winter sky. When he was angry, the shade deepened to the colour of a storm-tossed sea. At the moment, he was fixing Lucy with a look that had been known to make grown men break down in tears. His jaw was clamped shut, and his eyes looked like polished steel.

"That is a patently terrible idea."

We were in the Baker Street sitting room, with an unseasonably cold rain splattering against the windows and turning the city outside into a grey, dreary mess of snarled traffic and muddy streets. The setting reflected the mood of all three of us.

Lucy was sitting beside me on the sofa, her lovely face pale with concern. I tried to reason with her. I said, "What Holmes means is that the risks to you, Lucy—"

"Are not inconsiderable," she interrupted. "I know that. I have already outlined my plans for minimizing the possible danger."

She turned to Holmes again. "It is *not* a terrible plan. You and I both know it. Arkwright and whoever financed and orchestrated his escape from prison are still at large. Are we honestly imagining that they will give up now?"

Holmes took up his pipe. "I have cautioned you in the past against letting your emotions become an obstacle to logic and reason."

"I am *not* letting my emotions get in the way!"

Plainly that was not true.

Today was Friday, the second of July. The Duchess of Devonshire's grand ball—the social event of the century—was to occur tonight. I knew that was of less concern to Lucy than the fact that more than a week had passed since Jack had been shot and so far she had not been able to speak with him, not even once.

I was still keeping him sedated to manage the pain and stress of the wounds. A few times, while Becky had visited, Jack had come back to groggy consciousness and been able to speak with his young sister, at least a little.

But Lucy was required to be at Devonshire House for rehearsals every day, and whenever she managed to slip away to visit the surgery, she found Jack deep in a laudanum-induced sleep.

This morning when she had visited, I had been forced to tell her that Jack's temperature was slightly elevated.

Now my nurse was looking after Jack, and I would not have come with Lucy to Baker Street if there were any immediate danger.

Lucy leaned forward, her green eyes flashing. "The Prince's life is still in danger—as is the stability of our entire government. Tonight is the ball, a prime moment for an attack to occur, whatever His Royal Highness may believe to the contrary. We need to end this. Now. Not to mention that Mary's murder is also still unsolved and unavenged—although you will undoubtedly find that an excessively emotional appeal." Her shoulders squared up as she met Holmes's gaze.

Holmes looked at her a long moment. "I do not disagree. However, there are some victories that come at too high a cost to be considered victories at all."

"Now who is letting emotion get the better of reason?"

For a moment, I thought that indignation warred with a look that might almost have been embarrassment or self-consciousness in Holmes's grey eyes. Then—slightly to my amazement—his thin lips curved upwards in a flicker of a smile.

"I have expended a great deal of mental energy in accustoming myself to the presence of a daughter in my life. I should hate for the effort to be wasted by"—he cleared his throat—"losing you just when our association may be said to have begun to flourish."

Holmes's words seemed to penetrate the cloud of mingled fury and dread that had wrapped us all for the past few days. My own spirits seemed to lift. The room seemed brighter as I watched Lucy's reaction.

She returned Holmes's smile with a crooked one of her own. "In that case, it's a good thing that I have faith in you and Uncle John—and of course, in Toby's nose."

LUCY

56. DEVONSHIRE HOUSE REVISITED

Devonshire House was brilliantly illuminated, the street outside crowded with people hoping for a glimpse of the guests as they arrived.

Holmes eyed the front of the house, where a wreath enclosed an immense representation of a crown flanked by the letters V. R. on either side.

"I confess I prefer my own tribute to her gracious majesty."

Despite the worry that squirmed like snakes through the pit of my stomach, I smiled. "You should have offered to shoot the letters V.R. into the ballroom wall instead."

I, for one, would have paid handsomely to see the look on the Duchess of Devonshire's face.

"I should go in," I told Holmes.

We were standing in the shadows behind the carriage we had driven here, largely out of sight of the people vying for a look at the house. Though everyone would have likely ignored us in any case; we didn't look nearly important enough to merit a stir.

Uncle John and my mother were already inside.

It was only eight o'clock, and the ball wasn't due to start until half past ten, but there were the final preparations to be made for the D'Oyly Carte production of *The Yeomen of the Guard*—and my own plan to set into motion.

Holmes cleared his throat, his gaze fixed on the gas lanterns that blazed at intervals around the courtyard. "Watson has orders to stay at your mother's side at all times."

"I know."

I hesitated, looking up at the house. I had been searching for a chance to say this to my father, and I might not get another opportunity.

"I'm sorry that I dragged her into this. I'm sorry for asking her to come to London."

Holmes's shoulders twitched. I couldn't at all read the expression on his face. "She has been of not inconsiderable help in the investigation. Helping me at the Italian embassy, for example."

"Yes, but—" I stopped.

However many precautions we had taken, there was always the chance that I wouldn't survive tonight's ventures, which made it all the more important to me that I ask this question now. But my mind seemed to be coming up blank on finding the right words.

Holmes glanced at me. "You are wondering whether I have feelings of a personal nature in regard to her appearance here."

"Among other things."

Holmes was silent for a long moment. Then at last he said, "No one reading Watson's stories would suppose that I have ever wished to be more like an ordinary human."

I stared at him, shocked. "But you don't think—that wasn't why—" I stopped. I didn't usually inflict demonstrations of affection on my father, but in this case, I couldn't stop myself from touching his hand. "I didn't invite my mother to come because I wanted you to change or to be more like ordinary people. I don't *want* you to be ordinary—or to be anything, in fact, other than what you are. I asked my mother to London because I want you to be *happy*."

"Happy," Holmes repeated.

It was not often that I saw my father dumbstruck, but at the moment he was looking at me as though I had just spoken in Chinese.

At last he cleared his throat. "Yes, well. You will have heard the adage about old dogs learning new tricks, I imagine."

"Yes. I'm just not sure that it's *true*."

Holmes looked at me. He didn't actually make a sound, but his eyes held a look that was the equivalent of a resigned sigh.

"Perhaps this is a discussion that had best be tabled until a more opportune moment. I have already been inside to speak with His Grace about security measures for tonight, which means that I am now at liberty to disappear into the crowds."

Holmes had already changed inside the carriage into one of the old-fashioned livery costumes worn by the rest of the male servants in the house. Now, reaching into his pocket, he drew out a bristling gray mustache and affixed it under his nose.

I blinked. "You do realize it looks as though a wooly caterpillar crawled onto your upper lip and then expired from old age?"

"Quite possibly. However, few will look past the mustache to examine my features in any great detail." Holmes tugged on a gray wig to match the mustache.

"Do you think that Arkwright will be here tonight?"

"It is a possibility. His disfigurement would make it difficult to pass amongst an ordinary social gathering. But the occasion of a masquerade ball affords the option of a variety of costumes that could conceal his face."

I tried not to shiver.

An impatient bark came from inside the carriage beside us, and a lop-eared, brown and white dog jumped up, putting his paws on the glass window.

"Shhh, it's all right, Toby." I opened the door so that I could ruffle the short-legged dog's ears.

Holmes was silent a beat, then turned his gaze on me. "I have agreed to leave off trying to talk you out of this plan."

"Thank you." I had locked all my own doubts away, and I didn't particularly want them to be brought back again.

Holmes nodded. "So I will merely say that, should I lose sight of you, Toby and I will stand ready to find you at the proper time." His jaw tightened, his eyes turning the familiar gray of polished steel. "And should Arkwright or anyone else attempt to harm you, they will live just long enough to deeply understand the error of their ways."

LUCY

57. A DOORWAY

"Is Mr. Holmes here?" Captain Stayley asked. His eyes scanned the growing crowd in the ballroom. "I haven't yet seen him."

"He is. Somewhere." In addition to the waiter's costume, I knew that Holmes had several other disguises at the ready, though no one—not even me—knew which of them he might assume at any given time. "As you know, Mr. Holmes's methods are somewhat unusual."

Captain Stayley nodded abstractedly. We were standing near the head of the crystal staircase that led upwards from the entrance hall downstairs to the ballroom and other reception rooms. It was five minutes past ten o'clock, which meant that the ball had just started, the costumed guests were streaming in, and I could almost hear the Captain's thoughts running through a silent mental check of any task he might have left undone.

"Has Holmes made any progress, do you know?" Captain Stayley asked.

A man and woman were ascending the staircase. She was dressed in the fashion of the seventeenth-century French court, with a towering white wig and a gown stiff with pearls and jewels. Her companion wore the brightly colored knee breeches, coat, and hat of a medieval court jester.

I waited until they passed before lowering my voice. "I believe so."

I had had variations on this same conversation for the past two hours with every member of the Devonshire House staff I could find to talk to me.

Mr. Bellini was nearly rushed off his feet, but spared me a brief, hurried exchange near the stairs leading down to the wine cellar. I had also spoken to Eve Digby and several other assorted housemaids and footmen.

The conversation with Captain Stayley was easier, because I was actually free to mention Holmes's name and to speak openly of the investigation. With the others, I had merely said that I had heard a rumor that a traitor to the Crown was in attendance at tonight's ball and that the police were confident that they would be making an arrest.

"Holmes has discovered definitive proof as to the identity of the person behind the attempted bombings at the Jubilee," I went on. "He plans to reveal as much tonight."

Captain Stayley's eyebrows went up. "Indeed? That is good news. May I ask—"

I interrupted. "I'm sorry, I must go."

Another group of costumed guests was trailing up the stairs, and I fell into step beside them as they entered the ballroom.

The conversation with Captain Stayley might have been more open, but it was also very possibly pointless. He already knew the vital importance of Holmes' investigations, which made it unlikely in the extreme that he would spread the information I had just given him as gossip.

Although he might, of course, mention it to the Duke, his employer.

Or to a man of seemingly impeccable character, like Lord Lansdowne?

I shook my head and walked past the ballroom and the reception rooms, making for the servants' staircase at the rear of the house.

I had put the first part of the plan into motion, but it was highly unlikely that anyone would attempt to kidnap me in the midst of a crowd of revelers.

An hour later, I was giving up hope that anyone would attempt to kidnap me at all. I had sung a few numbers from the first half of *The Gondoliers* and would go back into the ballroom in another ten minutes to sing more from the final act.

Out of compassion for Mr. Harris's blood pressure, I had already made arrangements for one of the understudies to sing my part on the chance—or rather, *hope*—that I might not make it back.

I was standing in the shadows of a lilac bush in the garden behind Devonshire House, which had been transformed into a near fairyland. Lanterns twinkled in the trees, and the warm night air was thick with the smell of flowers. Costumed guests moved here and there, laughing, talking, and sipping flutes of champagne.

If my fingers hadn't been twitching with the urge to smash something out of sheer impatience, I might have found it an altogether lovely setting.

A waiter appeared at my elbow. Not Holmes. I had already spotted Holmes a moment ago, disappearing into the house to fetch more wine.

"Champagne, miss?"

I shook my head. "No, thank you."

Instead of turning away, the waiter passed a folded square of paper into my hand. "I was told to give you this."

My heart accelerated. "Who gave it to you? When?"

The waiter looked somewhat taken aback by the intensity of my voice. "I don't know, miss. A man just passed it to me a few minutes ago and asked me to hand it over to you."

"What did he look like?"

The waiter had probably assumed that he was helping a pair of lovers make arrangements for a romantic assignation. Now he looked as though he had no idea *what* to make of me.

"He had a costume with a mask on. Some kind of dark, hooded thing that came up over his head and covered his face."

Naturally. "Do you see him out here now?"

The waiter surveyed the garden and the assembled groups of ball guests, then shook his head. "No, miss. Will that be all, miss?"

"Yes, thank you."

The waiter sped away, and I looked down at the note.

The paper had been sealed with a blob of red wax, stamped with Mycroft's personal seal: the stylized M and H intertwined.

I broke the seal open and unfolded the paper.

To Lucy

Shock gripped me. The words were written in Mycroft's crabbed, cramped hand.

Come to rear of house garden. Urgent. Do proceed without delay. Vital information to convey before midnight.

Mycroft

P.S. Tell no one. You are being watched.

Seconds ticked by while I stared at the letters on the page, taking rapid stock of my options. Go back into the house ... find Uncle John or Holmes.

But there were those last five words. *You are being watched.* Fear dug into me, tiny crystals of ice that seemed to coat every inch of my skin.

The seal, of course, had been stolen from Mycroft's Whitehall office, and sorting out who might have had both access and the opportunity to use the seal on the note in my hand was something I didn't have time for now. But the handwriting—

The handwriting of the note wavered, the letters trailing slightly downwards, as though the author had been dazed ... or injured.

But I had been trained by Sherlock Holmes to recognize a forgery when I saw one. This was unquestionably, absolutely, Mycroft's hand.

I drew in a breath, crumpled the note up, and let it fall to the ground at my feet. Then I started to walk down one of the garden paths.

There were fewer and fewer lights as I moved towards the rear of the garden, and the crowds thinned rapidly. By the time I reached the row of lilac bushes that lined the garden fence, there was no one in sight.

Not that it would have mattered if there were, I couldn't have risked calling out or trying to summon help in any case.

This was exactly why tonight's plan had included backups and fail-safes.

Now I just had to trust my own life—and Mycroft's—to the hope that they would work.

I searched along the back wall of the garden until I spotted the gate Mycroft had mentioned in his note. Actually, it was less a gate than a door, set into the brick wall and doubtless bolted from the inside to make sure that no uninvited visitors trespassed on the Devonshire House grounds.

I set my hand against the metal latch ... and a shadowed figure stepped out of the bushes to my left. There was a click, and I felt the cold barrel of a revolver pressed against the back of my neck.

"Don't make a sound, Miss James. Unless you're hoping to die here, you're just going to walk through that doorway, nice and quiet."

LUCY

58. COLD AND DARKNESS

The voice was Arkwright's, though I couldn't see his face.

I should have been frightened—I *was* frightened, but not on account of the gun.

"Where is Mycroft? What have you done to him?"

"You'll find out soon enough." Arkwright prodded me harder with the revolver barrel. "Now *move*. And don't try anything."

We emerged through the back gate of the garden and onto a road. Before setting out tonight, Holmes and I had spent more than an hour poring over a map of the area, which meant that I could identify the street as Bolton Row.

At this time of the night, there wasn't a great deal of traffic, but a few carriages rolled by.

"If you shoot me out here, the odds are good that someone will see it," I said. "I assume that getting detained and arrested for murder isn't in your plan for tonight."

"Maybe not. But if I don't make it back in the next half hour, orders are that Mycroft Holmes is to be shot through the head. So unless you want to die knowing that you got your uncle killed, too, you'll step along quietly."

I felt him shift the revolver's position from my neck to pressing into the small of my back.

I gritted my teeth in frustration.

Duck, swing around, kick the gun out of his hand.

I could *see* the whole maneuver play out inside my mind. This was the perfect chance for me to get away from him. But while I might manage to escape, I couldn't guarantee that I could then overpower Arkwright and force him to tell me Mycroft's location.

I couldn't risk it, not when I had no idea where Mycroft was being held.

"How do you know that Mycroft Holmes is my uncle?"

I heard Arkwright snort behind me. "Your Doctor Watson. We drugged him when he was with you in Germany. He babbled like a brook—told us everything we wanted to know."

This was really only confirmation of what Holmes himself had already suspected, but my heart still sank. If something went wrong tonight, and Mycroft or I didn't survive, Uncle John would never forgive himself.

"Now no more talking," Arkwright growled.

* * *

The grass under my feet was wet with dew. Tree branches whispered and creaked above me as a soft spring breeze blew.

According to the mental map I had of the area, we were on the grounds of Lansdowne House, circling around towards the rear. I could see the house itself, white and imposing in the neoclassical style, looming through the trees on my left. But at the moment, with my whole attention focused on the man behind me, there was no space in my head to speculate on what Arkwright's presence here might mean in terms of Lord Lansdowne's possible guilt.

A small, single-story brick building loomed up out of the darkness ahead, appearing in shape something like a miniature version of a rural cottage. I halted, and Arkwright prodded me with the revolver again.

"Keep moving."

Three more steps forward and I could see a man—I assumed he was acting as guard—standing outside the building, his arms cradling a shotgun.

Spin, kick the gun out of Arkwright's hand, use it to disable the guard—

No, I still couldn't risk it. Even if I were positive that Mycroft was inside, there might be a second guard in there with him. My uncle could be dead before I even managed to reach the door.

There was little light out here, only the dim ambient glow coming from the windows of the house, which was largely in darkness, with only a few squares of yellow light showing here and there.

As we moved nearer, though, I caught a glimpse of the guard's face and realized with a jolt that it was Griffin.

He didn't speak as he moved aside to allow Arkwright to shove me through the doorway, but the leer he gave me told me that he hadn't forgotten our encounter at St. Paul's, in which I had first tricked him and then knocked him unconscious.

Not good.

I now had not only Arkwright to contend with—and any possible accomplices waiting inside—but an armed guard who would be extremely motivated not to let me get the better of him again.

I stepped through into the building and instantly felt the temperature drop. The air was damp and cold, with a smell of straw and sawdust.

"His Lordship's icehouse," Arkwright grunted behind me. "Makes for a good hiding place tonight. Not much chance anyone's going to come out here."

That was depressingly true. Lord and Lady Lansdowne would of course be at the Devonshire House ball, and their servants were probably taking a well-earned night off. The odds of anyone coming out to chip ice from the blocks stored here were practically none, besides which, the place would be well-insulated to stop the ice from melting in the summer heat. Even if I screamed for help, I doubted I would attract anyone's notice.

The interior of the icehouse was pitch black. I shuffled forwards, hands outstretched, and felt my toes collide against something hard.

I heard a click as Arkwright swung the door closed behind us, then the scratch of a safety match, and light flared.

I assumed that Arkwright had lighted a lantern, but I didn't turn around. My whole attention was caught by the big, motionless form that sat slumped in a corner, propped up against some of the straw-covered blocks of ice.

Mycroft's head was sunk on his breast, and the light picked out the crust of dried blood and the angry, purple bruise on his temple. His eyes were closed, his face slack.

My heart contracted painfully hard, though I drew a breath of relief as I saw Mycroft stir restlessly, his lips moving as though he were trying to mutter something.

His hands were shackled together, linked at the wrists with what looked like a pair of police handcuffs.

Arkwright let out a grunt of exasperation. "You wouldn't believe how much laudanum it takes to keep a man his size unconscious. I've given him enough to take down a horse, and still he keeps waking up."

Looking around, I saw that Arkwright still had the gun trained on me, though with one hand he had picked up a length of rope and a second pair of handcuffs.

"Sit down."

A single wooden hard-backed chair stood in the center of the small space, clearly set out in expectation of my arrival. I didn't move.

"Why on earth should I make this easy for you?"

Arkwright's ruined face quivered, a muscle twitching at the edge of his eye. "Because if you don't, I will shoot your uncle in the leg. And I will go on shooting him until you do as I say."

I sat down. Nothing in tonight's plans had included there being a second hostage here, and Arkwright looked as though he were balanced on the edge of exploding into violence. His hand shook slightly as he held the revolver, and sweat beaded his upper lip.

With his free hand, he rapped on the door behind him. It swung open a moment later to reveal Griffin.

"I'm going to tie her up," Arkwright said. He jerked his head at Mycroft. "If she tries anything, shoot him first."

Griffin didn't speak, but his mouth stretched in a slow smile.

In a way, it was flattering that Arkwright didn't make the mistake of underestimating me. But it was also extremely inconvenient.

Arkwright shackled my hands behind my back with the metal cuffs, and I worked at not recoiling when his fingers brushed against the skin of my wrists.

I strained my ears, listening. But I couldn't hear anything at all from outside.

"I hope you're not expecting the great Sherlock Holmes to rescue you."

I swallowed. "What?"

Arkwright moved on to tie my ankles to the legs of the chair. I tried to brace myself, but I still wasn't prepared for how horrible it felt when he drew the bonds tight. A clammy, sickening wave of helplessness slid through me. I couldn't move. Even ignoring Griffin, the shotgun, and Mycroft, fighting back was no longer an option.

At least after Arkwright had finished tying the ropes, he nodded to Griffin, and the big man withdrew, closing the door again behind him.

Arkwright's upper lip curled back. "Thanks to you and your father, I can no longer go out in public. My face is too *memorable*." His voice dropped to nearly a hiss as he leaned towards me. "You know what that leaves time for? Studying one's enemy. Reading. In particular, reading those disgustingly vainglorious stories of Doctor Watson's—which, whatever they lack in literary merit, they at least make up for in providing the occasional useful detail into how Sherlock Holmes thinks and operates."

His gaze dropped to my feet. "What did you dip the soles of your shoes in? Creosote? Anise? I've heard that's a scent easily picked up by dogs."

Ice shot through me. "What have you done to Toby?"

The Sign of Four was one of Becky's favorite stories, and she had come with me this afternoon to hire a descendent of the very same hound that Uncle John and Holmes had used to track down Jonathan Small. It hadn't made her *happy*, exactly, not in the same way it would have a week ago. But it had at least distracted her temporarily from her worry over Jack, and it had made her feel better about staying with Mrs. Hudson tonight while I came out to the ball.

Even Holmes had raised fewer objections to the plan, knowing that there were few places Arkwright could bring me where Toby wouldn't be able to track me down.

Now I pictured Arkwright finding the carriage where we had left Toby, yanking the whimpering dog out by the scruff of his neck and—

"Oh, don't worry." Arkwright's mouth twisted in a sneer. "Not that he didn't deserve it, but killing the mutt would have made too much noise. And poison might have been too slow. But did you know there's another use for your father's favorite, cocaine? Give it to a dog to sniff, and it numbs their nose. They can't smell a thing."

I stared at Arkwright, fighting against the knot of panic that was trying to tighten inside my chest. Panic wouldn't save Mycroft's or my life right now.

"Was it you who impersonated Police Commissioner Bradford and went to see Keenan Mulloy?" I asked.

"Yes." Arkwright gave a short, sharp bark of a laugh. "Good of the Commissioner to wear those preposterous mutton-chop side-whiskers and that bristling white mustache. They cover a multitude of facial scars." The unruined half of his mouth stretched in a smile. He mimed an empty sleeve, shrugging his left shoulder. "The idiot priest never suspected a thing. Thought he was doing his duty for God and country."

The sneer in Arkwright's voice made my fingers tingle with the wish that I could smack the gloating smile right off his mouth. Instead, I swallowed.

"Why are *you* doing this?" Partly I was trying to keep him talking, playing for more time. But a part of me honestly wanted to know how the man I had met last year had turned into the monster before me now. Or maybe the monster had always been inside him, just waiting to break free.

"Why?" Arkwright stepped back. The lantern's glow threw his disfigured face into a grotesque relief of shadow and light. A queer, ironic smile twisted his mouth, and his accent took on an Irish lilt. "Oh, let's leave my own feelings out of the conversation, at least for the moment. But I can tell you why my friend outside is doing this. And why Mr. Owens and his lot were waging *their* battle. Because the tree of liberty must be watered with the blood of tyrants."

People were more likely to speak unguardedly when they were angry. I had learned that much from watching my father work. And if I ever got out of here, we still needed to know what Arkwright's plan of attack was—and the identity of whoever was paying him. Arkwright was only an instrument; someone else, someone higher up, was pulling the strings.

I kept my voice calm, disinterested. "I was raised an American, remember? I already know that quotation; I had to learn it at school. Except Thomas Jefferson said it much better: 'The tree of liberty must be refreshed from time to time with the blood of patriots and tyrants.' "

"*Don't* patronize me!" Arkwright's voice was a snarl.

I raised my shoulders—as much as I could, with my hands tied. "Try not being wrong then? Though perhaps you wouldn't have studied the American Revolution in school, what with your country being the losers."

For a moment, I thought I had pushed him too far. Rage shivered across Arkwright's face, and his hand went to the gun he had slipped into his coat pocket.

Then he exhaled a hard burst of air. "As much as I would love to stay and teach you some humility, Miss James, I must save that pleasure for a later time. I have an appointment with more elevated company than yours." He stared at me, something hard and ugly moving beneath the surface of his gaze. "We will continue this conversation later, at which point you will tell me exactly what proof your father has in his possession and where. Otherwise, I will hurt you as I did your friend Mary Mulloy. Until you *beg* me to end your life."

LUCY

59. ELEVATED COMPANY

"Mycroft?"

The icehouse seemed soundproof; I couldn't hear a thing from outside, not a voice or a footstep or a rustle of breeze in the trees. But I still kept my voice to barely a whisper.

Arkwright was gone, but when he had opened the door, I'd seen Griffin still stationed outside, his gun at the ready.

"Mycroft?"

For the last few minutes, my uncle had been stirring restlessly, his head turning on the straw pillow.

At the sound of my voice, his eyelids flickered open, and his gaze, bleary and unfocused, found mine. "Lucy?"

He sat up with a jolt. "Lucy! *No.*" His words were slurred, but still thick with despair. "Tried to warn you—"

"I know you did. The part about wanting to see me before midnight—twelve o'clock—meant that I was supposed to pay attention to every twelfth letter in the sentences that came before. And those letters spelled out the word *trap.*"

Typical of Mycroft, even hurt and stupefied with a sedative, he had been able to spontaneously invent a message that would accommodate his code.

He blinked at me, shaking his head. "Then why—"

"Because I couldn't take the risk of your being killed before someone could get to you! Holmes and I took precautions for tonight, and I thought that at least if I walked into this *knowing* that it was a trap, there was a chance of saving us both."

Although our plans hadn't included Arkwright robbing Toby of his ability to track me down.

"Can you stand?" I whispered.

Mycroft's hands were shackled, but his ankles were unrestrained.

"Possibly."

He struggled to drag himself into a sitting position, but he was still weak and dizzy with the drug, and even at the best of times, his bulky form was nowhere near agile.

He was trying for the third time to get his feet under him when the icehouse door swung open, revealing Griffin. He glanced at Mycroft, smirked, and then his face split in a slow grin as his gaze landed on me.

"The boss said to make sure you stayed put here. But he didn't say I couldn't have some fun—"

He gave a sudden grunt and staggered forward.

Becky Kelly stood in the doorway behind him, both hands clutching a sizeable tree branch. She must have hit him in the back of the leg.

My heart stumbled in my chest. I couldn't even draw enough air to speak or cry out.

Griffin had only been knocked off balance; he hadn't actually fallen. He spun around and caught sight of Becky. His back was to me, but I saw his meaty hands clench. "You little—"

A tall figure stepped out of the darkness beyond the doorway.

"I believe that will be quite enough of that," Sherlock Holmes said.

His revolver was already leveled at Griffin. His jaw was hard.

* * *

"I'm sorry, Lucy. Please don't be angry with me!" Becky raised her tear-stained face to mine. We were standing outside the icehouse. Inside, Holmes was having a word with Griffin to determine what he knew of Arkwright's plans—which was something I didn't want Becky to see.

I wasn't sure how far my father would be willing to go to make Griffin talk, but I suspected his interrogation methods might be unfit for a child's eyes.

I put an arm around Becky and hugged her to me. "I don't understand. You were supposed to stay with Mrs. Hudson tonight."

"I know." Becky wiped her eyes. "But I was afraid something horrible would happen. So I had Flynn break into the house after Mrs. Hudson had gone to bed so that we could follow you here. I already knew the way."

"Flynn is here?"

"Yes. We were watching in the garden—you know, when you got that note and then dropped it on the ground?"

I nodded. I'd hoped that Holmes or Uncle John might find the note and at least have a direction in which to start searching.

"So when you left, we followed you," Becky went on. "You and that man. We saw him bring you in there"—she pointed to the icehouse—"and then Flynn ran back to fetch Mr. Holmes, and I stayed here." She glanced up at me. "*Are* you angry with me?"

"No. How could I be, when you may have just saved my life? But—"

The door to the icehouse opened, and Holmes emerged, with Mycroft leaning heavily against him. Behind them, I caught a glimpse of Griffin, handcuffed to the same chair I had been chained to.

He looked slightly white in the face, but he seemed unhurt, so maybe Holmes hadn't had to resort to bodily injury after all.

"He knows nothing." My father looked disgusted.

Mycroft was unsteady on his feet, and his eyes still had a slightly glazed, bleary look. But he raised his head at that. "I believe I ... intimated as much ... at the outset, Sherlock." His gaze focused on me. "Lucy." He shook his head. "Shouldn't have risked coming here. Not for me."

"Nonsense—" I still couldn't manage an *Uncle Mycroft*. But I said, "Isn't that what family is supposed to do? Save each other, if need be?"

I stopped short as I realized what I had just said.

Becky gave me a puzzled look. "What is it?"

"Nothing." This was hardly the time. I squeezed her hand, then turned to Holmes. "We need to find Arkwright. He spoke of watering the tree of liberty with blood. People will die tonight unless we can stop him."

Holmes's brows edged together. "Tell me exactly what Arkwright said."

"I don't think he told me anything of value. I tried, but—" I shut my eyes, trying to remember. "He said he was looking forward to teaching me humility."

I wasn't looking, but I heard a click, and imagined Holmes clamping his teeth together. "What else?"

"He must have arranged for the attack to happen at a very particular time, because he was threatening me, and then he suddenly said that he had to leave, that he had an appointment with more elevated company than mine." I stopped, realization striking like a bucket full of ice water dashed into my face.

"*Elevated* company. I thought he meant the Prince and the Duke and Duchess and everyone else with a title at the ball, but what if he meant—"

Holmes was already in motion, racing towards Lansdowne House with the long, easy stride that could eat up ground as rapidly as a professional athlete's sprint.

WATSON

60. N𝔸TUR𝔸L FORCES

We had come to Devonshire House on the night of the Duchess's ball, hoping to carry out Lucy's plan to entrap the assassin Arkwright. Holmes and I waited for word from Lucy as the guests arrived, but we had none until young Flynn came with news that Lucy was in the icehouse outside Lansdowne House, about fifty yards away.

We ran.

When we reached the icehouse, Holmes ordered me to stand guard outside and to come in only if he called for my help. Once again, I complied.

Now the door to the icehouse opened, and I saw Holmes running towards me and then past me. "Arkwright is on the rooftop!" he called over his shoulder, "Watson! Tell Lestrade."

Hearing his call and watching his lean figure running up to Lansdowne House, all my instincts urged me to follow.

But emerging from the icehouse were Lucy, Mycroft, and the child Becky. If Arkwright was indeed on the rooftop, they needed to be kept out of harm's way.

Which would mean I had to get them closer to the walls of the building, where they would not be as visible from the roof and where an assassin would not have a clear angle of fire. There was no moon, and the lights of Devonshire House were on the opposite side of Lansdowne House, so that the illumination of the Duchess's great social event hindered my vision rather than assisting. I watched Holmes's silhouetted figure come up to the shadowy doorway of the servants' entrance. I thought he would knock and wait. But he simply vanished.

Lucy said, "Arkwright's left the door open."

"The servants are all at the Duchess's event, or Arkwright has dispatched those that remained," said Mycroft.

"We don't all have to wait for Lestrade," said Lucy.

Becky said, "I don't want to stay here!"

"We will all go," I said. "We will keep to the shadows as much as possible. Lucy and I will enter. Becky, you and Mycroft will wait outside the doorway Mr. Holmes went through just now. You will keep a watch for Inspector Lestrade or Flynn. And if you see him, you will run straight away to him and tell him where the rest of us have gone."

We walked together. Through the windows we could see lights on the ground floor. The upstairs of Lansdowne House was dark. Two of the upper windows were open to the warm summer air.

From the direction of Devonshire House behind us came the music of a small orchestra. They were playing the national anthem.

"That will be the Prince and his party arriving," Lucy whispered.

We reached the servants' entrance. The door was open. On the hardwood floor, further into what was obviously the storage pantry, a man lay prone and motionless.

"Not Holmes," said Lucy.

She stepped back and held up a hand to indicate that Mycroft and Becky should remain outside. I felt for a pulse. There was none.

We heard faint voices coming from upstairs. Climbing soundlessly on the carpeted stairs, we could soon make out that the voices were those of Holmes and Arkwright.

We waited outside the door.

"Never came close to the Andaman Islands," Arkwright was saying. "Got off at the first port of refuelling. Wrote up my own interview at the garrison in Cape Town. Typed it myself. It went to the prison commander at Andaman with a fat wad of banknotes in the envelope, I should imagine."

"Why did you refer to Devonshire and Elswick?" asked Holmes.

"Following instructions."

"Whose?"

"Well that would be telling, now, wouldn't it? And if I did that, then you could shoot me. You're going to keep me alive and hope you can get me to tell. Just as I'm not going to shoot you until I'm good and ready."

Hearing those words, I drew my service revolver.

Lucy nodded.

The two of us burst into the room.

Arkwright was on a window seat across the room, holding a pistol trained on Holmes.

Holmes was on the seat at the window nearest us, holding a pistol trained on Arkwright.

Both windows were of the casement variety, and both extended up to just below the ceiling. Each had been opened wide. From Devonshire House the last few chords of the national anthem seemed to hang in the night air. Then came a smattering of applause.

On the floor beside Arkwright was a long webbed canvas bag, such as one might use to transport golf clubs.

Holmes lifted his free hand slightly in a gesture of caution.

Arkwright brandished his pistol. "I'll shoot him, you know. You may kill me, but I will be able to kill your friend, Doctor. So once again we are at something of an impasse. For a time."

"Until when?" Lucy asked.

"I will move at eleven-fifteen. That is in five minutes."

"You think you can shoot all three of us," I said. "But Holmes and I outnumber you."

"Indeed. But perhaps I am more agile than you imagine. Maybe. What do I care?"

"Then you might pass the time," Holmes said, "by telling us the name of your master. The man who is paying you. If you kill us, no will know. If we kill you, it will not matter."

Arkwright smiled brightly, a hideous effort with his ruined face. "Ah, but there is another possibility. You might merely wound me again. And if I were to give you the name of ..." He let the words trail off, toying with us. Then he smiled again. "If I were to give you the name of my protector, he might not protect me when I was on trial, as he did before. Something unpleasant might happen to me. Far more unpleasant than what happened last October."

He leaned back slightly against the edge of the tall window frame. "Now, shall I pass the time by satisfying your curiosity as to what is in this canvas bag? Very well, your silence gives consent. The bag contains a Chinese repeating crossbow. It has a range of three hundred fifty yards with normal ammunition. With the arrows I shall use, the range is reduced. But still I can reach the Duchess's tents over there"—he jerked his chin toward the open window—"with absolute ease and dispatch."

Holmes nodded. "How many arrows is your protector paying you to shoot?"

"I only need one shot, but I can take four shots if need be."

"Four arrows?"

"Well, this crossbow does shoot three arrows in one shot. But still, you may think that twelve arrows might have only a small impact on such a large gathering. However, I neglected to tell you that each arrow has been fitted with a thin tube of dynamite specially prepared for the purpose. Mr. Day's rubber adhesive surgical tape is very effective. Each tube of dynamite has a ten-second fuse, and I have plenty of matches. The apparatus has been tested on numerous occasions, even in rainy weather, at the appropriate elevation and distance. The range has been calculated; the tension of the crossbow has been properly adjusted."

Arkwright's face contorted into a hideous, leering grin of triumph.

"All I need to do is point the bow out this window, light three fuses, and pull the trigger. You see those bulky dark shapes out there amid the electric lights? Of course, none of you wants to take your eyes from me to look out the window, but you can take my word that one is the tent where they have the champagne, and the other—that's the supper hall. Most of the guests are inside, going through the reception line. Then they'll stroll into the grounds and get themselves a drink. And then ... boom! And boom again!"

"You will blame this attack on the Fenians, I suppose," said Holmes.

"The London papers will have a field day. Some of those guests are in medieval dress. Can you imagine how those knights will look, with their armour scattered about and their arms and legs in fragments?"

Arkwright seemed exultant in his cruelty. Yet his pistol never wavered.

"Best of all, I know the dearly beloved Prince of Wales has arrived to lend his gracious rotund presence to the drinking and feasting. Soon his too, too solid flesh will melt, eh? I will have finished the task that I began in Dover, and now there is no one to stop me. No one in this house is alive"—he gestured meaningfully at Holmes and his voice took on a tone of menace— "except you."

We heard footsteps on the stairs.

"That will be Lestrade," Holmes said. "You will not fulfil your mission. But if you tell us the name of your employer—"

A harsh voice from the hallway interrupted. "I wouldn't be so quick to bargain, guv'nor."

We turned and saw Griffin.

In his right hand he held little Becky like a rag doll. She was bound and gagged, though she was still fighting, furiously trying to kick her attacker's knees.

"Yer fat friend is on the ground out there," Griffin said. "I bet 'e won't wake up for a week—if 'e ever does."

He held Becky out before him, his prodigious strength lifting her off the ground with one hand. He turned to Holmes. "Let's put this little gal into the bargain."

He walked to the open window. He held the writhing and twisting Becky at arm's length, between the two open casements, with only air between her and the ground. "Put down your guns, or I throw the brat. She won't look very nice after she hits the pavement."

Lucy's face was white to the lips, her green eyes huge. She held herself motionless, though I could see her whole body quivering, fighting the urge to rush at Griffin.

Moving very slowly and carefully, Holmes grasped his pistol by the trigger guard and held it out at arm's length.

I followed Holmes's example.

Carefully, Holmes leaned forward, the pistol still pointing at Arkwright, but dangling from between his index finger and thumb. I saw his eyes move, first to Arkwright, then to Griffin holding Becky at the far window. "Pull back the child," said Holmes.

"Not bloody likely," said Griffin.

Almost simultaneously three things happened.

Holmes flung the pistol at Arkwright and dove at him.

Lucy dove at Becky.

I shot Griffin between the eyes.

Lucy caught Becky before she fell, pulling her into the room and holding her so that the child's face was tucked her shoulder, shielding her from the sight of Griffin's body.

I turned to the window.

Holmes stood alone.

WATSON

61. AT THE BALL

We made our way from the second floor to the ground level. Lucy supported Becky on the stairs, holding her tightly, although the child seemed more outraged than frightened by her ordeal.

"Teach me to fight like you," I heard her say to Lucy. "Because if anyone ever tries to tie me up again, I want to be able to kick them in the *head*."

Holmes went before us, anxious to find Mycroft. I carried the crossbow and the dynamite-laden arrows.

Mycroft was sitting up outside the doorway. Holmes gave him a long look and a brief pat on the shoulder. Then he moved quickly around the corner of the house to where Arkwright had fallen.

Lucy hung back, her arm around Becky. "You go, Uncle John. I don't want her to see."

I followed Holmes, and we looked down at what remained. Light from the ground floor window shone in patches upon the motionless mass of fabric and flesh. The body was face down, the hands and arms splayed outward on the pavement.

"Like Father Mulloy," I said quietly.

Holmes rolled the body over. The forehead had been smashed and crushed, all the way down to the lifeless eyes. But the remainder of the hideous face remained intact. Now there could be no doubt whatsoever as to the identity and the death of Adrian Arkwright.

An envelope had fallen from Arkwright's jacket. Holmes picked it up and looked briefly at the contents.

"Banknotes," he said. "These would have been payment for Griffin."

I gave a wary glance toward the street not far away, where the small crowd of curious onlookers still remained, watching the line of coaches turn the corner to Devonshire House and hoping to catch a glimpse of more distinguished arrivals.

Holmes said, "We cannot leave him here." His lips compressed into a grim smile as he looked around us. "We can put him in the icehouse."

* * *

The Devonshire House garden had been transformed for the Duchess's ball into a shimmering otherworldly spectacle of electric light, in colours of red, blue, and white. Thousands upon thousands of tiny glowing bulbs had been entwined around the shrubbery and pathways. Blue and green lanterns hung from the trees. As we approached the house we passed a tent for refreshments that stood at the centre of the garden, adorned with more coloured lights and lanterns. The tent was open on all four sides, revealing long tables that were crowded with libations. The coloured light shimmered on many bottles of champagne in their silvered ice buckets and on many more crystal goblets surrounding crystal bowls of sparkling punch.

Inside the tent, hovering behind the ring of tables, stood perhaps a dozen liveried attendants preparing trays. A few guests in costume were strolling through the garden carrying drinks.

"What funny clothes," said Becky. She still appeared remarkably unshaken, although I noticed that Lucy's hand kept involuntarily touching the child's hair or her shoulder, as though she wished to reassure herself that Becky was indeed safe and unharmed.

"No one's allowed in unless they're in costume," she said, "and the costumes have to be some historic figure from at least a century ago."

I wondered how any of the strolling guests would have reacted had they known how close they had come, only a few moments earlier, to being maimed or obliterated by a weapon that did not exist in the previous century. I wondered how they would respond if they saw the body on the second floor of Lansdowne House or the contents of the icehouse, where twelve arrows with their sticks of dynamite now lay soaked in water at the bottom of a wooden tub beside Arkwright's grotesquely smashed corpse.

The hour was eleven-twenty-five.

In the great courtyard at the front of Devonshire House the coaches were still arriving, processing in a long circle to allow their guests to alight and then moving on, each in turn, to make way for the next illustrious visitor.

Holmes strode up to the nearest guard.

WATSON

62. AN ACCUSATION

After a huddled discussion, Holmes was able to speak directly with Lord Lansdowne. Soon afterward, Holmes, Mycroft, and I were ushered into the Devonshire House library.

Becky Kelly had been sent off to wait with Flynn in the carriage outside, along with Toby. Unshaken the child might be, but she was exhausted enough to agree without argument.

Holmes had seen to it that a guard was posted to ensure their safety.

The Duke of Devonshire arrived soon after we did. I barely recognized him at first, costumed as he was beneath a soft velvet cap of the seventeenth-century style and cloaked in a fur-trimmed black cape. With the Duke was Lord Lansdowne, dressed as a white-wigged Austrian prince of the early eighteenth century, wearing a gold-trimmed white silk jacket, tights, and stockings.

Lansdowne nodded to Holmes, Mycroft, and me in turn, as did the Duke.

The two noblemen had been with us for only a few moments when the assistant to the Duke, Captain Stayley, arrived, escorted by Lucy James. He was dressed in a red coat as though for a foxhunt, with a white shirt, waistcoat, and breeches.

"I had just put on my costume and returned when this young lady dragooned me in the garden, Your Grace," the Captain said with an affable smile. "She said you needed me in the library at once."

"I'm afraid I didn't even give him time for a glass of champagne punch," Lucy said. She dropped a curtsey to the Duke. "Now I've just one more person to fetch. I'll be back momentarily, I'm sure."

"I trust you won't be kept from your refreshment for long, Captain," said the Duke. He gave Lucy a polite wave of his hand as she departed.

The Duke and Captain Stayley were plainly unaware of what had just occurred at Lansdowne House. They gazed impatiently at Sherlock Holmes.

"I will be as brief as possible, Your Grace," Holmes said, his tone diffident.

"We are indulging you out of respect for your skilful handling of the events of June 22, Mr. Holmes."

"Thank you. I would not interfere at this moment, if it were not important that we attend to this particular matter at once, without delay."

"What matter?"

"It is a matter of foreign relations, Your Grace," said Holmes. "A series of financial transactions. The representative of the foreign country involved will enter momentarily." Holmes indicated the open library door. "Ah, yes. May I introduce you to Herr Bernhard von Bulow, of the German Embassy."

Lucy James led the ambassador in. He was dressed in black, with a black-ruffed collar and velveteen hat. His moustached face was a polite mask. He showed no surprise at seeing the three British government officials facing him across the room. "Pray take a seat, Mr. Ambassador," said Holmes. "Miss James, you may leave us."

Lucy turned and walked away, but she did not quite close the door of the library.

Holmes remained standing. "Mr. Ambassador, we last met on a train bound for Cragside, and you asked about two of your associates. I still do not know where they are. However, a third—a Mr. Arkwright—is in England. He was killed this evening."

I was watching the other four men. Of course, Lansdowne and Mycroft, having been informed by Holmes, showed no surprise. The Duke and Captain Stayley evidenced only polite attention.

"On his person was found an envelope with several hundred pounds in banknotes."

Von Bulow shrugged. "What of it?"

"We are not following you, Mr. Holmes," said the Duke.

"You will, Your Grace. I promise. However, I must impart one tedious financial fact before I can come to the point. The fact is that the Bank of England keeps a record of the persons who sell foreign bonds—that is, documents from foreign persons or companies that represent the promise to pay certain sums at a future date. The bank pays the seller a cash sum that is less than the face value of the bonds. At the future date, the bank redeems the bonds for full value and collects its profit. Meanwhile, the seller of the bonds has the cash to use for whatever purposes he may choose."

At this, there was still no hint of concern or recognition from von Bulow, Stayley, Lansdowne, or the Duke.

"As I said, the bank records all such transactions. I have the bank's report. There are eleven transactions associated with the name of one gentleman that took place over a period of thirteen months, beginning in April of last year. The value of the foreign bonds involved totalled well over a million pounds sterling. The value of the cash disbursed to that one gentleman was over seven hundred thousand pounds."

"We continue to indulge you out of regard for your past performance, Mr. Holmes," said the Duke. "But you have promised to come to the point, and I do hope you will do so very soon."

"I shall do so now, Your Grace. The person who sold those foreign bonds to the Bank of England is your trusted assistant, Captain Hunter Stayley."

63. THE TRAITOR DIES

Stayley shrugged. "A personal matter, Your Grace. I had bought bonds from some foreign companies, and then I sold them. I fail to see the connection."

Holmes said, "The bank recorded the numbers of the banknotes you received in return for those bonds, Captain. Some were found on the person of a Mr. Hardcastle, who was an employee of the Waterloo and City Railway and also"—Holmes turned to the Duke—"in your Lordship's employ. He was in charge of security at the tunnel expansion of the underground near the Bank of England. I say 'was' because Hardcastle was found murdered several days ago. Other banknotes you received were found in the room of Keenan Mulloy, a priest, who died at St. Paul's on the morning of June the 8th. And I have little doubt that, when the banknotes found on the dead Mr. Arkwright are examined, their source will prove to be the same."

Another shrug from the Captain. "I spent the money. It went into circulation. I had no control over it after I spent it. And I have no obligation to say what I purchased."

Holmes turned to von Bulow. "Can you provide any information about the bonds, Mr. Ambassador?"

Von Bulow's face remained a mask. "I know nothing of this matter."

Holmes's manner was courteous, even courtly. "Nor, Mr. Ambassador, do we have any proof to connect you or your government with the bonds. From the names and signatures we can only point out that they represent the obligations of three reputable German companies. But that, of course, is inconclusive."

"At best."

"Even if it were conclusive, we would not be able to prosecute you, Mr. Ambassador. You have diplomatic immunity, as did your two now-vanished associates, Messrs. Dietrich and Richter."

"Of whom Her Majesty's government knows nothing," said Lansdowne.

Von Bulow said, "Is that a threat?"

Holmes shook his head. "Not at all. I merely provide notice to you that Captain Stayley here—to whom you gave those bonds as payment—will no longer be able to continue to serve as your clandestine agent."

"How dare you, sir!" cried Stayley.

Von Bulow ignored the outburst. "I admit no connection whatsoever with the Captain."

"It is as well for you and your Kaiser. The Captain will become a most unsavoury associate when certain evidence is made public at his trial."

Now Stayley sat up rigid, bracing himself with his palms on his thighs. "What trial?"

"You had an illicit alliance, Captain, with two young unmarried women. A Miss Maud Jones, a maid in this very house, whom the Duchess will no doubt remember, and a Miss Mary Mulloy, whose brother died at St. Paul's Cathedral."

"Rubbish. Slander."

"Both women were murdered. Mr. Arkwright committed the murders. He used your coach, Your Grace. It was seen in Whitechapel on the night of Miss Jones's murder."

"No connection with me," said Stayley.

The Duke was already beginning to turn away from his once-trusted assistant.

"Before he died, Mr. Arkwright admitted the murders," said Holmes. "Less than one hour ago. Less than one hundred yards from where we sit."

"He cannot be tried if he is dead," Stayley replied. "And his crimes have nothing to do with me."

"Mr. Arkwright had with him a substantial quantity of explosives—twelve sticks of dynamite, to be precise." Holmes turned to the Duke. "He was planning to murder you and all others here at Devonshire House tonight, Your Grace. He was particularly resolved on igniting the dynamite at eleven-fifteen this evening."

Stayley gave a sardonic smile. "You find the hour significant, do you?"

"The Royal party arrived just after eleven. I noticed, Captain Stayley, that you left Devonshire House shortly after conversing with Miss James on the staircase just after ten-thirty. You returned in costume, in a carriage, to arrive at eleven-thirty."

"I deny any connection whatever with this Arkwright person to whom you refer, whatever he may have said to the contrary."

"Your connection with Arkwright will no doubt become indisputable in due course," said Holmes. "As will your connection with the two failed attacks on June 22."

"Bluff and bluster!"

"Not at all. Six months ago, you witnessed an artillery demonstration near Cragside. Your name appears on the record of visitors. The shells used for that demonstration are identical to those discovered within St. Paul's Cathedral."

"Thousands of people have visited Cragside."

Holmes appeared to take no notice. He continued, "Your name also appears in connection with a deposit made on May 31, purportedly from the Deutsche Bank in Berlin into the vaults of the Bank of England: a pallet of gold bars, to be specific. However, the only gold in the bars was upon their painted surface. The bars themselves were made of lead. Within the pallet containing the lead bars, two large crates of dynamite were concealed. That dynamite was connected to a detonator in the tunnels outside the bank, which Mr. Arkwright was about to detonate at twelve-thirty on the 22nd of June, when Miss James and I interfered."

"You have no proof that I—"

Holmes held up his hand. "Whether or not I can prove your connection with the attacks of June 22 does not matter, Captain Stayley. At this very moment I have all the evidence required to send you to prison."

We all stared.

Holmes's voice took on a musing tone. "Captain Stayley, I asked the Bank of England to closely examine the bonds that they purchased from you and to verify their genuine nature with the German companies involved."

"And?"

"The bonds were forgeries, Captain."

The look of realization that came over Stayley's face is difficult to describe, even in retrospect. He stared in disbelief. His eyes bulged.

He was staring, not at Holmes, but at von Bulow.

His lips moved soundlessly.

Holmes continued, his words resonating like the chimes of a death knell, which indeed they were. "You, Captain Stayley, sold forged bonds. Selling forged financial instruments is a crime. You will be ruined and disgraced. You will be prosecuted and convicted and imprisoned." Holmes paused, and then said, his voice now silken, "You have a good idea what can happen to men of your class in prison."

Holmes turned towards the partially open library door and raised his voice a trifle. "Inspector Lestrade, if you would be so kind."

We all turned towards the door. Lestrade appeared, with Lucy and two constables behind him.

Stayley glared at Lestrade and then at Holmes, his neck turning scarlet and the veins on his forehead swollen.

Then, with a sudden leap, Stayley lunged, arms outstretched.

But not at Holmes.

Stayley lunged at von Bulow.

I caught a glimpse of something in the Captain's right hand. He would have crashed into von Bulow and borne him to the carpeted floor, but Holmes intervened. Grasping Stayley's right forearm he spun the Captain around, smashing him into the wall. Stayley fell, landing on his hands and knees. On all fours in his red coat and hunting outfit, Stayley glared at us with the desperation of an animal brought to bay.

A reddish fluid oozed from Stayley's right hand.

He whispered. "Von Bulow. Come here. I've got something important to tell you."

Von Bulow stood immobile.

Undeterred, Stayley lunged forward again, his bloodied right hand grasping for the leg of the German ambassador. I saw shards of glass glinting through the blood on Stayley's open palm as he stretched out his arm.

He would have connected with von Bulow, who remained transfixed in horror and revulsion, had not Lucy James been at the ambassador's side. Her foot lashed out in a savage kick that connected with a sharp crack on Stayley's chin.

Off balance, Stayley twisted around, supporting himself with his left hand. Then he reached for Lucy.

She kicked his left hand from under him. He fell onto his face. Then she stamped down hard on Stayley's outstretched right hand, grinding her heel into the metacarpal bones. Stayley screamed in pain.

Lestrade and his men encircled him.

"Help me!" Stayley cried out. "Doctor Watson, you are a medical man. Help me!"

"That's poison on his hand," Lucy said. "He wants to smear your face with it."

In a paroxysm of rage, Stayley twisted away, wrenching his stained and ruined hand out from beneath Lucy's boot, hauling himself up to his knees and, for a brief moment, clasping his hands together as though in prayer. Then with trembling fingers he began to pick at the shards of glass. Blood coated his wrists and discoloured his white shirt cuffs.

"A plague be on all of you," he said. Bloody saliva dripped from his mouth onto the carpet. Madness shone in his eyes. Lucy stepped back. She was pale and shivering, but her voice was steady. "What is it that makes you stare so, Captain? Do you see the world you are about to enter? Do you see Mary Mulloy? Do you see Maud Jones?"

Stayley opened his mouth as if to reply. Pink foam issued from between his lips. A great convulsion shook his frame. He pitched forward. His hands and arms twitched at his sides. Then he lay still.

Two of Lestrade's men came over and, at Holmes's instruction, stood above Stayley's body with their boots pressing down on each of his wrists. I felt below his ear for a pulse.

There was none.

Von Bulow said, "You saved me, Mr. Holmes." He turned to Lucy and bowed stiffly. "You and Miss James."

"Indeed," Holmes replied. "Perhaps you will return the favour now by leaving England."

* * *

Not long afterward, we made our departure from Devonshire House. We left through the garden, so as to direct Lestrade's men to what lay in the icehouse and on the second floor.

Passing the refreshment tent, we saw the Prince of Wales. He stood on a raised platform above a small coterie of costumed well-wishers. His garb was Elizabethan in style and black and silver in colour. A white Maltese cross was emblazoned on his chest, and white ostrich plumes adorned his black high hat. A long sword hung at his side.

Striking a theatrically noble posture, the Prince held up a crystal glass of champagne punch in a toast to our hostess the Duchess.

Catching sight of Lucy, he raised his glass a bit higher.

WATSON

64. AN EXPLANATION BASED ON EVIDENCE

We met Lansdowne briefly at Lansdowne House. Police had already cleared the upper floor.

"What made you go to the Bank of England?" Lansdowne asked.

"Because of our past history, Mr. Secretary," Holmes replied. "You will recall that two Novembers ago, we intercepted one million pounds in bearer bonds. Kent, the banker, was attempting to return them to the German Embassy here in London, since the assassination attempt they were intended to pay for had failed."

Lansdowne nodded.

"When we were in Germany last year, I mentioned the matter to Kaiser Wilhelm. We were in the presence of von Bulow. I said that the British government would overlook the assassination attempt if the Kaiser's government would overlook the financial loss. Of course the Kaiser pretended ignorance of the matter."

"As does von Bulow now."

"But it occurred to me that Wilhelm, having lost one million pounds in one attempt to destroy the British government, would not be willing to risk more."

"So you asked the bank to authenticate the bonds."

"I reasoned that Wilhelm would find it far less expensive to hire a forger than to supply another million pounds. Fortunately, my reasoning hit the mark."

* * *

The next morning we received the news that Scotland Yard had identified the poison in the vial that had broken in Stayley's hand, entered his bloodstream, and killed him. It was strychnine. There were two more vials in the pockets of Stayley's waistcoat. I still shudder to think of the consequences had Lucy not intercepted Stayley before he gained access to the punch bowls.

The same morning a search was made of Stayley's rooms. Hidden beneath the floorboards of his study was a journal. One of the pages of the journal had been torn out. The jagged edge of the missing page exactly fit the tracing of St. Paul's Cathedral that we had found hidden within the pages of *The Strand Magazine* in Lucy's flat.

In our Baker Street rooms that afternoon, Holmes showed the journal to Lucy, Zoe, and me.

Lucy examined the slim volume. "Poor Mary thought she was special," she said, setting the journal down on Holmes's desk. "There's not even a mention of her name."

One of the remaining pages displayed the names and dates of battles during the English Civil War. Beneath the list was written *16 December 1653. The Protectorate begins.*

On another page were two lists of names, arranged in two carefully ruled columns. On the left were the names of the principal offices in Oliver Cromwell's government, and in the corresponding spot on the right hand column, the names of contemporary men, presumably those whom Stayley would have chosen to fill those offices, had he lived to see his bizarre dream put into action.

"So that's why Arkwright referred to Stayley as his protector," said Lucy.

On other remaining pages of the journal were several speeches. One deplored a savage attack on the English clergy by "Irish renegades" at the Queen's Jubilee and called for war to be waged on Ireland forthwith. Another scornfully denounced the Duke of Devonshire as a traitor in league with the Fenians. A third proposed that the newly formed British government would take over the Armstrong munitions complex at Elswick in order to protect the security of the British nation.

" 'Devonshire' and 'Elswick,' " Lucy said.

"In Arkwright's falsified interview," Holmes said. "The two words were each intended to misdirect us. 'Devonshire' was to turn our attentions to the Duke, who was entirely innocent of treason, and 'Elswick' was to make us chase after a missing long-range gun intended for the Japanese, when the real weapons were common, readily available artillery pieces intended to be fired at short range."

Lucy went on, "But how could Stayley have imagined that England would choose *him* to lead the country?"

"As the assistant to the Duke, Stayley did wield considerable power," said Holmes. "Remember, he had also been granted access to the centre of political power for many years. Over time, he came to believe he was truly of importance. Perhaps his familiarity bred contempt for the abilities of those above him. But moreover, as you will see from what remains in the journal, I believe there were also more personal reasons at work."

Lucy and I examined other pages of the journal. Some concerned business matters, records of the payments to various members of the Fenians and to Owens, to Arkwright, and to Griffin, the City Police constable. Others described earlier transactions, dating back to the autumn of 1895 and making reference to an "LP" at the Bank of England who could convey funds to an organization or person referred to simply as "Worth." In retrospect, it was perfectly plain that Stayley had been the treasonous mastermind whom we had been seeking to identify.

Still other pages, more poignant, were addressed to Lord Frederick Cavendish, the brother of the Duke of Devonshire, who had been slain by Fenians in Dublin his first day in Ireland in 1882, fifteen years ago. There were poems. There was a paraphrase of a hymn. There were declarations of fidelity. There was a pledge concerning what would occur when they met one another in the next world.

In my memory, I can still see the words of Stayley's pledge. It read:

My dear Frederick,

I was not quick enough to throw my own poor body between you and those knife-wielding Irish villains, yet I know in my heart that when I see you again you will have forgiven me.

You shall be proud of me on that day, and you shall be proud of what I have accomplished.

Holmes closed the journal and dropped it into a file box. "The desire for revenge on the Irish was intensified by the Captain's wish to atone for his personal failure," he said. "Then both desires were magnified by his delusional self-importance. Gradually, his emotions drove him mad."

LUCY

65. FAREWELLS AND
NEW BEGINNINGS

I hugged my mother tightly. "You're really leaving?"

We were in the sitting room of 221A Baker Street. My mother's neatly packed and locked traveling cases sat ready by the door.

She nodded. "Yes. That position of first chair violinist in La Scala Theatre. I've had the offer. It's a wonderful opportunity."

It was. I knew that.

My mother drew back enough so that she could look at me. "Sherlock Holmes isn't going to change, you know. He's not going to settle down to a life of domesticity and marriage now."

"An old dog doesn't learn new tricks." I thought of what Holmes had said. "Do you ever wish that you had tracked him down when you were younger? If you had told him about me then, he might have—"

"Married me?" My mother's face turned a shade more wistful. "I know he would have. He's very honorable."

"Then why—"

My mother shook her head, taking one of my hands in hers.

"Even when we were young, I knew that Sherlock had already given me as much of his heart as he was capable of giving. And he had given me something more precious: you." She hugged me tightly again. "You'll come and visit me again in Rome?"

"Just try to stop me."

My mother let go and looked at me again. Her green eyes shimmered with tears, but there was a small twist of a smile on her lips as well.

"There is something more. I believe Sherlock Holmes would count me as a friend. No other woman on earth can say that." Her smile deepened. "Not even Irene Adler."

I smiled back at her. "True."

"Not every love story ends with the words *happily ever after*." My mother looked at me, squeezing my hands. "But that doesn't mean that *none* of them can."

* * *

"Why, Lucy!" Uncle John opened the door to his surgery. "I did not expect to see you today. So Scotland Yard let you out at last, did they?"

"Yes, finally."

I felt as though I had done nothing else for the past two days but give official statements and answer questions put by everyone from Lestrade and an assortment of other Scotland Yard inspectors to the Police Commissioner and the Prime Minister himself.

Attempts to destroy the government of England apparently brought out the full force of governmental bureaucracy in the aftermath.

Now evening shadows were falling across the street behind me. Shops were putting down their awnings, and laborers hurried past on their way home. Uncle John stepped back to allow me to enter. He seemed to hesitate a moment, clearing his throat in a way that made a sudden chill dash across my skin.

"Is Jack—"

"I'm afraid that Sergeant Kelly is gone."

My heart went dead in my chest. A huge hand seemed to have reached in and replaced the air in my lungs with ice.

"I mean that he is not here!" Uncle John took my hand. "I am sorry, my dear, I should have phrased that more clearly. He is perfectly well—much recovered, in fact. He was able to rise from his bed this morning. It is just—"

Uncle John stopped. He was looking at me with sympathy etched on his kindly, rugged face. He didn't want to tell me whatever it was he had to say next.

"Just—" I prompted.

Uncle John sighed. "He will need time to ... adjust to the limitations of his present circumstances. The nerve damage I spoke of, if you remember—"

"I remember." My heart was beating again, painful and slow. "You mean that Jack can't walk because of the damage to his leg?"

"With time, and rehabilitation, I believe that significant muscle function may be recovered in the injured leg. But for now—" Uncle John shook his head.

"And he hates it and doesn't want to see me," I finished for him.

Uncle John shook his head vigorously. "No, no, my dear. He didn't say anything about wishing to avoid seeing you, he just—"

"Left before he had to speak with me," I finished for him. "That seems a fairly clear message."

Did Jack blame me for what had happened? I would understand if he did. He'd never have been on the steps of Saint Paul's if it hadn't been for me.

He would never have been involved in *any* of this if it hadn't been for his meeting me.

Uncle John was saying something else, something about Jack needing time. The words washed past me as an all-but-meaningless drone in my ears. I patted Uncle John's hand, though, and thanked him.

Holmes was waiting for me in the street outside the surgery. I should have been startled to see him, but at the moment I seemed to be past registering things like surprise.

Without speaking, Holmes offered me his arm. I rested my hand in the crook of his elbow.

We walked in silence for the space of several blocks, and then my father opened his mouth.

I interrupted before he could say anything. "If you're going to tell me that this way of life is largely incompatible with personal attachments and family, you needn't bother. I already know."

Holmes looked down at me. There was understanding in his gray eyes. But he shook his head.

"That was not what I wished to say, in fact. I wished to say—" He stopped, his eyes on the street up ahead. "I wished to say that I hope you do not make the mistake of believing that I have all the answers to this vast complexity we call life." A faint

trace of a smile played around the edges of his mouth. "Life—
its meaning, its purpose, how it is best lived—that I know is
a mystery even I cannot fully solve."

I watched a pair of children chasing a hoop across a small
green at the end of the road.

"Uncle John said that Jack just needed time."

"He may well be right. Watson has a habit of being right
when it comes to affairs of the human spirit and heart." Holmes
glanced down at me again. "Just because I am alone does not
mean that you must—or even ought—to be. Indeed, it appears to
me that some of the highest risks are those most worth taking."

I looked up at him sharply. "Are you saying—"

If I had not believed it to be entirely impossible, I would have
said that a faint tinge of color had crept into my father's cheeks.

"Before leaving, your mother extended an invitation to me to
hear her play at La Scala in Milan."

I stared at him. "And you said …"

"I said that I would be *happy*"—Holmes voice lingered just
slightly on the word—"to give the invitation serious consideration."

66. A LETTER FROM DR. WATSON

Baker Street
December 2, 1897
My dear Holmes:
Today you received a card from Windsor Castle, including a colorful image of a stained glass window depicting the Nativity. The printed words are:

Gloria in Excelsis Deo.
With Hearty Christmas
Greetings and Best Wishes
from

It is signed

Victoria RI

and addressed by hand

To Mr. Sherlock Holmes.

A handwritten note appears on the reverse side:

With sincere gratitude
for your most diligent and competent service.

VR

I trust your travels continue to go well. Lucy appears to have become comfortably situated below us in 221A.

Faithfully yours,
JHW

THE END

HISTORICAL NOTES

This is a work of fiction, and the authors make no claim that any of the historical locations or historical figures appearing in this story had even the remotest connection with the adventures recounted herein.

However ...

1. On March 15, 1898, *The London Gazette* published an "Extraordinary" edition describing the events of Her Majesty's Diamond Jubilee that had begun in June 1897 and continued throughout the year. The level of detail in this publication is indeed extraordinary. One may read of the three committees responsible for preparations and the names of their members, the timetables for the hundreds of events, the names of the guests at each luncheon and dinner, the names of the occupants of the seventeen carriages in the Queen's parade to the thanksgiving service at St. Paul's Cathedral, and the names of the military men who escorted them. We drew inspiration from a note on the celebrations of June 22:

"Owing to the admirable police arrangements made by Colonel Sir Edward Bradford, K.C.B, of the Metropolitan Police, and Colonel Henry Smith, C.B., of the City Police, there was not the slightest disturbance or disorder during the day, which passed off almost free from accidents."

2. Details from the Duchess of Devonshire's ball would have been impossible for the authors to attempt without the fascinating and most informative book of that name by Lady Sophia Murphy, daughter of the Eleventh Duke and Duchess of Devonshire. Descriptions of the costumes at the event, including the costume of HRH the Prince of Wales, are taken from the text and photographs therein.

3. The description of Cragside is based on materials made available by The National Trust.

4. The Waterloo and City line was indeed constructing the Bank Station of the London underground railway during the time of this story. However, there is no record of any associated breach of security or attempt to compromise the structure of the Bank of England.

5. Part of Lansdowne House still stands near Berkeley Square in Central London. Since 1935, a portion of that structure has been the home of the Lansdowne Club. From its inception the club has admitted "members of social standing," including women.

6. Devonshire House was demolished in 1924. An office building named Devonshire House stands on the site. The wrought-iron entrance gates remain, standing between Green Park and Piccadilly.

7. Thanks to surface restorations and improved air quality in London, the exterior of St. Paul's Cathedral appears far brighter than it did in 1897. Within the crypt level there is now a fashionable café and restaurant.

A NOTE OF THANKS TO OUR READERS, AND SOME NEWS

Thank you for reading this continuation of the *Sherlock Holmes and Lucy James Mystery Series.*

If you've enjoyed the story, we would very much appreciate your going to the page where you bought the book and uploading a quick review. As you probably know, reviews make a big difference!

The other four adventures in the series are currently available in e-book, paperback and audiobook formats: *The Last Moriarty, The Wilhelm Conspiracy, Remember, Remember* and the prequel to the series, *The Crown Jewel Mystery.*

Watch for *Death at the Diogenes Club,* another Sherlock and Lucy book, to be released in 2017. In 2018, be sure to watch for *The Return of the Ripper,* and a collection of Sherlock and Lucy short stories!

ABOUT THE AUTHORS

Anna Elliott is the author of the *Twilight of Avalon* trilogy, and *The Pride and Prejudice Chronicles*. She was delighted to lend a hand in giving the character of Lucy James her own voice, firstly because she loves Sherlock Holmes as much as her father, Charles Veley, and second because it almost never happens that someone with a dilemma shouts, "Quick, we need an author of historical fiction!" She lives in Maryland with her husband and three children.

Charles Veley is the author of the first two books in this series of fresh Sherlock Holmes adventures. He is thrilled to be contributing Dr. Watson's chapters for this and future books in the series, and delighted beyond words to be collaborating with Anna Elliott.

CONTENTS

PART TWO
AND MOCK THE TIME

PART THREE
WITH FAIREST SHOW

PART FOUR
WHAT THE FALSE HEART DOTH KNOW

Made in the USA
Monee, IL
27 December 2021

87320128R10233